'Tis the Season for Sleuthing

"Sorry for bursting in on you like this," Diane said. "Only I thought you'd like to know I did send obits to the papers. You might want to tell Gillian, too. After all, both of you found his body."

I didn't see how finding a dead body required further involvement. Gillian refused to even mention the incident. And I had no business concentrating on anything but *A Christmas Carol*.

"Anthony resented his uncle," Diane went on. "At times, I thought he even hated him. I'd suspect foul play if Everett hadn't passed away at ninety-five. I still might."

I told myself to let this all go. But that was about as likely as telling Minnie to stop singing, "Ba-ba-ba ba-ba ba-ran."

"I agree there's something strange in all this, Diane. But we have no proof of foul play. Especially without an autopsy."

"Convenient, don't you think? Like the speedy cremation."

"We can't do anything about it. But to be honest, Everett likely died of natural causes. And Anthony is simply a greedy relative who will profit from his uncle's death." I lowered my voice. "If Anthony did kill his uncle, we can't prove it."

"We'll see about that." Diane turned on her heel and marched out of the store.

Books by Sharon Farrow

Dying for Strawberries

Blackberry Burial

Killed on Blueberry Hill

Mulberry Mischief

Hollyberry Homicide

Published by Kensington Publishing Corporation

Hollyberry Homicide

Sharon Farrow

KENSINGTON BOOKS
www.kensingtonbooks.com

For my sister, Susan Sarpa
We are the only ones who remember those annual trips
with Mom and Dad in search of the perfect Christmas tree.
And how, after hours of parental arguments, they finally
bought a tree. Only to have Mom announce the next day
that they had chosen the wrong one.

Acknowledgments

I'd like to thank my agent, John Talbot, a staunch champion of the cozy mystery. I also extend my gratitude to everyone at Kensington, especially my editor, John Scognamiglio, and the hardworking production and art departments. Finally, I send my thanks across the years to Charles Dickens. Without his wondrous *A Christmas Carol*, this book could not have been written.

Chapter One

"Jacob Marley is dead!"

I looked up to see Gillian Kaminski beside me. My friend looked too unhappy for someone surrounded by choo choo trains and toy Alpine villages.

"Don't get emotional about it." I smiled. "Jacob Marley's been dead for about a hundred and seventy years. Also he's a fictional character." I returned my attention to the Lionel train chugging along on the table before me. Every few seconds, the green-and-silver train emitted a charming whistle as smoke plumed from its stack.

I didn't add that I had been named after this character by my Dickens-loving mother. Like everyone else in Oriole Point, Gillian knew how I came by my name.

"You don't understand," Gillian said. "It's the old guy who plays Marley in the annual *A Christmas Carol*."

This time I gave her a closer look. She wasn't joking. "Everett Hostetter?"

"Yes. I discovered him sitting on a bench near the restroom. And I think he's dead. But I can't find anyone who works here." She scanned the crowd. "Where's Kit?"

"I introduced him to the president of the local model-train club. They went upstairs to check out the German antique trains. I'll run up there and get him."

"We don't have time for that." Gillian grabbed my arm.

She pulled me past the toy train layouts blanketing the Victorian house that had long been Oriole Point's Historical Museum. Once we reached the foyer, Gillian hustled me to the back of the building, It was almost closing time, with visitors making their way to the exit. Perhaps no one but Gillian had discovered the body so far.

As soon as we came to the end of the corridor, I saw the figure of an old man slumped forward on a walnut bench. I'd been in the museum enough times to know the bench was a replica of a Civil War–era piece on display in a roped-off room upstairs.

Gillian finally let go of my arm. "Is he dead?" she whispered.

I knelt before the motionless figure. No doubt Gillian viewed me as an expert on this subject. I had been close to more than one dead body this past year.

"Mr. Hostetter?" I asked in a loud voice.

Now that I was right in front of him, I could confirm that it was indeed Everett Hostetter. His head lolled to the side, eyes closed, as if he were napping. I put my hand an inch away from his lips, but felt no breath leave his body.

Next, I took his wrist. As I feared, he had no pulse. Because he felt warm to the touch, I guessed he had died within the hour. Maybe as recently as a few minutes ago.

To be certain, I placed my hand over his chest, searching for a heartbeat. I turned to Gillian, who hopped from one foot to the other.

"Call 911," I told her. "I'm afraid he's gone."

"How awful!" Behind her wire-rim glasses, Gillian's blue eyes filled with tears. "The poor man came here tonight to look at trains and now he's dead. It doesn't seem fair."

Death rarely was, but this wasn't the time to remind Gillian of it. "Call 911," I repeated. "Then go to the back parlor where the big Santa trains are set up. That's the last place I saw Diane Cleverly. She may still be there. As head curator, she needs to know ASAP."

Gillian pulled out her cell phone and hurried off.

Unlike Gillian, I was not unduly upset. Not only had I been in proximity to death several times, but Everett had had a good long run. He must have been at least ninety.

I took out my own cell phone and texted Kit. In addition to being a toy train hobbyist, my boyfriend was also an investigative detective with the sheriff's department. He would know how best to proceed with reporting Hostetter's death. Although I hated to spoil Kit's fun.

While I knew Kit loved trains, I had not been prepared for his exuberant delight at the sight of so many toy trains. I was glad I'd suggested we come to the opening day of the museum's toy train exhibit, even though we had to wait until our workdays ended.

Since Gillian worked for me at The Berry Basket, she overheard our plans and asked to come along. I had no idea Gillian was a toy collector, with Thomas the Tank Engine being her longtime favorite. Thankfully, the museum stayed open until seven on Wednesdays, and she eagerly accompanied us after we closed the shop.

I spent the first hour as a captive audience to Kit's tutorial about HO scale trains versus O scale trains. Not being his girlfriend, Gillian felt free to wander off on her own. While the train trivia was interesting, I was happy to hand Kit off to the president of the Lake Michigan Model Train Club. As fun as toy trains were, the elaborate layouts and miniature villages intrigued me far more. I'd also discovered the urn of hot cocoa and peppermint cake pops the museum put out for visitors. The evening had gone quite well.

Until Gillian found a dead body.

I straightened the collar of Hostetter's wool coat. It had been left unbuttoned. Leather gloves lay on his lap. Hostetter didn't look as if he had been about to leave the museum. Maybe he came here to use the bathroom, located just around the corner from the bench. And as an older gentleman, he probably felt the need to sit and rest.

Placing my hands on the bench, I used it as a support to stand up. This movement disturbed the folds of his coat, which sent one of his gloves to the floor. When I bent down to retrieve it, I spied a gingerbread man cookie on the floor. Or rather pieces of one. Crumbs and cookie fragments lay scattered on the polished wood planks.

I swept the pieces up in my hand. Not seeing a trash can, I dropped the cookie pieces into my jacket pocket.

A woman and little girl emerged from the restroom. Both looked startled by the sight of the motionless Everett.

"Mom, what's wrong with the man?" the girl asked.

The woman exchanged worried glances with me. I gave a small shake of my head, replying, "He's taking a nap. We should be quiet and let him sleep."

The girl pointed at the floor. "He dropped his bag."

As the mother led her young daughter away, I looked beneath the bench and retrieved a white paper bag. It held two gingerbread man cookies studded with dried candy and trimmed with white frosting.

A closer examination of Everett's face revealed cookie crumbs near his mouth. Given his age, a part of me envied Hostetter. I could think of worse ways to go than munching cookies as toy trains whistled from every corner.

Footsteps sounded on the wooden corridor. I looked up to see Kit striding toward me. "I got your text. Are you okay?"

"I'm fine." I pointed at the lifeless body of Everett Hostetter. "But he isn't."

I moved aside to let Kit examine the body. A second later, Gillian and Diane Cleverly, the museum's head curator, joined us.

Gillian still looked upset, while Diane appeared even more shaken. This surprised me. Diane was an elegant older woman who possessed a serene, unflappable temperament better suited to a Buddhist nun than a museum administrator.

"I've been expecting this." Diane choked back a sob.

"Was he ill?" Kit asked her.

"Everett had health problems, but he rarely spoke about them. And he didn't care for doctors." Tears sprang to her eyes. "At least he had a chance to tour the exhibit with me tonight. Although he felt too tired to go upstairs. Considering his age, I should have paid more attention to that. Perhaps questioned him more closely."

"Did he mention chest pains? Dizziness, maybe?" I asked.

She took a deep breath, struggling to get her emotions under control. "No. Only tiredness, which I understand. I'm seventy-six and in good shape. Still, there are days I feel like I've been around since the Great Flood. And Everett was much older."

"He did seem spry," I commented. "I rarely saw him use his cane."

"Chalk that up to stubbornness and pride," Diane said. "He should have used the cane, but he always pushed himself. And pushed other people, too."

"How well did all of you know him?" Kit asked.

Diane rummaged in the pocket of her burgundy dress, taking out a tissue. "I met Everett when I was twenty-six, shortly after I earned my PhD in history." She dabbed at her eyes. "My first position was archivist at one of Everett's companies."

"How many companies did he own?" I asked.

"A great number. Over the years, he sold off most of them. Three years ago, he accepted a buyout offer for the original company." She regarded the dead man with affection. "Everyone feared him. Except me. Maybe that was why we got along."

I'd always found Diane to be interesting, but now she intrigued me. I was seventeen when the museum board hired Diane as head curator, which was regarded as a real feather in our caps. Not many small regional museums boasted a newly retired history professor from MSU. One with critically acclaimed historical biographies to her credit.

I wondered about the relationship between Everett and Diane. As far as I knew, Everett was a bachelor. And Diane often spoke fondly of her husband, who died a decade ago. However, Everett came across as an unfriendly crank, while Diane Cleverly was one of the kindest, most charitable women I had ever known. What did these two dissimilar people have in common?

Kit looked at Gillian and me. "How about you two?"

"I knew who Everett Hostetter was," I replied. "But I never had any interactions with him. I don't think we ever exchanged a single word."

"Same here," Gillian said. "But everyone in town has read his cranky letters to the editor at the *Herald*." Gillian's father, Steven Kaminski, was the editor of the *Oriole Point Herald*, one of two weekly town newspapers. "Only he always signed his letters 'A Disgruntled Citizen.' "

"Those Disgruntled Citizen letters were all from Everett?" I asked.

"Yes. Dad didn't even print half of them. Mr. Hostetter never stopped being disgruntled."

"Everett did tend to be overly critical," Diane added.

"I recognize him as the guy who always plays Jacob Marley in *A Christmas Carol*," I said.

"Is this the production Oriole Point's amateur theater group puts on at the Calico Barn?" Kit was a recent resident along the eastern shore of Lake Michigan.

"They're called the Green Willow Players," I explained. "And *A Christmas Carol* has been one of their staples for decades. But Everett hasn't always played Marley. Someone new usually appeared as Jacob Marley when I was a kid. It was only after I went off to college that Everett Hostetter moved here and took over the role."

"Everett insisted on playing Marley," Diane said.

"I wonder why he didn't want the lead role," I mused. "Scrooge is the bigger part."

"To be honest, I don't know how he found the energy to act in *any* role." Diane sighed. "They even wrapped him in real chains. He rattled them as he walked about onstage. It's a miracle he didn't collapse during one of the performances."

The distant sound of EMS sirens greeted our ears.

Kit stood up. "His next of kin need to be notified

that his body has been taken to the hospital. Do you know who that would be?"

We all looked at Diane Cleverly, who said, "He lived with his nephew, Anthony Thorne. Their house is in the Vervain Grove subdivision, near the golf course."

Gillian bit her lip. "What do you think he died of?"

Diane, Kit, and I looked at each other. "He was an old man," I said. "It was his time."

The entry door to the museum opened as the EMS technicians arrived. When they rushed down the corridor toward us, nearby museum visitors reacted with surprise and alarm.

While the paramedics began their own examination, Diane cleared her throat.

"Everett's nephew is here." She nodded at the tall, stout man who paused in the museum's open doorway. "He's come to drive him home."

"Anthony!" She waved to grab his attention.

Anthony Thorne walked over. "What's going on, Diane? I'm here to pick up the old man, so I hope he's ready to—"

He stopped in midsentence at the sight of his uncle surrounded by paramedics.

"I'm sorry, Mr. Thorne, but your uncle has died," Kit said.

Anthony pushed past the paramedic team and shook the lifeless man. "Uncle Everett?"

"He's gone." Diane touched Anthony's sleeve.

He seemed confused. "I don't understand. He just died?"

"It happens, especially at this age," a paramedic

said. "He may have suffered sudden cardiac arrest, a stroke, even an aneurysm. How old was he?"

"Uncle Everett turned ninety-five last week," Anthony said in a dazed voice.

The two paramedics exchanged knowing looks.

"I guess I shouldn't be surprised, but he appeared fine when I left for work." Anthony looked over at Diane. "He said you were going to drive him to the exhibit today. How did he seem?"

"Same as always. He even brought a last-minute checklist of things he wanted to go over." Diane turned to us. "As our chief benefactor, Everett oversaw all museum business. He looked forward to this exhibit in particular."

"I got a call from him earlier," Anthony said. "He asked me to pick up crullers from the Drop Anchor Diner. They're in the car. Uncle Everett loved his sugar. One thing we had in common."

I held out the white paper bag I'd found on the floor. "It appears he was eating cookies when he passed away."

"Do I look like I'm in the mood for cookies?" Anthony snapped. "Throw them away."

Diane took the bag from me. "I'll get rid of them."

Up close, Anthony reminded me of a brown bear: big, lumbering, with a prominent nose. And quite hirsute. Looking at his thick brown hair and five-o'clock shadow, I guessed bristly hair also covered his chest and arms.

While Diane quietly spoke to Anthony, Kit informed the two EMTs that he worked for the sheriff's department. The trio exchanged words I couldn't overhear, except for the comment "It looks like a nat-ural death."

I gave an audible sigh of relief. I had seen far too much death recently, all of it unnatural. If the holi-day season had to be marred with a passing, at least this time it wasn't murder.

Chapter Two

Maybe I had overdone the "deck the halls" bit this year. I turned in a circle, searching for empty wall space in my shop.

I looked down at the white flocked wreath dotted with red hollyberries and glass ornaments. "Where can I hang this?"

Dean Cabot marched out from behind the counter. "Give me the wreath."

I handed it over. "Don't you dare stick it in the back room. And be careful. Those ornaments are blown glass from Austria. I'm selling the wreath for a hundred and ten dollars."

"Exactly. You're *selling* it, unlike the Styrofoam candy canes by the bakery case, the framed vintage Christmas cards behind the ice cream counter, the sleigh bells by the jams, the ropes of garland covering up the last bit—"

"You made your point." I stopped him before he could mention the seven-foot-tall spruce tree in the corner. "But you know I love to decorate for a holiday."

"All too well. We could barely move in here at Halloween." Dean rummaged through a drawer in the wooden hutch that displayed berry syrups, many of which I had created.

"Perhaps I had one too many hay bales in here, but customers love it when I decorate."

"Aha!" Dean held up a silver wreath hanger. "I knew we had one left."

He opened the door to The Berry Basket and slipped the wreath hanger over the top. After positioning the white wreath on the hanger, he bowed. "Voilà! And you're welcome."

I gave a nod of approval. "This is why I pay you the big bucks."

"Yeah, right." Dean straightened his blue chef apron. "You know I only work here for the gossip and my employee discount. Which comes in handy at Christmas. My cousins love our berry wines. Speaking of that, I need to finish unpacking the latest shipment of blackberry wine."

As he returned to the boxes behind the counter, I looked up at my strawberry-shaped wall clock. Beside it hung a hand-painted sign saying WE WISH YOU A BERRY MERRY CHRISTMAS. We opened in fifteen minutes. Time enough to add one more festive touch.

Even though lights already twinkled along store shelves and the front window, I had special-ordered a string of Christmas lights in the shape of hollyberries. They arrived before I left the house this

morning. How could I not find room for that in
The Berry Basket?

After all, Oriole Point lay smack in the middle of
west Michigan's fruit belt. And my shop specialized
in all things berry related: berry jams, jellies, wines,
salsas, vinegars, pastries, baking mixes, teas and coffees,
as well as dinner sets decorated with berries, aprons,
berry cookbooks, strawberry hullers, and much, much
more. I also hosted berry-themed events, which
prompted a glance at the wooden table by the window.

Spaced out over the red tablecloth were jars of
berry jam, covered baskets of crackers and crumpets,
small serving plates, and silver spreaders. I had
scheduled a free jam tasting at eleven.

"Best get these up before customers start to arrive." I sat cross-legged on the floor and began to remove the lights from their box.

"You're incorrigible. I'm shocked you haven't
hired someone to play Santa in the shop."

"Despite the sarcasm, that's not a bad idea. At least
for the weekend Hollyberry Festival. Santa always
draws customers with children. And I can give away
the blueberry lollipops we sell. I also saw a Santa suit
at the secondhand shop."

"Why didn't I keep my mouth shut?" Dean shook
his head.

"But I'd have to scramble at this late date to hire
someone to play Santa."

"Don't look at me. And Andrew will be busy over-
acting in *A Christmas Carol.*"

"You're both too young and snarky to pull it off.
What about Gareth Holmes?"

"The guy who carves duck decoys?"

"Yes. He's always in a good mood. And he has a bushy white beard." The more I thought about it, the better this sounded. During lunch, I'd run over to the secondhand shop and snap up that Santa suit. Gareth seemed amiable, so I was sure he'd agree to play Santa.

"He does look like Kris Kringle," Dean said. "Even his cheeks are ruddy."

The shop door opened, letting in both a blast of wintry air and Gillian.

"Hi, girl," I said. "You do know you're not on the schedule today."

Because Gillian was on college break, she was available to work during the week, something she normally did only in the summer.

Gillian shut the door behind her. "I had to warn you about *A Christmas Carol.*" She took a deep breath. "That play is cursed. Just like the barn."

Dean and I exchanged confused glances. "Is this about Everett Hostetter dying?" he asked. "Marlee told me what happened last night at the museum."

"The man was in his nineties," I reminded her. "It was old age, not a curse."

"You don't know the whole story." Gillian sat down at one of the bistro tables by our ice cream counter. "Andrew texted me an hour ago and asked me to come to the Calico Barn as soon as I could. Suzanne called the whole theater group in for an emergency meeting."

Andrew Cabot, my remaining Berry Basket clerk and Dean's younger brother, had been cast in the production of *A Christmas Carol.* No surprise there. His mother, Suzanne Cabot, a longtime member of the Green Willow Players, had snagged the director's job this season. This no doubt played a factor in Andrew landing the role of Ebenezer's nephew.

"The actors probably learned about Hostetter's death this morning," I speculated. "Since you were the one to find him, did they ask for details?"

"No. They wanted me to join the cast." Gillian yanked off her white wool cap, sending a mass of wavy blond hair tumbling about her shoulders. She looked at Dean. "Your mother was quite upset when I got there."

He shrugged. "Mom's always upset."

"With reason this time. She'd just heard about Everett's death and had a panic attack. Your brother had to give her extra Valium."

Dean snickered. "Next Christmas I should buy Mom a fainting couch. One for Andrew, too."

Not a bad idea. Andrew and Dean Cabot were prone to drama and exaggeration. They came by it naturally. Their mother was not only a member of our amateur theater troupe, she was the receptionist at the police station, where she had a front-row seat for every crime and misdemeanor in town.

"Was Suzanne fond of Everett Hostetter?" I asked Gillian.

"I have no idea. But she is upset a cast member died the first time she'd been asked to direct a production. Especially *this* cast member."

"Hostetter didn't seem like a warm, fuzzy fellow," I observed.

"Mom didn't care for him," Dean said. "He criticized everyone, including her. However, Hostetter was the Green Willow Players' biggest donor. For the past nine years, the group hasn't made a move without his approval. They depend on his money to keep them afloat, Especially with the mortgage payments on the Calico Barn."

"I always thought the theater group should have rented the barn, not bought it outright," I said. "Real estate is so pricey along the lakeshore."

"That's why everyone there kowtowed to Hostetter," Dean said. "And he threatened to withhold his sponsorship of the theater group if he didn't play Jacob Marley every year."

"When did Jacob Marley become such a sought-after role? I could see wanting to play Ebenezer, but Marley?" I frowned. "And Suzanne has to stop overreacting to everything."

"There's more," Gillian said. "Suzanne freaked out because she's now lost *two* actors."

Alarmed, I looked up from the tangled lights. "Another actor died?"

"Don't say such a terrible thing!" Gillian said. "No. They rushed Andrea Shipman to the hospital last night with a burst appendix."

Our town was small enough that I knew Andrea Shipman was the twentysomething daughter of Oriole Point's favorite plumber and the middle school art teacher.

"Poor girl," I said. "That takes weeks to recover from."

"Exactly. Which is why they asked me to replace her as the Ghost of Christmas Past. Suzanne wants a young woman with long, pretty hair for the role. She says none of the company's wigs are attractive enough."

I grinned. "When did the Ghost of Christmas Past

spend so much time on hair care? Maybe Suzanne is confusing the character with Cher."

"My brother's behind this," Dean said. "He apparently added boho-chic elements to the Cratchit family costumes. Andrew always goes for style over substance."

Talk about the pot calling the kettle black. Neither Cabot brother was the Dalai Lama.

Although born eleven months apart, the brothers looked like twins. Both were tall, auburn-haired, attractive, and obsessed with fashion and Instagram. The only difference between them was that Andrew was gay, and Dean preferred women. Although Dean's standards were way too high. I didn't think he would be satisfied until he found a girl who was a cross between Gigi Hadid, Misty Copeland, and Ruth Bader Ginsburg.

"Why aren't you taking this seriously?" Gillian said in obvious frustration.

"What do you want us to do?" I asked. "Dean and I have nothing to do with the play. But Suzanne is right. You would make a lovely Ghost of Christmas Past."

"There is no way I'd be part of this production. First, a death. Then a medical emergency. All on the same night!" Gillian shuddered. "Who knows what terrible thing will happen next?"

"When did you become superstitious?" Dean asked.

"This isn't superstition. This is fact. Everyone knows the Calico Barn is unlucky."

"Because of the farmer who got murdered there? That happened about a thousand years ago." I gave her a reassuring smile.

The Calico Barn once belonged to the Van De

Bergs, a family of dairy farmers. It stopped being a working barn in 1951 when the farm and everything on the property was auctioned off. That was when local entrepreneur Fred Calico bought the picturesque barn.

While the exterior kept its white paint and weathervane rooster, the building had been moved from its original location to a spot just within town limits. Since then, the rechristened barn had been a restaurant, antique shop, and theater. And despite Gillian's fears, nothing bad had happened there since it had been sold.

However, a disgruntled farmhand did murder Ethan Van De Berg during the Depression. Rumors claim the deadly dispute involved unpaid wages. And I had heard stories about a young boy who tragically fell to his death from the hayloft.

"The murder happened in 1932, not centuries ago," Gillian said. "And what about the little boy who died in the barn a decade earlier? Also don't forget the Van De Berg woman. Two years before the family moved, she cut her hand on a rusty tool in the barn and died of tetanus!"

"The Van De Bergs owned the barn for decades," I told her. "Of course bad things happened there over the years."

"All of them in the barn?" She shook her head. "That building is unlucky. I've always hated to see plays there. And my parents insist we attend *A Christmas Carol* every year. I had to force myself to even enter the barn today. I left as soon as I could. Everett might still be alive if he hadn't spent so much time there."

Dean laughed. "You're funny, Gillian."

"Nothing about this is funny. And I'm staying far away from the barn and the Green Willow Players. I hope you do the same, Marlee."

"Aside from buying a ticket, I've never been involved with the Green Willow Players or their *Christmas Carol.* I even missed most of those years when Everett played Marley."

Although I was born and raised in our beautiful lakeshore village, at eighteen I left Michigan to attend New York University. At the same time, my parents moved to Chicago. After graduation, I produced cooking shows for the Gourmet Living Network in NYC. Then, three years ago, I wisely decided to come home to Oriole Point for good and open a berry-themed shop. Not only did I love berries, but it gave me a connection to the generations of Jacob ancestors who once owned berry orchards in the county.

Dean walked over to the shelves of berry wines, cradling a half dozen bottles in his arms. "A shame you chopped your hair to shoulder length, Marlee. Otherwise, you'd be a shoo-in for the Ghost of Christmas Past."

"Lucky me." After my broken engagement to Ryan Zellar this past summer, I'd cut a good six to eight inches off my long dark hair. I changed hairstyles after every major life transition. I hoped my hair had a chance to grow out before the next one.

I glanced up at the clock again. "Gillian, it's ten. Can you put the OPEN flag outside? Along with the sandwich board advertising the jam tasting."

While she did so, I finished untangling the lights. Weekdays in December were busy as locals and visitors took care of last-minute Christmas shopping. The Berry Basket did well in the run-up to the holidays. Even without free jam and crackers.

With Christmas a week away, I didn't have time to mourn a man who had enjoyed such a long life. Particularly since I had no reason to be fond of him. Nor could I do anything other than send a get-well-soon card to Andrea Shipman.

I stood up, shaking out the string of lights. Last year I hung so many lights in the store, I blew a fuse three times. I hoped to keep my lights to a reasonable wattage this year. I spied a nice spot for this latest string along the shelf that held berry muffin mixes and granola. As I dragged a stepladder over, Gillian stomped back into the store, looking even gloomier.

"I've thought of some locals who might be good in the roles of Jacob Marley and the Ghost of Christmas Past." I climbed the stepladder. "How about Rowena Bouchet to replace Andrea Shipman? Rowena has beautiful long hair."

"She's also drop-dead gorgeous," Dean said with feeling. When they were in high school, Dean had a serious crush on Rowena Bouchet, who was now the owner of the downtown yoga studio. And the fiancée of a local sculptor.

"As for Jacob Marley," I continued, "Old Man Bowman does love an audience. And he's the right age for the role. Only Suzanne has to keep him from talking about Bigfoot."

"Suzanne doesn't want Old Man Bowman for that role. She wants you."

I almost fell off the stepladder. "Me?"

At that moment, Andrew Cabot burst in. I admired his gray winter ensemble: North Face jacket, fur-trimmed boots, leather gloves, earmuffs, cable-knit scarf. And a gray plaid tote bag slung over one shoulder. As always, he was ready for his close-up.

"Mom wants you to play Jacob Marley," he announced.

"Gillian just told me. And the answer is no."

"It makes perfect sense," Andrew said. "After all, look at your name."

I rolled my eyes at him. "You must be kidding."

The expressions on Andrew's and Gillian's faces told me otherwise.

Casting me as Scrooge's former business partner because my name was Marlee Jacob seemed the height of whimsy. Then again, that's how I came by my name. My mother, an English literature professor at Northwestern, was rereading *A Christmas Carol* when she went into labor. After I chose to enter the world on Christmas Eve, Mom decided that since our last name was Jacob, no other first name but Marlee would do. My mother has conceded that hormones and exhaustion may have played a role. However, her favorite author is Charles Dickens, and I think she remains quite pleased to have given me a Dickensian moniker.

"Jacob Marley is an old dead guy." I draped the lights along the sides and top of the shelf. "People will think it's a joke if I turn up as Marley. I'm also the wrong gender."

"In Shakespeare's time, men played all the roles. Even Juliet," Dean said.

"Last year, Glenda Jackson performed as King Lear on Broadway," Andrew added.

"Maybe you should see if Ms. Jackson is available," I suggested.

Andrew went over to the coffeemaker, where I'd brewed cranberry-nut coffee. "Our mayor has been cast as the Ghost of Christmas Present. Dickens didn't describe him as a six-foot-four African American, but Lionel is fantastic in the role."

I had no doubt of that. Oriole Point's mayor, Lionel Pierce, not only boasted an imposing presence, he possessed a deep, rumbling voice that my baker, Theo, likened to thunder.

"Leave Marlee alone," Gillian said. "She doesn't want to do it. And you should drop out of the play, too. The play has a cloud hanging over it. A big unlucky cloud."

Andrew chuckled. "You sound like Professor Trelawney from *Harry Potter*."

"Don't treat this as a joke." Gillian glared at Andrew. "An actor died. Another actor is now in the hospital. The play is as cursed as the barn."

"I don't believe in curses," I said before things grew too heated. "I simply have no desire to appear in the most popular theatrical production Oriole Point throws all year."

"This isn't the Goodman Theatre's *Christmas Carol* in Chicago," Andrew said. "We're all amateurs. And everyone will come to see Marlee Jacob playing Jacob Marley. You'll be in costume, too. With lots of makeup to give you a deathly pallor. And a cloth that winds around Marley's head. What they used in Victorian times to keep the corpse's jaw closed."

Dean chuckled. "A festive touch."

"Since the previous Marley just died, I'm not sure how festive the audience will be."

"Don't be a spoilsport." Andrew joined Gillian at the table, having had the courtesy to bring her a coffee. "By the way, you have too many lights. You'll blow a fuse again."

"I have less lights than last year. It will be fine."

"Maybe Marlee is worried about stage fright." Gillian decided to take a different tack to dissuade me. "If she's shy about going onstage, you shouldn't force her."

"Shy?" Andrew asked. "Marlee? You two *have* met?"

He and his brother enjoyed a good laugh.

"I'm not shy," I said. "Or nervous about being onstage. In high school, I belonged to the drama club. During my senior year, I played Chava in *Fiddler on the Roof.*"

It had been a lively production, and I had been quite good in it. If I hadn't majored in marketing, I might have pursued a drama degree. Good thing I hadn't. My life had seen more than enough drama this past decade. I didn't need the added theatrics of an acting career. It was one reason I'd left my career as a TV producer in New York City and returned to my hometown. And what I hoped would be a calmer life. So far, that hadn't been the case.

"We're in a bind, Marlee," Andrew said. "Opening night is in less than a week."

"Everyone in town knows you," Dean chimed in. "They'll want to see Marlee Jacob perform as her namesake. And I'll promote it big-time on Instagram and my blog."

"You only appear in the beginning of the play," Andrew added. "After you warn Scrooge about the other ghosts, you can relax backstage until it's time for the curtain call."

"How am I supposed to learn all my lines by Tuesday?" I replied, surprised that I was considering it. "Not to mention the staging?"

"You appear in just one scene. And you have thirty lines, tops. See for yourself." Andrew pulled a script from his tote bag.

Gillian jumped to her feet. "If something happens to her because of this play, I'm going to blame both of you. And, Marlee, you'll regret not taking my advice." She stormed past me.

After Gillian slammed the door behind her, I turned to the Cabot boys. "Wow. I've never seen her like that."

"The dead body last night rattled her." Andrew took another sip of coffee. "If she'd found as many as you have, the poor girl would need to be hospitalized."

"You should do it, Marlee," Dean said. "Hostetter's death throws a shadow over the production. Casting a young woman with your name in the role serves as a distraction."

Despite my mother's fondness for Dickensian names, I also was a fan of *A Christmas Carol*. I loved every incarnation of the story, from the classic movie with Alastair Sim to Bill Murray in *Scrooged*. A woman as Jacob Marley would be one more tweak to the famous tale.

"Fine. Only don't blame me if the town thinks this is the height of miscasting."

The two brothers high-fived.

"Okay, everyone." I went over to the switch by the front door. "Prepare to be dazzled."

I flipped the switch. The shop blazed with hundreds of sparking lights. Then they flashed off. I clicked the switch several times. Nothing.

"You blew a fuse again," Dean announced, stating the obvious.

"I love Christmas, too," Andrew said. "But you overdo it."

"I refuse to believe there is such a thing as too much Christmas."

"I beg to differ," Dean said. "As one example, your latest blown fuse."

"Don't forget the five pounds I'll put on after eating my way through all the holiday parties." Andrew looked happily resigned to that pronouncement.

I didn't bother to mention another example of what might also be termed too much Christmas. Or at least too many Christmas cookies. The death of Everett Hostetter.

Chapter Three

Determined to hang my hollyberry Christmas lights, I convinced the shopkeepers on either side of The Berry Basket to allow me to use their outdoor outlets. I already had too many exterior lights plugged into mine. Now, thanks to their neighborliness, tiny red lights twinkled along my window boxes and decorative wooden shutters.

When I stood back to admire my handiwork, snowflakes began to fall. Denise Redfern, owner of the Tonguish Spirit Gallery next door, knocked on her front window to get my attention.

She pointed at the drifting snow and mouthed, "Snow!" She looked delighted.

I gave her a big thumbs-up. The past week had brought falling temps, but this was the first real snow. A brief dusting two weeks ago didn't count.

Every retailer in Oriole Point looked forward to this. Our downtown had been decked out with garlands, lights, Christmas trees, illuminated menorahs, and wreaths since Thanksgiving weekend. As always, the decorating committee did a wonderfully extravagant job. The annual Christmas tree put up in the village square near city hall was taller than any in my memory. Yet the early December days often reached fifty degrees, with accompanying sunshine. This made it difficult for my fellow Michiganders to get in the holiday spirit.

But once snow blanketed our village, it became a scene worthy of Currier & Ives. One that encouraged visitors and residents alike to begin shopping in earnest.

As the wind blew from the lake, I tightened my knit scarf. Today was the first time I'd worn my thick winter parka this season. Up to now, a light quilted jacket had sufficed.

I looked up and down Lyall Street, pleased at the number of shoppers who strolled along the main thoroughfare of Oriole Point. And on a Thursday, too. The village only held four thousand inhabitants, but our scenic location on the shores of Lake Michigan made us a prime tourist destination, especially in summer. Oriole Point boasted one of the most beautiful coastlines in all the Great Lakes, drawing beach lovers and boaters from around the world.

It was also a favorite spot for Midwesterners. Chicago was a two-hour drive south, and countless others visited from the other side of the state. Not surprisingly, most people who relocated to Oriole Point originally hailed from the Windy City or metro Detroit.

The snow drifted down, covering my wooden planters filled with evergreens and pinecones. If the weather predictions were correct, we were in for

HOLLYBERRY HOMICIDE   29

days, if not weeks, of lake-effect snow. I stuck out my tongue, trying to catch snowflakes as I had when I was a child.

"A word of advice," a mocking voice said. "Standing outside your shop with your tongue stuck out won't drum up business."

I turned to meet the sardonic gaze of Officer Janelle Davenport. That in itself was amazing. We didn't often catch a glimpse of her eyes. Janelle liked to wear aviator sunglasses, even on cloudy days. She once remarked that it made her look intimidating.

"Merry Christmas to you, too," I said with little enthusiasm.

Aside from Chief Gene Hitchcock, Janelle was the only full-time member of our small police department. A competent officer, Janelle had earned the respect of our police chief. However, I found her abrasive, suspicious, and irritating. I suspected she held the same opinion about me.

She gestured at my shop exterior. "Overdecorating as usual, I see."

"Everyone else likes it." To prove my point, I smiled at three women with shopping bags who now approached.

One of them called out, "The store looks fantastic."

Although the three ladies lived in suburban Chicago, all of them kept second homes here. We'd gotten so friendly, we sometimes met for lunch when I went to visit my parents.

"Even prettier than last year." Another woman nodded at my lights, garland, candy-cane decals, and Christmas gift baskets on display in the front window.

"Thanks." I gave them all a quick hug.

"Love your toy soldier, Marlee," the third lady added. "Is it new?"

"Found it at an estate sale last month."

The six-foot-tall nutcracker soldier who stood guard beside my shop entrance had cost a small fortune. But I couldn't resist, even though the red-garbed figure weighed so much, it took four of us to put him into place. I feared I might have a problem finding volunteers to help remove him when the holidays were over. On the positive side, not even the strongest gust from the lake would knock him over.

"You've all arrived at a perfect time. Our free jam tasting begins in ten minutes. And Theo baked crumpets for the event." I gave them a welcoming smile as they trooped inside. I heard Dean call out a greeting before the door closed behind them.

I threw Janelle a smug grin. "Told you. People love my decorations."

"Looks garish to me." Janelle took a sip from her thermos. She spent a lot of free time downing caffeine at Coffee by Crystal, our local version of Starbucks. I marveled that her hands didn't shake.

Since she wasn't in uniform, Janelle must be off duty. I wondered if she was getting her Christmas shopping done. Although I had never seen her with a single shopping bag from a downtown store.

"In town to check items off your gift list?" I asked.

"No. I returned late last night from driving my sons to Milwaukee. My ex has them until Christmas Eve, then he flies them back Christmas morning. And he better not be a day late. Or I'll have him up before a judge before he can say 'Happy New Year.' "

If I were Janelle's ex-husband, I'd make a special effort to have those boys home in time. "It's a great opportunity to finish your Christmas shopping. All the downtown shops are running holiday sales."

She took another sip from her thermos. "I do my shopping online. Who has time to wander in and out of stores?"

"I'm glad not everyone agrees with you." Although I also did a brisk business online via The Berry Basket website. But I didn't blame Janelle. She was a single mom with two sons and a full-time job. Running my business left little opportunity for me to go shopping as well. And while I didn't have children, my talkative parrot and energetic kitten required a healthy amount of attention.

An uncomfortable silence followed.

"My jam tasting starts soon," I said finally. "Come in and sample a few. I have several less common jams, including lingonberry and thimbleberry."

"No thanks. I'm sure they're as overpriced as everything else in your store. I'll stick to Smucker's." But she made no move to leave.

Okay. I'd done my best to be civil. "Well, I guess I'll finish setting up my overpriced jams. Maybe mark them up a dollar or two." I didn't bother to conceal my sarcasm. "Unless you had another reason for stopping by. Maybe you'd like to criticize my haircut."

"Calm down. I happened to be across the street when I saw you putting up more lights. I haven't checked any town ordinances, but you might have exceeded your limit."

From her expression, I sensed she wasn't entirely joking.

"Come back when you find out." I slapped my hands together to warm them up. "For now I intend to enjoy the holidays and my decorations."

"Oriole Point goes mad over Christmas. And that tree is a danger to the public." She glanced at the Christmas tree in the village square.

The town viewed our annual live evergreen as Oriole Point's version of the Christmas tree at Rockefeller Center, which meant it had to be of an impressive size. This year, the committee had been too ambitious. The gargantuan tree fell twice during installation. And had fallen twice since. It towered over the other downtown buildings, leaning precariously with every gust from the lake.

"It is larger than our normal tree," I admitted. "But you know Piper. Anything to top the last event she put together."

"The woman is as much a hazard as that tree," Janelle grumbled.

"Piper might have gone overboard this year," I reluctantly conceded.

A member of Oriole Point's founding family, Piper Lyall-Pierce held a lot of sway. She was also married to the mayor. And as the head of the Tourist and Visitor Center, Piper never stopped finding new ways to celebrate the lakeshore and our town. I viewed her life as an endless series of committees, task forces, and holiday festivals. To paraphrase: this was Piper's town; we just happened to live in it.

"If that tree falls on a tourist, Oriole Point will be

in for a major lawsuit. All because you people can't stop decorating." Janelle's expression turned scornful. "And you're one of the worst offenders. Since you're so crazy for Christmas, I'm amazed you aren't performing in *A Christmas Carol* at the Calico Barn. Seems right up your alley."

"Actually, I am. The Green Willow Players drafted me this morning. They needed an emergency replacement for one of the actors." I shrugged. "I don't blame them, given my name."

She looked wary, as if I were trying to put something over on her. "What are you talking about?"

"Marlee Jacob. Jacob Marley. I'm surprised Suzanne and her amateur theater group didn't think to use me before this."

"I've lived in Oriole Point for nine years, and every year Everett Hostetter plays Jacob Marley. Did Suzanne finally decide it was cruel to expect such an old man to be part of the production? If so, it's about time." Janelle tipped back her head to enjoy a long sip from her thermos.

"His time was up, but not in the way you think. Everett died."

Janelle did a perfect spit take, and I tried not to laugh.

"Are you serious?" she said, ignoring the coffee she had spilled over her jacket.

"Of course I am. He was found dead last night."

"Found dead! Where? How did he die?"

News of Hostetter's death had startled her.

"Gillian, Kit, and I went to the historical museum for the opening of their toy train exhibit. Right before closing, Gillian spotted Everett unconscious on a bench by the restroom. We called EMS, but he was already gone. Since he was in his nineties, his heart probably gave out."

She looked off into the distance and murmured, "Everett dead. *Everett?*"

Then she surprised me by laughing.

"You find this funny?"

Janelle shot me a sharp glance, as if for a moment she'd forgotten I was here. "I guess I thought he'd live forever. The man acted as if he would, too." The hint of a smile appeared. "But he was wrong, wasn't he?"

"He almost did live forever. In five years, he would have turned a hundred." A blast of wind from the lake made me shiver. A four-block stroll down Lyall Street led you right onto the Lake Michigan beach. "How well did you know him?"

Those suspicious eyes narrowed at me. "I don't see how that's any business of yours."

"Seems a natural question, given your reaction to his death."

"My reaction?"

"You acted shocked by the news." I paused. "And amused."

Janelle shook her head. "I don't know why I waste my time talking to you."

Before I could respond to this unfair remark, Janelle brushed past me. She hurried down Lyall Street toward the white clapboard building housing the police station. More than one shopper stepped out of her way.

I had never been able to figure Officer Davenport out. Today she had confused me more than ever. She reacted too strongly to the death of a man who had not been a beloved figure in town. A man I wasn't even aware she knew well.

Even worse, she seemed happy to learn he was dead.

Chapter Four

I didn't often order a cheeseburger at The Wiley Perch. Because the Great Lakes supplied the beach towns with some of the best perch in the country, most restaurants had it on their menus. But no one served up the delectable lake fish better than The Wiley Perch.

Tess Nakamura, my best friend, looked at me with surprise after I ordered a cheeseburger and truffle fries. "You always have the perch strips and smashed garlic potatoes."

"Feeling in the mood for red meat." I handed my menu to the server. "Anyone like to split an appetizer?"

Tess turned to David Reese, her longtime boyfriend. "Breaded Parmesan zucchini with the herb dip?"

David nodded. "Sounds fine to me. Don't know what Marlee and Kit want."

"I never turn down anything with breading or Parmesan on it," Kit replied.

I laughed. "Lucky for him he's dating a girl who's half-Italian."

"Oh, I know exactly how lucky I am." Kit hugged me close.

Tess gave a mock sigh. "Young love. We were like that once, weren't we, hon?"

"Don't listen to her. We still have our moments." David ruffled her hair. "Lots of them."

Tess and David Reese met as students at the Rhode Island School of Design twelve years ago. They'd quickly become a couple, professionally and romantically. The gifted pair of glass artists now owned Oriole Glass, which operated as their studio and gallery. They also owned a home a few blocks from my lake house. Although not married, I didn't know of a couple more committed to each other. David and Tess were my role models when it came to romance. And this time I may finally have chosen right.

I watched with an air of contentment as Kit joked with David and Tess about whether they should order a pitcher of craft beer. It made me happy to see the three of them get along so well. That hadn't been the case with my last boyfriend. Instead, Ryan Zellar preferred spending most of his time at the family orchards, surrounded by relatives. I was one of the few outsiders he and the Zellars had admitted to their circle. A circle far too suspicious of outsiders.

Despite a few misgivings, I surprised myself last winter by accepting Ryan's proposal of marriage. I soon learned I'd been right to have doubts about Ryan as a trustworthy life partner. Our breakup this past summer had been painful, but inevitable. However, I didn't nurse a broken heart over it. At the same time, I discovered I had feelings for a slightly husky investigative detective with curly brown hair and chocolate-brown eyes.

While Atticus "Kit" Holt didn't possess Ryan's movie-star looks, he was far more attractive to me in every way. Even better, his mother had named him after her favorite fictional character: Atticus Finch. Our respective moms would finally meet at Christmas. I was certain the two bibliophiles would get on splendidly.

"Now that we've got our food order out of the way, I want to run something by both of you," Tess began. "David and I came up with a great idea today while we were at the studio."

"As soon as the lake-effect snow began to fall," he said.

Although we could see nothing but darkness and snow, we all glanced out the window beside our table. If visibility had been better, we would have had an excellent view of the Oriole River and the marina. On clear nights, we could also see the stone lighthouse at the end of the river channel, which emptied into the huge expanse of Lake Michigan. Even with all the snow, I caught a glimpse of its red rotating light.

"What's your idea? Something Christmas related?" I perked up.

"Is there anything Christmas related you haven't done yet?" Tess eyed my Rudolph the Red-Nosed Reindeer sweater. "Except for playing Santa and performing in *A Christmas Carol?*"

"Knock one of those off the list. Andrew convinced me to play Jacob Marley in this year's production at the Calico Barn. You know my mother's obsession with *A Christmas Carol.* They'll be thrilled to learn I'm appearing in it. Too bad they won't get here until Christmas Eve. Luckily, our last performance is a matinee that day."

Tess looked skeptical. "You're really in the play?"

"A last-minute thing. Now I have to scramble to learn my lines. Opening night is Tuesday." I glanced up as our server approached with a pitcher of beer. "That was fast. Especially on such a busy night."

The two big dining rooms of The Wiley Perch were packed, and the noise level high. I spotted owner Hiram Wasserman speaking with a table of customers by the bar, while his daughter Amber played hostess. Like every other business in town, the place had been lavishly decorated for the holidays. Being Jewish, Hiram included both Christmas and Hanukkah decorations. I loved the plethora of white lights twinkling along every cornice and window. He must have more fuse boxes than The Berry Basket.

We devoted the next few moments to pouring pale Michigan ale into our pint glasses.

Once I enjoyed my first taste, I asked, "Can I hear about this big idea?"

"David and I thought the four of us should take a trip together right after the New Year," Tess explained. "Things slow down then. It's a perfect time to head somewhere warm."

"How about Mexico?" Kit said. "My sister and Greg honeymooned at the Solmar Resort in Cabo. Greg claims they ate their weight in ceviche while they were there."

"I love ceviche." Tess sighed. "Especially with shrimp and avocado. We should go."

"But not only for the appetizers," David added. "I've heard Cabo is fantastic for snorkeling."

"I'm in. I've never been to Mexico." Scarfing down ceviche while sunning on the beach sounded perfect. Especially in January. I gave everyone a questioning look. "Should we do this?"

Kit lifted his glass. "Cabo San Lucas gets my vote."

Tess grinned. "We're headed for Cabo and a mountain of ceviche."

"That was easy," David said. "Now we just have to coordinate our work schedules."

Tess leaned over the table. "Before we get sidetracked by the trip, I want to know how you came to be playing Jacob Marley."

"Did they choose you because your name is Marlee Jacob?" Kit's eyes crinkled in amusement. "Because you're too young and beautiful to play Jacob Marley."

"And you're not a man," David said. "Just saying."

"The entire Cabot family believes my casting will drum up interest. Not that the play needs it. Tickets always sell out for *A Christmas Carol.* I'm a bit of extra trimming. Like tinsel."

"But Everett Hostetter has played Marley every year for almost a decade." Tess seemed puzzled. "How did they get him to step aside?"

"I'm relieved," David said. "Rehearsals and performances must have exhausted him."

"He seemed in good shape for his age," I said.

David didn't look convinced. "I thought he looked frail."

"That man is indestructible," Tess announced. "He'll bury us all."

"He wasn't as indestructible as you thought," I said. "Everett Hostetter is dead."

"Dead!" David looked almost as surprised by this news as Janelle had.

"Are you sure?" Tess asked.

Kit sent me a curious look. "I didn't grow up in Oriole Point, so enlighten me. Do all residents expect to live an unusually long time?"

"Except for the occasional murder victim," David said in a wry tone.

Kit frowned. "Yes, except for that."

"Everett Hostetter did seem spry for his age," I told him.

"I don't think he missed a single city council meeting," David said. "Same with school board meetings. He always had a grievance to air."

"Gillian told me that Hostetter was the one who wrote all those letters of complaint to her dad's paper. The ones signed 'A Disgruntled Citizen.' "

"That was Everett Hostetter?" Tess asked me. "Although I don't know why I'm surprised. He had such a cold, unfriendly expression. I never saw him smile."

"And he seemed to have about as much personality as our lighthouse," I added. "Not that Everett ever shed much light. A gloomy guy."

I described how Gillian found him at the museum, with Kit adding a few details. "He appears to have been eating gingerbread cookies when he passed," I concluded. "At least he died happy. Assuming Everett Hostetter ever felt happy."

"What was the exact cause of death?" Tess asked.

"I'm guessing his heart gave out." I took another sip of ale. "Kit and the paramedics didn't think there would be an autopsy. Unless the family asks for one."

David looked at Kit. "Why no autopsy?"

"Depends on the circumstances," Kit said. "Under Michigan law, the family can request an autopsy if they believe the death appears suspicious. Relatives usually want answers if a death occurred during a medical procedure. An autopsy also takes place if the death raises legal issues. Often families want to know if death resulted from a genetic problem they should worry about."

"An autopsy must be required sometimes," Tess said.

Kit nodded. "In cases of a possible suicide or murder. Deaths resulting from an injury, fall, poisoning, et cetera. When a healthy child or adult not under a doctor's care suddenly dies. Or if doctors suspect a person died from a disease that might serve as a threat to public health."

"None of which seems relevant to the death of Hostetter." I sat back as our appetizer arrived. "Which means it's unlikely there will be an autopsy."

Everyone spread napkins over their lap and prepared to share the breaded zucchini.

"Better for the family." Tess reached for a zucchini. "An autopsy is not something you want to deal with during the holidays."

"Or ever," David muttered.

"How much family did he have?" I wondered. "Aside from his nephew."

"Anthony Thorne moved to town with his uncle nine years ago," David said. "I remember because they bought the house my cousin Neal was interested in. From what I can see, it's only the two of them. Although I've seen Anthony with a fair number of women."

"What does the nephew do for a living?" Kit asked.

"Financial consultant," David replied. "My friend Craig hired Anthony Thorne several years ago to help him with his portfolio. I asked Craig about it because I considered talking to a financial advisor, too."

"Because we're so rich." Tess giggled. "I convinced David it was a waste of money."

"Was Anthony Thorne any good?" I asked.

David made a face. "My friend said Anthony's fees were exorbitant. And some of the investments Anthony made for him lost a great deal of money. To make things worse, Craig's credit card information got stolen around that time. He suspected Thorne had something to do with it, but couldn't prove it."

Kit and I exchanged troubled looks.

"Anthony can't be the only relative of Everett's," Tess said.

I thought a moment. "I should ask Diane Cleverly. She got quite upset last night over Everett's death. She also implied that she and Everett were on friendly terms. I'm wondering if it was romantic."

"Sweet, kindhearted Diane Cleverly with that stony-faced old man?" Tess shook her head. "I don't believe it. Unless she took him on as a charity case. No one in Oriole Point volunteers for as many charitable causes as Diane."

"The Hostetters aren't from around here," David said. "A long time ago, Everett came to our studio to see if we could repair a stained-glass transom window.

He said it came from his former home in Grosse Pointe Shores. The house he grew up in."

"I remember that window." A dreamy look came into Tess's eyes. "An exquisite piece dating back to 1910. Everett mentioned how every room in the mansion contained at least one window of stained glass. And, yes, he used the word *mansion*."

As everyone in Michigan knew, Grosse Pointe was home to some of the most impressive mansions in the metropolitan Detroit area. A place where the giants of the automotive industry such as Henry Ford built their estates. Premier among the Grosse Pointe suburbs was Grosse Pointe Shores, known as the wealthiest town in Michigan.

"If Everett lived in a Grosse Pointe mansion, he probably had a pile of money." I turned to Kit. "Maybe the police *should* request an autopsy. To make certain there was no foul play."

"Even if he was rich," Kit replied, "there's nothing suspicious about his death. The man was ninety-five."

"Rich elderly people do die," Tess said in a stage whisper. "They're not all murdered."

I sighed. "You're right. Too many recent murders have skewed my thinking. If I'm not careful, I'll start sounding like Gillian. She believes the play is cursed."

"That was true four years ago when Carl Fitzbaum played Ebenezer," David remarked. "He forgot all his lines."

"Carl finally brought his script onstage and read from it," Tess said. "At one point, the actor playing Bob Cratchit hit Carl on the head with Tiny Tim's crutch."

Kit laughed. "I'm sorry I missed that production."

"Me too," I added. "I might like a little slapstick to go with my Dickens."

"Especially this year, with our perennial Jacob Marley dead," David said.

"A shame he didn't get the chance to take his final curtain call." I did not pretend to mourn the passing of Everett Hostetter. Still, any death is a loss. I now understood Gillian's shock and dismay. Everett hadn't expected to die last night. A disturbing reminder that death could come for any of us without warning.

Kit speared a zucchini. "His nephew said he'd inform the rest of the family."

"Whoever they may be." I enjoyed my own Parmesan zucchini. "And it's not beyond the realm of possibility that one of those relatives might request an autopsy."

"If so, I'll be the first to hear about it," Kit said. "The Hostetter death has been assigned to me. Not that I expect there to be anything to do but fill out the report regarding the death."

"Why wouldn't Hostetter's death be assigned to the Oriole Point police?" I asked. "The historical museum is within town limits. Doesn't it fall under their purview?"

"Let's just say there's a conflict of interest involving your local police."

This startled me. "What do you mean?"

"It's Officer Janelle Davenport." Kit hesitated before adding, "She's Everett Hostetter's daughter."

Chapter Five

"Tie me kangaroo down, sport!"

I looked up from the script of *A Christmas Carol.* "Be quiet, Minnie. Mommy's trying to learn her lines."

I was also trying to figure out how none of us had realized Janelle Davenport was Hostetter's daughter. How frustrating to learn Kit had no further information on the subject.

"Be quiet!" came Minnie's reply. "I'm the boss. Kiss, kiss."

With a resigned laugh, I got up from the loveseat and went over to the perch where my voluble African grey parrot held court. Smoothing her feathers, I planted a kiss on her beak.

She responded with several lip-smacking noises, then added, "Give me cashew."

"You've had too many this morning." I tapped the silver dish of raw vegetables attached to her tall perch. "Eat a few veggies first."

Minnie let loose with a catcall whistle, her attention drawn to the black kitten who pounced onto the cushioned seat of the bay window. "Kitty, kitty, kitty!" Minnie exclaimed before doing her best imitation of Panther's meow.

I returned to my comfy seat on the loveseat, determined to focus on the play.

Andrew lied when he said I only had thirty lines. I counted fifty-seven. Some lines long enough to qualify as paragraphs. I hoped to memorize half of them before rehearsal tonight. So far, I had committed ten to memory. But I'd forgotten how distracting my animal companions were. Almost as distracting as the revelation that Hostetter was Janelle's father.

Minnie broke my train of thought by imitating the ringtone of my cell phone.

She was always at her loudest and most talkative in the morning. I adopted Minnie in June from an Australian family moving back to Brisbane. I quickly fell in love with the avian charmer and couldn't imagine parting with her. However, Minnie required a lot of attention and endless cashews. Along with a cautious eye to make certain she didn't hop about the house pulling on loose threads of fabric. If I didn't keep her wings clipped, heaven knows the damage she'd inflict on the house—and my Christmas trees.

While Panther didn't speak, the kitten made up for it by batting around toys, knocking down ornaments, and climbing up the drapes bordering my bay window. I found the kitten right before Halloween— fittingly in a pumpkin patch. Orphaned after his mother had been killed, he'd been left to run wild. How could I not take this adorable fur baby home? But I couldn't break him of the habit of playing with every ornament on my trees. Since I put up four artificial Christmas trees, this provided lots of feline activity.

And next week I had an excursion planned to the tree farm to chop down a live Scotch pine. I knew five decorated trees might seem excessive, but I had a house big enough to hold far more. And I waited all year to smell the delectable fragrance of a fresh pine tree in my house.

For the moment, all my trees were safe as Panther stared out the window. I wasn't sure at what. Lake-effect snow had fallen all night, and was predicted to continue through the weekend.

After taking a big sip of French-roast coffee, I announced, "Now back to the script."

There had been no need for Andrew to give me a script. When I compared it to my battered old copy of *A Christmas Carol*, I realized the theater group had lifted every line of Jacob Marley's from Dickens's story. At least no one could criticize the playwright.

As Minnie launched into a chorus of "Jingle Bells," I focused my attention on the longer passages of my part. I closed my eyes and recited, "'It is required of every man that the spirit within him should walk abroad among his fellow-men, and travel far and wide; and if that spirit does not go forth in life, it is condemned to—'"

A high-pitched bark broke my concentration.

"Marlee, where do you put *obraztsy kraski*?"

I counted to ten before turning my attention to Natasha Rostova Bowman, my Russian friend and current houseguest. She stood in the entrance to the living room. At her feet sat Dasha, her Yorkshire terrier, who added an affronted bark.

Although I didn't speak Russian, living with Natasha for the past two weeks had acquainted me with her most often-used phrases.

"I do not know where your *obraztsy kraski* are. And they're called paint swatches in English. You need to refer to them as that when you get around to speaking to the painters."

"*Obraztsy kraski.* Paint swatches." She rolled her large almond-shaped eyes at me.

Despite the early hour and that she still wore silk pajamas and a fleece robe, she was already in full makeup. It was like living with a Kardashian. "Painters do not care as long as I pay them. So where is big box of swatches?"

Minnie's singing grew louder, almost drowning out Dasha's barks. I would never learn my lines if this kept up.

"I don't know. You're the one always carrying them around. You and your friend with the fanciful decorating ideas."

"Katrina is not fanciful." She gave me a suspicious look. "What is *fanciful*?"

"Unrealistic, exotic, too imaginative."

"Imagination is good! Exotic, too. People say I am exotic." She tossed back her lustrous mane of dark brown hair. If Natasha had a better command of the English language, Suzanne would probably cast her as the Ghost of Christmas Past. "I cannot have person with dull ideas help me with Peacock. It will be best spa in Michigan."

I didn't know if her spa would be the best, but it might be the most costly. For the past few months, I'd heard constant updates about the construction, design, and decoration of Peacock. I thought she should rename the spa Versailles.

"Then you may want to hire someone focused only on decorating. Not a former Miss Washington/feng shui specialist/psychic medium."

Natasha held up a manicured finger. "Is good to be so many things. Shows she is *raznostoronnly*. What you call versatile. You must be *raznostoronnly* to win beauty contest. I know this. I am beauty queen, too."

Natasha never tired of reminding people of her beauty pageant past. It wasn't vanity. She regarded her contest victories to be as crucial to her success as other women might regard a college degree. And who could blame her?

At twenty, she came to Chicago to compete in Miss World. A wealthy older man on the judging panel happened to be in the market for a trophy wife. That man was Oriole Point native and real estate magnate Cole Bowman. Cole and Natasha married soon after, but the union turned as sour as Cole's business dealings. The larcenous Cole moved back to Oriole Point with his young wife, where he was subsequently murdered. This left twenty-eight-year-old Natasha a wealthy, beautiful, and merry young widow. One who planned to open a spa called Peacock. A venture that had so far required about five hundred paint swatches to agonize over.

"And Katrina has experience in decorating," Natasha went on. "She once have boyfriend who own spa in place called the Head of Hilton."

"Hilton Head," I corrected her.

"This Head of Hilton," she said, ignoring my comment, "is resort for rich people. And he ask Katrina to use feng shui to design their salt caves."

"Impressive." I'd heard about Katrina May's qualifications before, but I still didn't know what a salt cave was. "Although I'd rethink her plan for the cactus scrub room."

Katrina had advised Natasha to turn one of the treatment rooms into a facsimile of the Mojave: a sand-strewn floor, potted cacti, and lighting fixtures that rivaled the wattage of a baseball stadium.

"A cactus scrub room must be like desert," Natasha insisted. "One hundred degrees! For clients to sweat out *primesi.*"

I assumed she meant "impurities". "Make sure clients don't sweat out every drop of moisture in their bodies. Or you'll need to revive them when the scrubbing is done."

She waved my comment away. "I now must change color of cactus scrub room. Is too orange. Is why I need my *kraski.*"

"Try the sunroom. That's where your moving boxes are. And I made coffee about ten minutes ago. It's strong today. I need the caffeine to help me memorize my lines." I held up the script, hoping she'd get the hint.

"*Nyet.* I only drink tea on mornings it snows." She gestured at the white vista outside the expansive bay window. The snowfall had finally slowed down.

"What does tea have to do with snow?" I asked.

But Natasha and Dasha were on their way to the kitchen. Panther scampered after them. The kitten adored Natasha's Yorkie. Even if it did take a week of cautious observation before Panther regarded the small dog as a playmate rather than a threat.

I loved Natasha. After Tess, I regarded her as my closest friend. Naturally, I invited her to stay with me after she sold her house before her luxury condo was ready to move into. Only I didn't think it would take the entire month of December. At times it felt as if she and Dasha had been underfoot for months.

I began to repeat, "'It is required of every man that the spirit within him should walk abroad among his fellow-men, and travel—'"

The doorbell rang. Dasha raced out of the kitchen, yapping at the top of her lungs. Minnie responded with her favorite line: "Whassup?"

"Whassup indeed," I muttered.

Who could be at my door unannounced at nine in the morning? During a snowstorm, no less. Whoever it was deserved to have me greet them in my Snoopy flannel pajamas and Santa socks. Although maybe one of my neighbors wanted to borrow a snow shovel or needed a jump start for a car battery.

Instead, Oriole Point's power couple, Piper Lyall-Pierce and her husband, Lionel, stood on my covered porch. I swung open the door.

"Hi, guys. Did we have an appointment no one told me about?"

Ignoring my question, Piper stamped the snow from her boots. "Don't keep us standing out here. It's freezing."

"Sorry for showing up on your doorstep like this," Lionel said as I ushered them inside, "but my wife insisted we come straight over after breakfast."

As Dasha's yapping reached frenzied heights, Piper removed her gloves, teal-blue coat, and cashmere scarf. Piper flung the outerwear at me as if I were a servant in *Downton Abbey*.

"Stop barking this minute!" she commanded Dasha.

The Yorkie turned tail and ran. No one had imperious down like Piper. Trying to be a gracious hostess, I hung their coats in the foyer. Then led them into the living room.

"You have far too many Christmas trees, Marlee," Piper announced with disapproval.

"I have plans to bring in another. A real one. And at least none of my trees are the size of a redwood." I gave her a pointed look.

She pretended she hadn't heard me.

"We wanted to see you before you opened the shop for the day," Lionel explained as Piper took her customary seat on the glider rocker.

I gestured for Lionel to sit on the adjacent leather club chair.

"I'm not going in until noon. Gillian's on the schedule to open. Would you like coffee?"

"Don't trouble yourself." Lionel still looked sheepish about their visit.

"Coffee would be perfect," Piper said. "Cream, one sugar. Stevia, if you have it. Lionel prefers tea. Earl Grey, cream, no sugar."

Before she put in a request for Belgian waffles, I hurried into the kitchen. I was now grateful Natasha drank tea on snowy days. Her electric teakettle had just finished heating the water.

"We have guests." I noticed Dasha had taken refuge beneath a stool at the kitchen island.

Natasha frowned. "Who comes to house?"

"Piper and Lionel."

"I like Mayor Lionel." She lifted the lid of the cake dish on the counter and removed a slice of cranberry coffee cake. "He has manners of *dzhentl'men*. But Piper act like czarina. And hair dye is wrong for skin. Make her look like scarecrow."

"Keep that observation to yourself." I removed a few slices of coffee cake, too.

"That took long enough," Piper remarked when I returned.

Even though I regretted answering the door, I handed them their cups of tea and coffee, then pointed at the tray of pastries I'd placed on the coffee table. "Theo made extra coffee cake for the shop yesterday. He knows how much Kit loves it. And this cranberry-cream coffee cake recipe is the best I've tasted."

"Day-old pastry?" Piper said in a reproving tone. "Is the coffee reheated, too?"

"Say one more rude thing and I'm kicking you out." I smiled. "Just you. Not Lionel."

Piper knew me well enough to keep quiet. I was one of the few people in town unimpressed that the Lyall family had founded Oriole Point. Or that she was the richest person I knew, her fortune increasing ten years ago when she married Lionel Pierce, a wealthy retired executive. She wasn't normally this obnoxious. Entitled? Yes. But something must have happened to amp up her patrician attitude. I wondered if her upcoming fiftieth birthday played a factor.

I sat on the loveseat, letting them enjoy the first sips of hot coffee and tea. Lionel handed a fork and dessert plate to his wife, then did the same for himself.

Minnie launched into her Beach Boys tribute, "Ba-ba-ba ba-ba ba-ran," as Piper took a cautious nibble of cake. A delighted smile followed.

"Good, isn't it?" I asked her.

"A shame Theo refuses to work for me. My personal chef has no talent for pastries."

My mouth fell open. "You tried to hire Theo away from The Berry Basket?"

"I may have broached the topic. The young man should be commended for his loyalty."

"Unlike you, Piper, I thought we were friends."

"We are. Why else do you think Lionel and I came here this morning?"

"Is this about the Hollyberry Festival? Please don't ask me to volunteer for anything else. Not with the play to study for."

Lionel finished his bite of cake before saying, "We haven't come here for that. And the town appreciates your offer to serve free hot chocolate at your booth in the park."

"Berry-flavored hot chocolate. My store doesn't stock plain hot cocoa. But free samples are a nice way to introduce people to berry cocoa." I grew suspicious. "If you're not here about the Hollyberry Festival, what's the problem?"

Piper answered with another question. "Is your detective boyfriend upstairs?"

"No. Kit's at his apartment in New Bethel."

She looked disappointed. "I assumed he often spent the night here."

"Once or twice a week. But he spends a lot of time

in New Bethel, where the county sheriff's office is." I glanced at the script beside me. At this rate, I'd never learn my lines. "Is one of you going to tell me what this is all about?"

Lionel cleared his throat. "Everett Hostetter."

"What about him?"

"It appears he had something to do with an associate of your houseguest," Piper said. "Is Natasha here?"

"She's in the kitchen."

The sound of the microwave being turned on confirmed this.

"And Katrina May?" Piper asked. "Is she a houseguest, too? I assume that's her car in the driveway. No one else I know drives a red Miata with a SPIRITED vanity plate."

"Katrina felt anxious about driving back to Grand Rapids in the snowstorm, so I asked her to spend the night."

"Where is she now?" Piper looked around the room, as though she expected to glimpse Katrina behind one of the Christmas trees.

"Upstairs bathroom. If Minnie stops singing her fifth chorus of 'Barbara Ann,' you'd hear the water pipes rattling."

Lionel leaned forward. "Do you keep anything valuable upstairs?"

"Designer bags?" Piper asked.

"Where do you keep your jewelry?" Lionel said.

"Are you serious?"

"Are you serious?" Minnie repeated my question. This was how my parrot had acquired a vocabulary of three hundred words. With more added every time someone spoke in her presence.

"You know I don't own anything worth stealing," I continued, "except for this house."

My three-story Queen Anne overlooking Lake Michigan with its own private beach was indeed valuable; the house and lakeside property were worth over a million dollars. Not that I would ever sell it. My great-great-grandfather Philip Jacob built the house in 1895 as a wedding gift for his bride, Lotte. He even painted it robin's-egg blue, her favorite color. The family had kept it the same color since then. Just as we had cherished and maintained every turret, balustrade, and gable. It had been handed down to a Jacob female for generations. I was the latest grateful recipient.

"What is this all about?"

"Ms. May is a fraud," Piper informed me with an air of satisfaction.

"How so? When Katrina was still a teenager, she won Miss Washington. She became a certified feng shui consultant in her twenties. And she has an office in Grand Rapids where she gives psychic readings."

Piper snorted. "Quite the Renaissance woman. Does she plan to add juggler to her résumé next year?"

"You thought highly enough of Katrina two months ago when you asked her to give a feng shui workshop at your Harvest Health Fair."

Piper's sharp gaze grew steelier. "I had an entire week of workshops to fill. And Councilwoman Mims suggested I ask Katrina to take part. But I never even spoke to the woman. My assistant contacted Katrina to arrange for her appearance."

"I didn't hear any complaints about Katrina's workshop. That's how Natasha met her. Natasha hadn't even heard of feng shui before then. Now Natasha is almost as fascinated with feng shui as she is with interpreting her dreams every morning."

"I'm not surprised Russian Barbie would be taken in by that woman."

"I don't get this, Piper. What is your beef with Katrina?"

"We believe Ms. May is not to be trusted," Lionel announced in his booming voice.

I gestured at him to keep his voice down. "Shhh. The pipes have gone silent, which means she's done in the bathroom. Natasha is within earshot, too." Although I heard the TV go on in the sunroom, which meant Natasha had taken her tea and cake to another part of the house.

"She's a fraud," Piper repeated.

"Because of the psychic medium thing? I think she's the real deal. Do you know she sensed I have a ghost in my house?"

"Of all the ridiculous things I've ever heard!" Piper exclaimed.

Lionel shook his head. "Don't be taken in by her, Marlee."

"You don't understand. I've always known about the ghost. All the Jacobs have stories to tell about her. She was my great-grandparents' cook." I nodded in the direction of the kitchen. "I hear Mary in there sometimes. That was her name. Mary Cullen."

"Katrina no doubt encouraged this delusion." Piper frowned.

"It's not a delusion. Besides, Mary's a friendly ghost. Like Casper." I smiled. "When she wants to remind me she's here, Mary makes the pans hanging over my kitchen island clang together. It's rather sweet. Not frightening at all."

Lionel and Piper looked as if I had just disrobed in front of them.

"Katrina mentioned Mary last night," I continued. "She does seem to have an intuitive gift."

Piper pursed her lips. "You can't be serious."

"I am. Some people are gifted with psychic abilities. My Grandma Jacob, for instance. Last night at dinner Katrina gave me a message from Grandma. She told me things only my grandmother or I would know." I had been most impressed, and a little freaked out.

"I never took you for a gullible young woman," Lionel said.

"Gullible, gullible, gullible," Minnie murmured. "Give me cashew."

"I'm not gullible." I didn't bother to conceal my exasperation. "But I am impatient. Please get to the point of this visit."

"I told my wife we should wait before speaking to you. Especially since I was going to see you at rehearsal this evening." Lionel took a sip of his tea. "No need to rush over here."

"I disagree," Piper said. "Marlee should know about Katrina."

My glance fell on the script beside me. "I don't think I should. If I don't learn my lines in time for dress rehearsal, Suzanne's next panic attack will land her in the hospital."

"And I had a panic attack when Ginger Ferris called me this morning."

"Ginger arrived a little early for her annual holiday visit," I remarked.

Ginger Ferris moved away years ago after marrying an executive for Chrysler. Since then she split her time between their homes in metro Detroit, Kauai, and Santa Fe. We only saw Ginger at Christmastime when she returned to visit family. And to remind the rest of us that we were chumps for spending winter in a place where it snowed.

"Ginger is here to attend her niece's wedding," Piper informed me. "When she had lunch yesterday at San Sebastian, she spotted Natasha and Katrina sitting at a table by the bar."

"San Sebastian is the most expensive restaurant in town. Natasha eats there all the time. As you and Lionel do." I finished my coffee. "Although I didn't realize Ginger knew Natasha."

"She knows *of* Natasha," Piper said. "But she recognized Katrina. Ginger called this morning to ask how long Katrina May had been in Oriole Point."

"Why does she care about Katrina?" I asked.

"Because she's a criminal!"

"She's a criminal!" Minnie screamed.

"Quiet, please." I was ready to put my hands over Piper's mouth and Minnie's beak.

"I don't care who hears. You need to know what Ginger told me. And that was before I realized that woman spent the night here. You are far too trusting, Marlee."

"And I trust you have something to back up this accusation."

"We only want to make certain you're not putting yourself in danger," Lionel said.

"Am I in danger?" I asked.

"I certainly hope not. I'd hate for anything to happen to Marlee," said the woman who observed us from the entrance to the living room.

"Piper, Lionel." I waved my hand in her direction. "This is Katrina May."

Chapter Six

"Good morning." Katrina gave us a pageant-perfect smile. "Of course I recognize both of you."

"*Do* you?" Piper asked.

"Everyone knows the mayor of Oriole Point." Katrina nodded at Lionel, who got to his feet.

"Pleased to meet you, Ms. May," he said.

"Can you fly?" Minnie asked of the room at large.

"And your wife invited me to appear at her health fair in October." Katrina turned her attention to Piper. "A shame we never got to speak while I was there. I wanted to thank you for the opportunity. I received several new clients out of it."

"I'm thrilled my fair allowed you to shill for customers." Piper took a long sip of coffee. "A pity I didn't ask for a finder's fee."

"Piper can be so droll." I threw her a warning look.

Katrina shut her eyes. "Don't be alarmed, but I sense an older male figure standing beside you, Mrs. Lyall-

Pierce. I believe he's your grandfather. First letter of his name is *H*. Henry, perhaps?"

"The Lyalls founded Oriole Point and continue to be its most important family," Piper said in a bored voice. "It's hardly surprising you know my grandfather's name."

"He has a message." Katrina cocked her head to one side, as if listening. "He wants you to know he's pleased you married a politician. And one who is African American. It was time for the family to become more diverse."

Lionel raised an amused eyebrow. "The afterlife has had quite an effect on Grandpa," he said to his wife.

"Indeed," Piper said. "My grandfather had little use for anyone who wasn't a descendant of a founding Dutch family. This change of heart is illuminating."

"The Other Side is a more evolved place," Katrina said.

"Apparently." Piper sniffed. "He also had no use for hucksters who pretend to speak with spirits."

"I don't pretend." Katrina's smile didn't waver. "But the spirits of your ancestors tell me that you do."

"Tell your ancestors it's a shame they never taught you manners," Piper shot back.

Katrina appeared not to hear her. "Your mother asks forgiveness for the harsh words she spoke to you the week before she died."

Piper's mouth fell open.

"It is something she regrets. She was angry because you broke off your engagement to the man she thought perfect for you. A man with a name that sounds like Jonathon, or Jefferson."

"Enough!" Piper visibly trembled. "How dare you mention my mother!"

I held up my hand. "I don't think we need more messages from the Great Beyond today."

Time to derail this meeting before Piper turned into a real-life version of the autocratic Miranda Priestly from *The Devil Wears Prada*. As someone named after a Dickens character, I often equated people with their fictional counterparts. Miranda Priestly seemed a doppelgänger for Piper; even their hairstyles were identical, except Piper kept her stylish bob ash blond, not white.

Then again, although I had only recently met Katrina, it was long enough to realize she could hold her own with anyone, even Piper. Katrina reminded me of Mary Poppins: determined, firm, and gifted in cheerfully ordering people about.

Katrina demonstrated that when she said, "Agreed. Some people are not prepared to hear the truth. Perhaps the mayor's wife will contact me when she is ready."

"I heard you get up while I was still in bed," I said to forestall Piper's response.

"I wanted to brush the snow off my car before taking a shower and getting on the road."

I smiled. "Since you put your coat and boots on, I guess you're leaving now."

"Best to take advantage of the break in the weather. The sooner I'm back home, the better." Katrina pulled a fuzzy cap out of her coat pocket. "I have clients to read for in Grand Rapids this afternoon. I also promised Natasha I'd work out the feng shui placement for her lobby by Monday. And I received a psychic message that must be passed on to my accountant."

"Such a busy girl." Piper's tone of voice revealed that she had recovered from the shock of Katrina's reading. "Is it true you also passed on psychic messages to Everett Hostetter's sister?"

I sat up. "What?"

Katrina took the question with aplomb. "That was a long time ago."

"A little over nine years." Piper's expression turned smug.

"Did you know his sister?" I asked Piper.

"No, but Ginger did. Everett lived in Grosse Pointe before coming here. As did his sister, Sarah, who was married to Dr. Franklin Thorne, an ophthalmic surgeon. Ginger met the Thornes at a charity function, although Franklin has since died." Piper looked at Katrina. "You probably know when."

"He died eighteen years ago, but I met Sarah much later," Katrina answered in a brisk voice, as if she were discussing how best to organize your sock drawer. "And I didn't technically work for her. After she and I became acquainted, I helped her as much as my gifts allowed."

"I assumed you passed on messages from the deceased Dr. Thorne," Piper said. "Did you feng shui her kitchen, too? Maybe reorganize the cupboards."

"Give it a rest, Piper." My patience was growing thin.

"I did both." Katrina turned her stern nanny vibe way up. "After her husband's death, Sarah became a recluse and allowed the house to fall into neglect. I am skilled at reading the energy in a room, which involves far more than reorganizing. There's a spiritual dimension to feng shui, an ancient Chinese practice which goes back even further than the Lyall family in Oriole Point."

Piper glared at her. I didn't need to be a feng shui specialist to read her energy.

"Some people don't understand the benefits of clearing the energy around them," Katrina continued. "Sarah realized her surroundings had allowed grief and fear to overwhelm her. I helped release the negativity in her home."

"Did that include any unwelcome ghosts?" Piper said with scorn.

"Whether ghosts are welcome or not is not my concern. I am only a conduit. When spirits have a message to pass on, I do as they ask."

Piper smirked.

"How did Everett's sister and you meet?" I asked.

"I met her through Everett."

"Are you saying Everett Hostetter was interested in feng shui?"

Katrina waved her hand as if to banish the idea. "He thought it was nonsense."

I felt a bit confused. "Then Everett believed in ghosts?"

She hesitated. "Everett believed in only two things: the power of money. And the existence of ghosts. Of a life beyond the grave."

"Hah!" Piper cried with derision.

"I'm sure you had only a passing acquaintance

with him. Too passing for you to realize where his fears lay."

"Fears?" I asked. "He was afraid of ghosts?"

Katrina sighed. "Aren't most people afraid of ghosts?"

"Not you, of course," Piper shot back.

"Sometimes even I am afraid of them." A shadow passed over Katrina's face. "Ghosts know so much about us."

There didn't seem to be an adequate response for that. "How did you meet Everett?"

"I appeared weekly on a local TV morning program to talk about feng shui. On occasion, I did psychic readings for the anchor team, particularly around Halloween. My segments were quite popular with viewers."

As a former TV producer, I could see how Katrina would be an asset to any program. She was a pretty brunette: articulate, polished, relentlessly confident.

"Everett saw me on the morning show. A segment where I passed on messages from the weatherman's recently deceased father. His office contacted me."

"How did Everett Hostetter become interested in ghosts?" Lionel asked her.

"He had experience with the paranormal. Several prophetic dreams, a grandmother who appeared to him the night she died. His sister and mother were believers, too. Growing up, the family lived in what he claimed was a haunted house."

I sat back. "Wow."

"Exactly," Piper said. "If ever there was a man who seemed immune to the supernatural, it was Everett Hostetter."

"That proves you didn't know him," Katrina replied. "Then again, he didn't allow people to get too close."

"Except for you." Piper suddenly looked like a cat who has caught sight of a bowl of cream. "Ginger mentioned that you were briefly married to Everett."

I dropped what was left of my coffee cake.

Katrina pursed her lips. "This Ginger person had a lot to say about Everett and me."

I couldn't keep the shock out of my voice. "You were Everett Hostetter's wife?"

Katrina nodded.

"How long were you married?"

"Only a year. The age difference was too great for the marriage to continue."

"Yes. A husband who's a century older than his wife might present problems."

"Piper, really," Lionel chided her.

Katrina shrugged. "I understand your shock. Everett was eighty-five when he proposed."

"How old were you?" I asked, still trying to wrap my head around all this.

"Twenty-nine."

I couldn't help cringing.

"It was all rather whirlwind. He proposed on our fourth dinner date. Everett had isolated himself for many years. He wanted a companion." Katrina paused. "I also had abilities he was intrigued by."

Piper gave a harsh laugh. "I'm sure you did."

"I resent your implication." Katrina's eyes flashed with anger.

"How did you come to work for his sister?" I asked before a quarrel broke out between the two women.

Katrina shifted her attention to me. "As I said, I

never worked for her. Sarah and Everett were estranged. Something he regretted. Everett realized I could help his sister."

"With psychic readings or feng shui?" I asked.

"Both. I regarded myself as a peace offering. Fortunately, after some resistance to the shock of our marriage, Sarah welcomed my help. After all, I was family now. I'm glad she did. I convinced her to let go of the negative energy in her home. And her life. The spirit world also had messages for her that I was able to relay."

"If you passed on messages from her dead husband," Piper said with disapproval, "you took advantage of a widow's grief."

Katrina stiffened. "That wasn't how Sarah saw it. Our sessions provided closure and solace. I like to think we became friends. Sarah was as lonely as her brother."

"She did have a son," Piper reminded her.

Katrina raised an impeccably shaped eyebrow at Piper. "Who spent all his time in California. Of course Anthony did finally show up." Her voice hardened. "For her funeral."

"When did she die?" I asked.

"A little over nine years ago. The day before she died, I'd given her a reading over the phone. She seemed fine. The next morning she was dead from a sudden heart attack." Katrina shook herself. "Why are we talking about Sarah? This is not a topic for casual conversation."

She was right. However, I was intrigued by this latest weird connection with Everett Hostetter. First, our village policewoman turned out to be his daughter. Now, I learned he'd been married to the local psychic.

"You didn't keep his name after the divorce," I observed.

"It didn't seem right. The marriage was so brief." Katrina glanced out the window. "I do need to go before the lake-effect snow starts up again." She turned to leave.

"Katrina," I said, "do you mind if I ask when you moved to Grand Rapids?"

For the first time I saw her firm resolve waver. I'm no mind reader, but I suspected she was undecided about whether to be honest.

"Nine years ago," she said finally. "Now I must be on my way."

Her confident smile back in place, she gave us a royal wave and left.

The three of us remained silent until after the front door shut. Minnie muttered, "Katrina, Katrina, Katrina," as Panther scampered into view, batting a plastic ball.

"How strange," I said finally.

Piper looked vindicated. "Isn't she? And I haven't even told you what Ginger said."

Lionel looked closer at me. "I think Marlee is troubled about something else."

"Everett Hostetter and his nephew moved to Oriole Point nine years ago," I began. "Katrina came to the area then as well. And Janelle Davenport relocated from Wisconsin at the same time. It's too coincidental. And I don't believe in coincidences."

Piper looked confused. "Why should we care when Officer Davenport moved here?"

"Janelle is Everett's daughter."

"His daughter?" Piper shrieked as Lionel choked on his cake.

I explained how the death of Everett Hostetter was being handled by Kit and the sheriff's department since one of the Oriole Point police officers was a child of the deceased.

"I don't think I ever saw Everett and Janelle together," Lionel said.

"Were you friends with Everett?" I had a hard time imagining Everett with friends.

"No. But Everett attended every meeting of the city council. Armed with a list of complaints, suggestions, and grievances. Sometimes he stopped by my office with recommendations as to how I could be running the town better."

"And he never mentioned Janelle?"

"He never talked about anything personal."

I looked at Piper, who appeared lost in thought. "You're awfully quiet."

"I'm upset something like this escaped my notice. I pride myself on knowing how everyone is connected in Oriole Point. Somehow I've dropped the ball."

"Don't blame yourself. I bet both of them agreed to keep their father/daughter relationship secret. What's weird is that I was the one who told Janelle her father died."

Piper looked at me with wide eyes. "How did she take it?"

"Shocked at first. With no sign of grief. Instead, she seemed to find it funny. She never mentioned he was her father."

"I wonder who Janelle's mother is," Piper said.

Lionel looked thoughtful. "And I wonder why they kept their relationship a secret."

Piper snapped her fingers. "Speaking of secrets, I haven't told you about my conversation with Ginger. She says Sarah Thorne wasn't the only rich client of Katrina May. Ginger knows of three others, all with stories to tell."

"Since you asked if I had anything valuable upstairs, I assume they accused Katrina of theft."

"One of Katrina's first clients hired her as a feng shui consultant for a vacation home. At the end of the job, she discovered several expensive designer handbags missing, two of them Birkins." An outraged Piper looked down at her own teal handbag; she never left the house without one of her color-coordinated Birkins. For anyone to steal a Birkin ranked high on Piper's list of most heinous crimes.

"Did she call the police?"

"This particular socialite and her husband had a fondness for cocaine." Piper lowered her voice. "And Katrina gave them a psychic reading. She warned them to revert to clean living or the police would enter their lives."

"The couple viewed it as a veiled threat," Lionel said. "They worried if they reported Katrina to the police about the handbags, she might tell them about the stashes of cocaine hidden in the house. Which she must have discovered during her feng shui organizing."

"The woman is a liar and opportunist," Piper declared.

Or she's the real deal, I thought. "Is this all Ginger has on Katrina?"

"Tell her about Robert Swann," Lionel suggested.

"Robert Swann is an exclusive jeweler in downtown Birmingham," Piper said, mentioning a tony city in metro Detroit's Oakland County. "After an attempted robbery in his showroom, he hired Katrina to do her feng shui thing for him. That's how he learned she was also a psychic."

"I don't see the problem."

"She began to give him readings," Piper went on. "And the spirits knew a great deal about his extra-marital affairs. Since Robert was only successful because he married into a wealthy family of jewelers, he couldn't risk losing everything if his affairs came to light." Piper's smile turned knowing. "And after she finished working for Swann, Katrina was seen wearing a number of highly expensive pieces of jewelry."

"You're saying she blackmailed the jeweler?"

"She, or her devious ghosts. And I bet the contents of her jewelry box would dazzle."

"Maybe he had an affair with Katrina. The jewels could have been a gift."

"Don't be obstinate." Piper looked frustrated. "She used her spirits to threaten him."

"Her next client was a rich widower in his seventies," Lionel said. "He had moved into a condo, but didn't want to give up all the stuff from his previous residence. His daughter hired Katrina May to convince him to let these possessions go."

"Let me guess. Something went missing."

"Worse," Piper said. "He died."

I started. "Did the police suspect Katrina of murder?"

"No, he died of complications from pneumonia." Piper seemed disappointed. "But after his death the family learned his will had been altered. The widower collected art. And he left a valuable painting to Ms. May. A Basquiat."

"Interesting." Jean-Michel Basquiat was one of the most famous contemporary American artists of the past fifty years.

"The family accused Katrina of conniving to get the painting, which his daughter was especially fond of. They claimed Katrina passed on messages from his deceased wife, casting his relatives in a negative light. The family tried to prevent Katrina from taking possession of the Basquiat, but she hired an attorney and threatened to sue for slander. Clever girl." Piper's voice held a note of grudging admiration.

"What about Everett's sister? Did Katrina steal from her, too?"

Husband and wife looked at each other. "Not that we know of," Lionel said finally.

"Let me get this straight. Katrina is suspected of stealing handbags. She may have frightened a cheating jeweler into handing over some baubles. And you believe she conspired with a dead wife's ghost to nab herself a Basquiat." I crossed my arms. "Do we also think she kidnapped the Lindbergh baby?"

"After you're done with the sarcasm," Piper said, "I think you'll agree there's something fishy about our feng shui psychic."

I shrugged. "Possibly. But don't be alarmed on my

behalf. I don't own a Birkin or a Basquiat. And my most expensive piece of jewelry came from QVC."

Lionel sighed. "We can't help but be worried, Marlee."

"She's been living in Grand Rapids for years," I said. "Less than an hour's drive away. Have you heard any rumors about dubious deeds committed on this side of the state?"

Piper perked up. "I googled Katrina and found out she's dating Randall Gorman, the man who owns half the radio stations in west Michigan. There are lots of photos of them attending black-tie events along the lakeshore."

"Doesn't surprise me. Katrina's pretty, smart, successful."

"Oh, she's successful. One of the online articles said Katrina met Randall when he and the former Mrs. Gorman hired her to feng shui their lake house. Six months later, the Gormans divorced. The article mentioned there were financial indiscretions on the part of Mrs. Gorman, causing Randall to divorce her."

"And you think Katrina and her spirits told Randall about these indiscretions?"

"Absolutely. Randall is so impressed by Katrina's feng shui and psychic skills, he plans to give her a daily radio show." Piper gave me a knowing look. "For him to be impressed by Little Miss Psychic, she must have given him a demonstration. I bet her spirits revealed his ex-wife's mishandling of their money. Which led to the divorce."

"Perhaps. Only there's more than one explanation

for everything you've told me. But this does all sound a little shady."

Piper sat back with her arms crossed. "*Shady* is the word for it. You need to warn Natasha. I may not think highly of the Russian Tornado, but I don't want to see Natasha robbed by that sly snake."

"Natasha is convinced Katrina has wonderful ideas for her spa. She won't believe me. Not without proof." I bit my lip. "And if Natasha learns we suspect Katrina of being unethical, she might say something to her. Not deliberately. But Natasha is nothing if not indiscreet."

"I wish Natasha would tell her," Piper said. "And she should do it when she fires her."

I ran over the possible consequences in my mind. "I'll advise Natasha not to trust Katrina with too much responsibility. And I'll find out if Katrina is passing on any ghostly messages that might take advantage of Natasha. But I don't want to overreact and put Natasha in the middle of a deadly situation."

"Deadly?" Lionel asked. "Katrina is likely a thief and a liar, but there's no evidence she ever physically harmed anyone."

"All I know is Everett Hostetter, his nephew Anthony, Janelle, and Katrina all showed up in Oriole Point around the same time. And that there's a connection between them."

"So?" Piper asked.

"So I'm wondering if Everett Hostetter was murdered."

Chapter Seven

A row of ducks watched me as I made my way into Holmes Duck Decoys.

Although Gareth Holmes opened his store six months ago, I'd never made the time to stop by. I also had no use for a wooden decoy since I didn't hunt.

I took a deep breath. The building smelled of fresh paint and new wood. A fragrance I wish they could bottle.

For a moment, I wondered if ducks were the only occupants of the shop until a door opened near the back, revealing Gareth Holmes. He held an unpainted wooden duck, examining it with concern.

"Hi, Gareth," I said softly, not wanting to startle him.

He looked up with a wide smile. "Hello there, young Marlee."

Gareth invariably greeted me with "young Marlee", which I found rather sweet.

As he frequently did, Gareth wore a rumpled flan-

nel shirt tucked into faded jeans held up by suspenders. Those jeans were tucked into scuffed work
boots. In addition, Gareth boasted a Santa-like girth,
the shirt stretched tight over his stomach. As Dean
had noted, Gareth's cheeks were ruddy above his
thick, white beard. I expected him to greet me with a
"Ho, ho, ho."

"Are you here on OPBA business?" He set the
duck decoy beneath the counter.

The town shopkeepers belonged to the Oriole Point
Business Association, otherwise referred to as OPBA.
As members, Gareth and I attended the monthly meetings. I was also membership secretary, which involved
more paperwork than I cared for. I knew Gareth pri-
marily from these meetings. But we were no more
than casual acquaintances.

"No, I had a favor to ask. Also I've never been inside your shop." I scanned the shelves of painted decoys and framed photographs of ducks on the walls.
"You have ducks in here I haven't seen in Michigan.
And I'm a member of the Lakeshore Birders."

He winked at me. "I bet you thought I spent all my
time carving mallards."

"I assumed you'd sell bufflehead decoys, too.
Along with goldeneyes, scoters, greater scaups, ring-
necks. But you have duck species not native to the
state."

"My customers come from all over the country,"
he said with a note of pride. "Sportsmen who appreciate the craftsmanship of a handmade decoy. Here,
let me show you."

Since I knew they were used to lure actual birds
into the line of fire, I didn't mention that I found

duck decoys disturbing. However, I didn't want to dampen his enthusiasm.

Luckily, the shop was small, with only so much room for all those decoys and Gareth's portly figure. I listened for the next fifteen minutes as he gave me the name and details of each duck decoy, down to what shade of paint he had used.

When he began to describe the type of ribbon epoxy he recommended for the duck eyes, I broke in, "I don't want to take up your time, especially in the middle of a workday. I haven't even been to my own store yet. Gillian opened at ten, but I promised to be there by noon."

In the distance, the tower clock above city hall began to toll the eleventh hour. I couldn't help but smile with relief at the gentle sound. The previous bell in the tower had been louder than Big Ben. After its destruction this past autumn, the town insisted the new bell be less deafening.

He gestured at his empty shop. "Until the snow slows down, neither of us is likely to see many customers."

Although the lake-effect snow had stopped earlier, allowing Katrina to head back home, the white stuff was back. Not blizzard strength, but strong enough to discourage cautious drivers.

"I still have to get ready for this weekend's Hollyberry Festival." My glance fell on one of the festival posters Piper's assistants had distributed around town.

"I heard The Berry Basket is serving free hot chocolate at the Hollyberry Market." His smile turned even more benevolent. "That's kind of you."

This year Piper added an open-air market to the long list of festival events. For five hours on Sunday, local vendors agreed to sell winter-themed products in the park along the river.

"It promises to be a busy weekend," I said. "Theo and I also have to decide on recipes for Christmas cookies. All berry flavored, of course."

Gareth chuckled. "Of course."

"And I ordered lanterns to put outside for the festival. They arrive today. As soon as they do, I'll paint berries on them. Finally, Dean and I agreed to take part in the street caroling Sunday evening. When the festival mercifully comes to a close."

"You're more ambitious than I am." Gareth returned to the front counter. "I'm content to carve my decoys and run the shop. Even then, I'm open shorter hours than everyone else."

"Actually, that's why I'm here. You always close at three o'clock, even on weekends. I assume you're doing the same for the festival."

"That I am." Gareth sat down on the metal stool behind the counter. Above him hung a large glossy photograph of a merganser duck. "Most of my regular customers are sportsmen or wooden-decoy collectors. All early risers. I don't see much traffic later in the day."

"I wondered if you'd be willing to come to The Berry Basket on Saturday after you close. Just for an hour or two." I hesitated before going on. "You see, I bought a Santa suit and can't think of anyone in Oriole County who looks more like jolly Saint Nick than you. There will be children here because of the parade. Since you resemble Santa so much, I thought it would be fun if . . ." My voice trailed off. This may have been too presumptuous even for me.

Gareth looked puzzled. "I look like Santa?"

Oops. Did the man not know he was Santa's twin? Embarrassed, I opened my mouth to speak, when he burst into a hearty laugh.

"I'd love to play Santa for the kids. And it won't be the first time."

"Really?"

"I've dressed as Santa every year since I retired. In fact, I only came alive after I retired and met my wife. That's when we moved to South Haven."

South Haven was another beach resort town along Lake Michigan, just a few miles south.

"My wife was delighted when the local VFW asked if I would play Santa at their annual Christmas party for kids. Didn't see how I could refuse."

"I'm sorry. I didn't know you had a wife."

"Annette died last year." His voice grew husky. "After that I relocated to Oriole Point. Too many memories in South Haven. And I've always found Oriole Point charming. That's when I also decided to make a little money woodworking. It's been my hobby for decades."

Although his shop did fit in with our eclectic commercial mix, I marveled he had enough customers to keep it solvent.

He picked up the decoy he'd held earlier and gave it a gentle pat. "Besides, I don't do it for the money. I like working with my hands and watching ducks. Not a bad way to spend the rest of my life. And Oriole Point is special. A perfect place for a fresh start."

"Oriole Point does have a quality about it that few

places do. The energy here embraces you." Katrina probably knew the feng shui explanation for it.

Gareth suddenly looked taken aback. "I can't believe I've had you here all this time and not offered you anything. I keep a half-gallon jug of apple cider in my fridge." He pointed at the back room. "Also have a plateful of Christmas cookies brought to me by a widow in town. She's taken a fancy to me. Given my figure, she must hope the cookies will grab my attention."

"No thanks. I'm sure I'll eat my weight in cookies by the time Theo and I bake our batch for this weekend."

"You wouldn't believe the people who stop by to drop off cookies. I must look like I enjoy them. I might have to cut back before I burst out of my suspenders." He took a bag of cashews from beneath the counter. "Can't see myself giving up cashews though. Not even to slim down my Santa figure."

"Speaking of that, I'll bring the Santa suit over today. I'm confident it will fit. And thank you for agreeing to play Santa for me."

"My pleasure. And I mean that. Who doesn't love Santa Claus?"

I chuckled. "I have a hard time seeing you in a business suit. Where did you practice law before you retired? Chicago? Grand Rapids?"

"The Detroit area. My law office was in Bloomfield Hills, which means my clients had far too much money. Along with the determination not to part with a cent of it. Sometimes that determination led their accountants to push boundaries."

"Prompting the necessity for a lawyer," I guessed.

"And often the IRS."

We laughed.

"Even with all their money, they still tried to push the limits of the law," he went on. "Many hid assets from family members and business partners. I kept my own clients from going to prison, but it wasn't easy. I was happy to retire. Although I wonder what happened to a few of my greedier clients."

"Still planning tax-evasion strategies with their accountants and lawyers?"

"No doubt." He opened the bag of cashews and held it out.

I took several. Like Minnie, I found it hard to resist cashews.

"I do know what happened to at least one of my clients before he died." Gareth tossed back a couple cashews. "Since you live here, you probably knew him."

"Who?"

"Everett Hostetter."

Five minutes later I had pulled up a spare stool to the front counter, a glass of cider in one hand, a fistful of cashews in the other.

"Please tell me what you know about Everett," I said.

"You look serious. Did the two of you have a disagreement?"

"I didn't know him personally. But after Gillian and I found his body at the museum, I've discovered some strange coincidences."

I quickly related what I had learned about Everett's sister, Janelle, and Katrina May.

Gareth's expression grew worried.

"Don't you find it odd that Everett, Janelle, Anthony, and Katrina all moved here nine years ago?" I concluded. "Katrina said his nephew lived in California before this. Janelle moved here from Milwaukee. Katrina relocated from Detroit. What brought all of them to the area at the same time?"

He crossed his arms over his belly. "I don't know about the others, but Everett moved to Oriole Point because of Diane Cleverly, the curator at the historical museum. And I was the one who told him that she was here."

"When?"

"Shortly after I moved to this side of the state. There was an article in one of the local papers about your historical museum, and I saw Diane's name. I knew Everett would be interested."

"Were Everett and Diane a romantic couple?"

"Depends on how you define romance. And I don't know how Diane viewed the situation. In 1970, Everett took over a steel company. Diane was hired to archive the corporation's documents."

"Diane mentioned it was her first job after earning a PhD."

"She was almost twenty years younger than Everett and made a strong impression. Everett always spoke of her highly. Something he did with few others. Back then, there weren't a lot of women in the workforce with PhDs. He admired her."

"Because she was an early feminist?"

Gareth laughed. "No. Because Diane was an orphan. Raised by the state. Yet she worked her way through university all on her own. With honors, too. He was struck by how nice she was. Kind and generous. Everett didn't understand that."

"Why?"

"He wondered why she wasn't angry and bitter at the world. Like he was."

"What did Everett Hostetter have to be bitter and angry about? I heard he once lived in Grosse Pointe Shores. I assume that meant he was rich."

"Oh, yes. Born rich, too. But he believed his father neither respected nor loved him. From what I know of his father, I suspect that's true. It made Everett cynical. Hard. He thought anyone who tried to be his friend only wanted his money. The same with women. Everett never trusted people, not even me." Gareth ate another cashew. "Only I think he trusted Diane. And she trusted him, which I thought unwise. Everett was not a nice man."

"It sounds like Beauty and the Beast."

"There was even a mansion that looked like a castle. Everett let her get as close as anyone could. I think he was in love with her." Gareth frowned. "As much in love as a man like Everett Hostetter could be."

"I wonder why they never married."

"He did propose. Diane turned him down. She left the company right after. I was there the day she packed up her office. I tried to convince her to stay. She was the only cheerful person in the building. Things got much grimmer after she left."

"And Everett?"

"He got much grimmer, too."

"No wonder he was obsessed with *A Christmas Carol.*

Except Scrooge seems a better fit for him than Jacob Marley. In the story, Scrooge lost his first love as well."

Gareth shook his head. "You're wrong. Scrooge is a changed man in the end. Jacob Marley is the character who died loveless and alone."

He impressed me with his close reading of Dickens. "You're right," I said. "It's Marley whose life was ruined by the love of money. How sad."

"And I was like him for most of my life. It cost me two marriages. I'm still estranged from my children." Gareth sighed. "With reason."

"I never would have guessed such a thing. You're such a jolly person."

"Oh, I was a terrible workaholic. If a person or endeavor didn't put money in my pocket, I ignored them. Thanks to my third wife, I got off that joyless path." He smiled. "It is a shame Everett couldn't persuade Diane Cleverly to marry him."

"Maybe that's why he proposed to Katrina May. Because he regretted losing his chance with Diane."

"Katrina May," Gareth said with an actual curled lip. "How did you even learn about that?"

"Piper told me."

He rolled his eyes. "That woman should work for the CIA."

"It's interesting that he moved to Oriole Point because of Diane. It shows Everett didn't only think about money."

Gareth grabbed more cashews. "Everett had a change of heart after his sister died. He took her death hard. That's when he retired."

"Seems long past due. He would have been eighty-six."

"If you knew what tight control he kept on his business empire, you'd appreciate how shocking it was when he handed over the reins to a new CFO and board of directors."

I thought back to my recent conversation with Diane. "He must have known Diane's husband had passed away by then. Do you think he hoped to make a life with her?"

Gareth looked skeptical. "Everett could only change so much. Certainly not enough to persuade a woman like Diane Cleverly to marry him."

"They appear to have been friends."

"Her good opinion was important to him. I only knew one other person he valued that highly. His sister."

"Anthony's mother?"

He nodded. "The Hostetter clan were a cold-blooded bunch, except for Sarah. A shy woman, but high-strung, nervous. Prone to panic attacks, heart palpitations. Too sensitive for the family she was born into. Luckily, she married a decent man. Although Everett was disappointed she chose a doctor, rather than someone with a portfolio to match the Hostetters'."

"Then Everett and his sister were close at one time."

Gareth considered this. "Sarah was much younger than Everett, and he felt protective of her. Until his controlling instincts took over."

"How so?"

"When Everett offered her husband a position in

the family business, Dr. Thorne turned it down. To make it worse, Sarah took her husband's side. Everett never forgave her for that."

"Seems harsh."

"Everett was a harsh man. It galled him when his baby sister chose love over money. Only he couldn't ignore her. Everett and Sarah owned controlling shares in the family corporation. He hesitated to alienate her too much. Shortly before she died, he convinced her to sign those shares over to him. So he got what he wanted." Gareth smirked. "He usually did."

"Since he moved here with Anthony, I assume he took her son under his wing."

Gareth wore an inscrutable look. "The past is a hard thing to make amends for. Everett tried. In his fashion."

I glanced up at the decoy ducks, their dark eyes cold and lifeless. It appeared Everett had had much in common with them. "As his longtime attorney, the two of you must have spent a lot of time together. And you both retired to the same lakeshore. Did you view him as a friend?"

"He remained my client, never my friend."

"Everett lived with his nephew for almost a decade. There must have been familial feeling between them."

Gareth leaned over the counter. "I suspect it's a case of mutual guilt over Sarah. Anthony was a neglectful son. Everett, an unfeeling brother."

I munched on some cashews. Nine years was a long time to share a house out of a sense of guilt. And we had forgotten another member of the Hostetter family.

"Did you know Janelle Davenport was his daughter?" I asked.

"I knew. More than that, I am not comfortable telling you. Even if he's dead, Everett Hostetter was my client. I must honor client/attorney privileges."

We munched cashews silently for a few minutes. "Is it really fair to say Everett was like Jacob Marley," I said finally, "that neither of them could change their lives? Everett gave up his Grosse Pointe mansion and moved to a modest house in a small village. What if he brought Janelle here? And his nephew. Katrina, too."

Gareth topped off my glass with cider. "Everett's dead. None of this matters now."

"Do you think it was a natural death?"

He spilled some of the cider on the counter. "The man was ninety-five years old. Of course he died of natural causes."

"I don't know. There's something funny about all this."

"Don't even mention the idea to anyone. I'm serious, young woman. You've stumbled into enough trouble this past year. Don't go chasing after trouble now."

"So there is trouble if I go looking for it?"

"There's always trouble around. And Everett Hostetter caused his fair share of it."

"How?"

"It doesn't matter." Gareth threw back his glass of cider as though it were a shot of whiskey.

When he put his glass down, he turned to me with his usual jovial smile. "I think it's time for you to move along to your shop. I have Christmas cards to write."

Except the mood no longer seemed jolly. And I feared the upcoming Christmas might feature far too many ghosts. Not all of them on the stage of the Calico Barn.

Chapter Eight

"I miss Minnie," Gillian announced as a customer left, laden with purchases. "Why haven't you brought her to the shop this month?"

Focused on painting berries on the new white lanterns, I didn't look up from my work space behind the front counter. "In the beginning, I let Minnie stay home because I knew Natasha would keep her company. Now Natasha has grown fond of her. The feeling seems mutual. They talk to each other all the time. The other day Minnie kept repeating '*ptashka*.' " I smiled. "That's 'pretty bird' in Russian."

"Exactly how long is Natasha staying with you?"

"Until her condo by the river is finished." I sat back after painting the last blueberry on the lantern. Only five more lanterns to go.

"I heard the new condo complex might not be complete until spring."

"I have no idea." I wiped my paintbrush on a cloth. "Anyway, I offered Natasha a place to stay until her new home was ready. And I didn't put an expiration date on the offer. I don't mind. My house has three floors and lots of rooms. We're not sharing a small apartment."

"You don't find her a bit much?" Gillian asked. "I like Natasha, but she exhausts me."

"She's no more exhausting than Minnie. Although that Yorkie of hers needs to chill out."

When my streaming-music service sent the first notes of "God Rest Ye Merry Gentleman," over the shop speakers, I hummed along. Time to forget about Everett and why Katrina, Anthony, and Janelle followed him to my beautiful village. I had lanterns to paint, customers to wait on, another tree to buy, gifts to wrap, and a play to learn.

The script lay on the counter before me. For the past hour I'd alternated memorizing lines, painting berries, and cashing customers out. Thank goodness, Gillian was here to handle the pastry and ice cream counters. Despite the snow, we'd had a steady stream of customers. Unlike Holmes Duck Decoys, The Berry Basket offered a wide variety of goods. I suspected foot traffic was light at Gareth's store even in the best of weather.

Gillian straightened the bistro chairs. "Does Kit mind that Natasha is staying with you?"

"Not at all. Kit likes Natasha."

"But the two of you must want time alone. You've only been dating a few months."

"And everything is going great. But I am in no hurry for this to progress any faster."

She didn't look convinced. "You've admitted that

you love him. And it's obvious he loves you. It's only natural—"

"That we continue to enjoy each other's company," I finished the sentence for her. "And take it slow. Don't forget I broke off my engagement to Ryan in August. I have no intention of rushing into anything serious. Not even with a man as wonderful as Kit."

The shop door swung open and four customers hurried in. While Gillian greeted them, I took the lantern into the back of the building, which held my cramped office and the kitchen.

Theo came in every morning before 4:00 a.m. to bake our daily pastries. Because he often left before the store opened, I always found the kitchen gleaming and spotless, as my meticulous baker preferred it. This morning he also left trays of raspberry brownies, triple-berry crumble bars, glazed blueberry muffins, and cranberry tarts.

He'd be pleased to learn Mrs. Berkenbosch purchased the entire batch of crumble bars in the first hour. She pronounced it the perfect dessert for the meeting of her mah-jongg club today.

After setting down the lantern on the stainless-steel counter, I picked up the handle of the next one I needed to decorate. Once I inserted flickering candles, the foot-high lanterns were sure to look festive on the sidewalk in front of the store.

I returned to the shop to find Gillian serving tarts to the ladies, who also sipped today's complimentary tea: blackberry ginger spice.

I opened my little pot of red paint. Strawberries for

this lantern. Strawberries required a bit more attention to detail than blueberries. With a sigh, I looked down at my open script beside me. I had memorized twenty lines so far. And rehearsal was tonight.

A women who enjoyed a tart at a bistro table asked, "What smells so wonderful?"

"This red-currant cranberry candle." I pointed at the three-wick candle flickering on the front counter. "You're also by our candle section along the wall. You may be picking up on those scents as well."

"Mandarin berry is my favorite." Gillian held up a jar candle.

"Smells like raspberry pie." I dipped my paintbrush into the red paint. "If you love berry fragrance, all our soaps are berry scented. Quadruple-milled, too."

This sparked a conversation among the ladies as to which scents they preferred: floral or fruity. Meanwhile, two more customers came in, stomping snow off their boots. When the door opened again, I put aside the paintbrush. With Gillian helping customers and the ladies ready for more tea, I had no time to paint or learn lines.

But when I looked up, Diane Cleverly came toward me.

"Hi, Diane. Good to see you. Here to do a little Christmas shopping?"

Her smile was brief and perfunctory. "Don't have time for shopping this week. Not with several schools scheduled to tour the toy train exhibit before Christmas break."

"Great exhibit, by the way. The kids will love it."

"Hope so." She undid the top button of her coat, then carefully removed her wool hat, covered in snow. "It's coming down again. The snowplows will never be able to keep up."

"Typical lake-effect snow. Once the lake freezes, we'll just have regular snow."

"You say that like it's a good thing." I knew Diane had spent most of her adult life in Lansing, where lake-effect snow was the stuff of rumors.

"Are you okay?" I asked, curious at her troubled expression.

Although I didn't know Diane well enough to read her expressions. The museum hired her while I was living in New York. She'd replaced the garrulous and beloved octogenarian Helen McAvoy, who promptly moved to Naples, Florida.

Because Diane was in her sixties when she was hired, some people wondered that the curatorial position didn't go to a younger person. But I'd worked at the museum one summer when I was in high school, and I knew how little the museum employees were paid. Including the curator. We were lucky to find a retired history professor from Michigan State willing to take on the position.

Diane looked over her shoulder. The women at the bistro tables chatted among themselves as Gillian greeted a couple with young children.

She turned back to me. "I thought you'd like to know the latest about Everett Hostetter."

"The latest? Is this about his funeral?"

"If only I had news of his funeral." Diane looked as if she was trying to control her anger. So much for that serene, unflappable temperament I had credited her with. "I'm sure you've noticed there's been no obituary in the papers for Everett."

To be honest, I hadn't noticed. I didn't make a practice of perusing the obits in the local papers. "So?"

"Anthony should have taken care of the death announcement. After all, the man died two days ago. I realize Everett had few friends." She stopped herself. "Actually, I don't think he had any friends. Only there are basic procedures that are to be followed after any death. Procedures his nephew should have seen to."

She must have no idea that Everett had an even closer relative. His daughter, Janelle.

"I called Anthony to ask about the funeral." Diane's expression turned even more disapproving. "And he has no plans for a funeral or a memorial service. But as soon as I hung up, I placed obituaries for Everett in all the papers."

Over her snow-dusted shoulders, I saw the door open again, letting in another customer. I didn't have time to be concerned about Everett Hostetter, living or dead. "That's his nephew's choice, not ours. Besides, more families than you realize forgo funerals. They settle for a cremation and a memorial service. Maybe a little ceremony for the scattering of the ashes. Some families do online tributes."

"That's another thing. Anthony has arranged for Everett to be cremated tomorrow." Her voice shook with anger. "Barely forty-eight hours after his death."

"Is that unusual?"

"I find it unusual when the family member insists the body be cremated as soon as legally possible. Michigan law mandates a two-day waiting period. Anthony didn't waste any time."

I gave her a closer look. "Even though you claim

he had no friends, you're upset. Maybe he did have one friend. And I'm sure he was grateful for your friendship."

"Everett viewed the world in a hostile manner. It wasn't in his nature to let anyone become close." Her voice shook. "But I do think we were friends."

I hesitated, not wanting to upset her more. "I spoke with Gareth Holmes earlier. He mentioned that Everett proposed to you many years ago. And that you turned him down."

Diane shut her eyes. "That man. He puts himself in the middle of everything."

"I'm sorry. This is none of my business."

"It's not your fault. Gareth is like the last guest at a party who won't leave." She sighed. "Yes, I turned down Everett's proposal. But that was a lifetime ago. Since he moved here, we did spend time together, but always concerning museum business. As a major sponsor of the museum, Everett helped us to stay open all year. And he underwrote the toy train exhibit. The museum and I were extremely grateful for his help."

"He seems to have thought a great deal of you. I don't blame you for being upset."

"It's not right for Anthony to act as if his uncle never existed. Especially since he might inherit everything. If so, I doubt he will be as generous to the museum as Everett."

I began to understand Diane's turmoil. Without proper funding, the museum would cut back on hours, exhibits, and employees.

Diane suddenly realized the shop had filled up with people. "Sorry for bursting in on you like this.

Only I thought you'd like to know I did send obits to the papers. You might want to tell Gillian, too. After all, both of you found his body."

I didn't see how finding a dead body required further involvement. Gillian refused to even mention the incident. And I had no business concentrating on anything but *A Christmas Carol.*

"Anthony resented his uncle," Diane went on. "At times, I thought he even hated him. I'd suspect foul play if Everett hadn't passed away at ninety-five. I still might."

I told myself to let this all go. But that was about as likely as telling Minnie to stop singing, "Ba-ba-ba ba-ba ba-ran."

"I agree there's something strange in all this, Diane. But we have no proof of foul play. Especially without an autopsy."

"Convenient, don't you think? Like the speedy cremation."

"We can't do anything about it. But to be honest, Everett likely died of natural causes. And Anthony is simply a greedy relative who will profit from his uncle's death." I lowered my voice. "If Anthony did kill his uncle, we can't prove it."

"We'll see about that." Diane turned on her heel and marched out of the store.

Great. Now I had to worry about the play. And the safety of Diane Cleverly.

Chapter Nine

My reception at the theater felt chillier than the winter air.

I hoped no one would notice I was late. But when I entered the auditorium, the entire company turned to look at me. Even the actors rehearsing onstage, one of whom was Andrew.

"You're fifteen minutes late, Marlee!" Suzanne Cabot shouted from the stage.

I slunk into an aisle seat. "Please accept my apologies. I couldn't find my script."

Postmistress Jennifer Hamelin, who sat in the row in front of me, looked over her shoulder. "You need to be on time. It's rude to keep the company waiting. I had the good manners to arrive early."

Jennifer had been cast as Bob Cratchit's wife. I hoped she came across warmer in the role than she was now.

"I honestly couldn't find the script."

"No excuses," Suzanne shot back. "Cast members

have been emailed rehearsal times and I expect everyone to comply. You've also interrupted the scene."

"We're working," Jennifer hissed. "Respect that."

I sank down farther in my seat. I felt as unwelcome as Jacob Marley's ghost. At least our mayor winked at me from across the aisle. Although this wasn't a dress rehearsal, Lionel wore a voluminous green velvet robe that could only belong to his Ghost of Christmas Present character.

All the actors were in partial costume. A mobcap sat atop Jennifer's curls, with a plaid shawl pinned about her shoulders. Andrew wore a Victorian blue frock coat over his designer jeans. The fellow playing Scrooge sported a nightcap.

With a clap of her hands, Suzanne turned to the actors onstage. "Again, please. Take it from just after Scrooge says to his nephew, 'What reason have you to be merry?' "

Local building contractor Ed Wolfson had been cast as Scrooge. A longtime member of the Green Willow Players, Ed always appeared in comic roles. Last year he'd enjoyed great success as Oscar in *The Odd Couple*. Ebenezer might prove challenging for him. I also hoped he'd be made to look older for the performance. In his late forties, Ed sported a muscular physique and appeared the picture of health.

As I pulled the script out of my bag, Ed/Ebenezer said in a cranky voice, "What right have you to be merry? You're poor enough."

Andrew replied, "What right have you to be dismal? You're rich enough."

Their exchange told me they were only at the beginning of the play. Therefore my late arrival had made no difference. And the blame for my tardiness lay with Gillian.

She'd made an attempt this afternoon to once more discourage me from taking part in *A Christmas Carol*. When I laughed her fears off, she said no more about it. But as we were closing the shop, she took my script when I wasn't looking. After she left, I found it tucked between two of Theo's cookie sheets.

While I studied my highlighted dialogue in the script, I heard Ed bark in his affected old-man's voice, "Every idiot who goes about with 'Merry Christmas' on his lips should be boiled with his own pudding, and buried with a stake of holly through his heart."

I feared I might feel the same way by the time we got to opening night.

Intent on learning my lines, I jumped when Suzanne yelled, "Marlee! Onstage please!"

I'd done my best to memorize the script during the scenes where Bob Cratchit asked for Christmas Day off, and Scrooge rebuffed the gentlemen asking for charitable donations. The set now switched from Scrooge's office to his bedroom.

With a heavy heart, I climbed the three steps leading to the stage. I should have taken the afternoon off and stayed home to memorize.

As Ed adjusted his nightcap, Suzanne described how a video of Marley's ghostly face would be projected on Scrooge's front door during the performance.

"So you have to film me as Marley?" I asked.

"Don't be silly. We'll use the video of Everett as Marley, as we have for eight years."

"No one will notice that I'm a completely different Jacob Marley?"

"We don't have time for these questions. You're here to act." Suzanne steered me behind the new backdrop rolled onstage. "Stay here until your cue."

"My cue?"

She pointed at the script clutched in my hand. "Wait until the bells in Scrooge's house stop ringing. Kevin will then make loud sounds offstage to sound like Marley banging his way up the steps to Scrooge's bedroom."

I followed her gaze to Kevin Watts, who held a baseball bat. In real life, Kevin worked for the sanitation department.

"When Kevin is done banging, you appear."

"Right after Scrooge says it's humbug." I remembered that much.

Local grocer Stan Lufts interrupted us. "Excuse me, Suzanne. But I have to run to the store. A shipment of Brussels sprouts arrived late. I'm the only one who can sign for it."

She sighed. "As long as you're back in time for your scene."

"Don't worry. Fezziwig doesn't appear for another half hour." He pointed at his cravat and waistcoat. "And I'm ready to go onstage as soon as I return."

"Why is everyone in partial costume?" I asked as Stan disappeared backstage.

"Costumes help actors stay in character." Suzanne fussed with her large blue lapis necklace. She collected statement jewelry with the same passion that Piper did Birkins. "Only most of them are too lazy to get fully dressed for rehearsal. They behave like rank amateurs."

I wanted to remind Suzanne that everyone here was an amateur, including her.

"Let's get through this rehearsal!" Ed bellowed. "I have an early appointment tomorrow to pull out the bathroom sinks at the public library."

Suzanne patted her mass of teased hair. She loved big hair so much, she could have been a Texan. "Temperamental actors," she sniffed, before leaving me alone behind the backdrop.

The scene began. Ed grumbled and said, "Humbug," followed by an audiotape of ringing bells. I heard Kevin grunt and looked over in time to see him whack a piece of plywood on the floor with his bat. Again and again.

Then I was on.

A wave of nerves washed over me. And not because twenty actors stared up at me from the audience seats. I wasn't prepared. In fact, I had a hard time recalling the lines I *had* committed to memory.

Ed Wolfson regarded me with mock horror as if I already looked like his cadaverous business partner. He asked what I wanted with him.

I opened my mouth. Nothing came out.

"What do you want with me?" he repeated.

My mind raced. It was an easy first line. *"Much!"* I finally shouted.

"Not so loud," Suzanne instructed me from the wings. "Scrooge is old, but he's not deaf."

Ed asked for my name in his shaky Scrooge voice.

My lines were coming back to me. "Ask me who I *was*," I said with relief.

We made it through the next few lines without incident. Then Scrooge asked Marley why spirits walked the earth and why they came to him.

I'd memorized this passage only this morning. It was the first long passage I committed to memory. But nothing came to me now. Not one syllable.

"Repeat the line, Ed," Suzanne said.

I still had nothing to say after he did. Ed said the line yet again.

Admitting failure, I looked down at the script in my hand. I read aloud the passage that began, "It is required of every man that the spirit within him should walk abroad among his fellow-men."

Ed said his next line: "You are fettered. Tell me why."

With an air of defeat, I read, "I wear the chain I forged in life" from the script.

How could I not remember one of the most famous lines in *A Christmas Carol*?

My scene with Scrooge—the only scene I appeared in—at last came to an end. Most of the lines belonged to Jacob Marley, and I dutifully read every one of them from the printed page. And in a monotone I hadn't heard myself use since I awoke from wisdom teeth surgery.

Someone in the audience said, "I feel like I'm watching Carl Fitzbaum all over again."

My mood plummeted even more. The other night at dinner, Tess and David said that the worst *Christmas Carol* production took place four years ago when Carl Fitzbaum's Scrooge forgot every line during the performance. And how a frustrated actor hit Carl on the head with Tiny Tim's crutch. If I had that crutch now, I'd clobber Andrew for letting me think playing Jacob Marley would be easy.

After my last line, both Ed and the actors in the audience looked stunned.

"Sorry." I clutched the script to my chest. "I haven't had time to memorize all the lines."

I expected a dramatic response accompanied by hand-wringing and sighs, but Suzanne only nodded. "We expected too much of you. Our mistake."

I felt even worse.

"At least Rowena is up to snuff in her role," Suzanne continued. "She came to the theater earlier today and ran lines with me. I'm grateful she's such a quick study."

Everyone looked at Rowena Bouchet, in the second row. Given her lustrous long hair, it came as no surprise that she had replaced Andrea Shipman in the role of the Ghost of Christmas Past. But who knew our town yoga instructor was a budding Judi Dench?

Rowena blushed. "I have a good memory. Thanks to my daily meditation."

"If only all my actors meditated." Suzanne glanced my way.

"We can do the scene again," I said. "I might remember more lines this time."

"That would not be fair to the other actors. We have an entire play to get through."

Andrew sent me a mock-aggrieved look. I glared back at him.

"But I'd like you to go downstairs and spend the

rest of rehearsal studying your lines," Suzanne continued. "We cannot have a repeat of this performance."

Like a chastised schoolchild, I made my way offstage. I suddenly envied Everett Hostetter. Yes, he was dead. But at least he had an excuse to not act in the play.

Before the barn had been moved to its present location, construction crews excavated a basement, which the hundred-year-old barn now sat atop. But given the bone-chilling temperature down there, I wondered if I'd been sent to the catacombs instead.

Even if I hadn't known the barn had been sold in 1951, the retro basement would have been a giveaway. Someone with questionable taste had covered the walls with knotty pine, and the floor with aqua linoleum. The fluorescent lights overhead made me think of a steno pool in *Mad Men*. An ancient refrigerator hummed loudly by the restrooms. I suspected if I looked inside, I'd find Jell-O molds and iceberg lettuce.

The freezing temps didn't help. I spotted at least six space heaters, all switched on. But it still felt like a drafty root cellar. On either side of the basement ran partition walls, their knotty pine covered with posters from past productions at the theater.

I peeked into the communal dressing room for men, easy to tell from the costumes hanging on the racks inside. The women's dressing room lay directly across. Both had identical long makeup tables and illuminated mirrors. And more space heaters.

Voices overhead reminded me that everyone else in the Green Willow Players knew their lines. I'd be wise to use my time in the basement to study. I sat on one of the chairs before the makeup table in the women's dressing room. Combs, brushes, hair dryers, cosmetic cases, and bottles of adhesive lay scattered about. A pile of wigs sat in the center. I wondered if one was mine.

Determined to focus, I read each line from the script, closed the pages, and recited it aloud. When I successfully remembered the passage that began with *I wear the chain I forged in life*, I let out a sigh of relief.

All I had to do was not allow any distractions to get in the way. Except I couldn't help being distracted by the sound of someone coming downstairs.

"Welcome to the Green Willow Players, Marlee." A statuesque redhead appeared in the open doorway of the dressing room.

I jumped to my feet. "Mrs. Madison!"

The last person I expected to see was my high school biology teacher. Due to her height and flaming-red hair, students had nicknamed Christine Madison "Big Red," after the famous red lighthouse in nearby Holland. Now in her sixties, the retired schoolteacher still used the same copper-red hair dye. And continued to wear her thick mane twisted in a casual chignon.

"When did you join the Green Willow Players?" I asked after we hugged. "I've never seen you in any of their plays."

"Nor will you." She peered at me over her trademark green eyeglasses. "But after I retired from teaching, I felt a little bored. My husband hired Ed Wolfson to remodel our kitchen, and he suggested I help out with the players. Now I take care of the costumes here."

"You're the wardrobe mistress?"

"That makes it sound fancier than it is. I haul costumes out of trunks and put them back at the end of the season. The fun part is hunting through garage sales for old clothes."

"Are you here to give me my costume?"

"In a way." She took a key from her cardigan pocket and handed it to me.

"And this belongs to . . . ?"

"Your dressing room."

I waved at the long table behind me. "I thought this was the women's dressing room. And the men's is along the other wall."

"Two lucky actors get their own private dressing room. I'll show you."

I followed her to the farthest end of the basement, which held two rooms.

She pointed at a half-open door. "That one is reserved for the lead performer. Since Ed Wolfson is Scrooge, it's his for this production."

A quick glance inside revealed a dressing table, chair, and mirror. Scrooge's frock coat and nightgown hung on a wheeled clothes rack.

Christine Madison unlocked the room next to Ed's. "This is yours."

"Why do I get my own dressing room? Jacob Marley only appears in one scene. It makes more sense to give it to the actor playing Bob Cratchit."

"This dressing room was set aside for Everett Hostetter to use during the annual *A Christmas Carol*.

He insisted on having a private dressing room. One he liked to keep locked."

"I heard he was one of the biggest donors to the Green Willow Players. I guess that bought him some perks."

"Not much of a perk. Too bad he didn't use his money to spruce up the basement."

"It does have a *Leave It to Beaver* vibe." I shivered. "A chilly one, too."

"We have a dozen space heaters down here, which must be a safety violation. Please remember to un-plug yours when you leave." She pushed open the dressing-room door and switched on the dim ceiling light. "Here you are."

It was larger than Ed's dressing room, and the cos-tume that hung from a clothing rack could belong to no one but Jacob Marley. Beside it dangled the infa-mous chain I'd be required to rattle. Up close, I real-ized it contained more than simple links. And looked heavy.

"You lucked out. This is the only dressing room with a private bathroom." She gestured to a half-open door near the makeup table. "Another reason Everett claimed it for his exclusive use. Not that he didn't have the right. He's kept the theater company financially afloat for years."

Along with the historical museum, I thought. I took a peek at the white-tiled bathroom, which boasted an overhead light bright enough to illuminate the stage upstairs.

"You lucked out with the costume, too. You're the same height as Everett. And he lost so much weight this past year, the costume had to be taken in. I think that's why Suzanne wanted you to replace Everett. She figured you'd fit in his costume."

"Here I thought it was because of my name." I went over to examine Jacob Marley's pale gray stovepipe pants, waistcoat, and matching Victorian jacket.

"That, too. I know your parents always buy tickets for *A Christmas Carol*. I'm sure your mom will appreciate you performing as your namesake."

"I'm sure she will." I suddenly felt uneasy about putting on the clothes last worn by a dead man. "Has the costume been cleaned since Everett died?"

"No. If it makes you feel better, Everett only wore it twice this year. Once during the fitting when I took it in. And during his last rehearsal." She peered at me again over her glasses. "Suzanne does love to get the actors into costume."

I touched the frock-coat sleeve. The fog-like color brought to mind a phantom. It unsettled me to imagine Everett now as an actual phantom. Perhaps haunting this basement.

"Could I have it dry-cleaned?"

"Don't tell Suzanne if you do. Also dress rehearsal is Monday night. You'd have to make sure it's back in time."

It was Friday evening. The chances of getting the costume dry-cleaned on Saturday were slim to none. I wondered how the costume would hold up in my washing machine.

"Having second thoughts about taking on the role?" Christine asked. "I remember your performance in *Fiddler on the Roof* during senior year. You were such an extrovert. And you never stopped talking with your friends during my class."

I did love to chatter, especially in a class I had little interest in. "Sorry. Biology was not my favorite subject. And I hated the dissections."

"Ah, yes. You set my dissection frogs free." She shot me an irritated look. "You deserved the six-month detention."

I grinned. "I'll let you in on a little secret. My best friend, Tess, set the frogs free. I just took the fall for her."

"Tess Nakamura? That polite, straight-A student who never broke a single rule?"

"She did that day. Tess hated the idea of killing a frog. But afterward, she became so upset about being punished, I told her I'd take the blame." I shrugged. "No big deal for me. I used the after-school detention to do my homework."

"I never guessed." Christine laughed. "I hope she felt guilty about the whole thing."

"I've been using it as leverage for years. Whenever I need a favor, I mention the frogs."

"Still the same Marlee. Pushing limits, taking risks, smack in the middle of everything. So why do I get the feeling you're nervous about taking on the role of Jacob Marley?"

"Maybe it's because Everett Hostetter died two days ago. I feel funny about stepping into his role *and* his clothes." To be honest, I recoiled at the idea of donning that costume. "It creeps me out. I also think it's odd that Everett kept his dressing room locked. Why?"

"Hard to tell. Everett preferred his own company. It amazed me that he wanted to act in the play every year. Although he was good in the role."

That made me even more nervous about my upcoming performance.

She gestured at an old-fashioned rocking chair in the corner, a floor lamp beside it. On the other side of the rocker stood a wooden bookshelf. "He had all that brought here. As you can see, he was quite the Dickens fan."

I scanned the titles. "They're all Dickens's works, or books written about Dickens."

"Like I said, Everett was a fan. By the way, he mentioned that there was a first edition of *A Christmas Carol* on that shelf."

"Is that why he always locked the dressing room?"

"Could be. But why keep it in the dressing room and not in his home?"

Perhaps because he didn't trust the nephew who lived with him.

"All I know is he spent a lot of time alone in this room throughout the year. And not just on rehearsal days, or when business meetings were scheduled upstairs. I think he looked on this as a second home." Christine pointed beneath the makeup table. "It may have served as his office, too. Those locked metal boxes probably contain legal papers."

I crouched down to get a better view of the three metal boxes hidden in the shadows beneath the table. "Has Suzanne contacted Everett's next of kin? All of this belongs to the estate. Which I guess means Anthony Thorne."

Christine made a face. "Suzanne dislikes Anthony.

Every time he attended *A Christmas Carol,* he disparaged the cast during intermission. Especially her performances. And he referred to her as Miss Piggy."

I winced.

"You can imagine how Suzanne reacted to that," she went on. "Last year, things got so bad, she smacked him across the face with a program."

"Looks like I've been attending the wrong performances of *A Christmas Carol.*"

"Things do get dramatic around here. But I don't think Suzanne is in any rush to hand a thing over to Anthony. I doubt he knows anything belonging to his uncle is even in the theater. Except for the costume."

"Anthony didn't visit his uncle at the theater?"

"Oh, no. He only showed up at the Calico Barn when his uncle performed as Marley." Christine gave a rueful chuckle. "I got the feeling Everett forced his nephew to attend, as if he were a child and not a man in his forties. And Anthony fled as soon as the curtain rang down."

"They didn't like each other?"

"Not from what I observed. Strange when you realize they shared the same house for almost a decade. Whenever Everett spoke of his nephew, it was in the most disapproving terms."

This could explain why Anthony Thorne wanted his uncle cremated at record speed. And why he didn't bother with a funeral or even an obituary in the papers.

"Perhaps Everett spent so much time here to avoid being with a nephew he didn't like." I shrugged. "I've heard Everett found fault with everyone. I'm sure he wasn't easy to live with."

"Even I might have found fault with his nephew."

"Why?"

"I learned something about him from my daughter in Los Angeles. Alyssa has been a TV reporter there for almost twenty years."

I had a vague memory of the Madison girl going to California, which was where Anthony spent much of his life before moving to Oriole Point.

"What did she tell you about Anthony?"

My former high school teacher looked like a student caught smoking in the bathroom. "Forget I said anything. It's all in the past. Only Everett died so unexpectedly. Then Andrea was rushed to the hospital with a burst appendix. All of us involved with the play this year feel stressed-out. I'll be glad when *A Christmas Carol* is behind us. In January we begin rehearsals for *Pygmalion.* That can't come soon enough."

I followed her out of the room. She locked the door and handed me the key. I didn't mention that I had no reason to lock the dressing room. Although if there were first editions in there, I suddenly felt protective of them.

"Can you at least tell me if what Anthony did was criminal?" I recalled what Piper and Lionel had told me this morning about Katrina May. "Is he a thief?"

"No." Christine peeked at me again over her glasses. "He killed a man."

Chapter Ten

I'd never tasted soup made from pickles, barley, and beef kidneys. But Kit and I were already on our second bowl and enjoying every drop of it. Along with thick slices of black bread, slathered in country butter.

Natasha had been the perfect houseguest and cooked a pot of *rassolnik*, a Russian version of meatball soup. The kind of soup that sticks to your ribs. The weather demanded some real rib-sticking power, too.

Even though this might be a heavy meal to dig into late in the evening, neither Kit nor I had made time for dinner until now. Suzanne would have blown a gasket if I'd asked to leave rehearsal early, especially since I arrived late. And this afternoon, Kit had been called in to investigate a triple homicide at the eastern edge of the county. A case sure to require his full attention for the foreseeable future.

He did make time to come to my house afterward for a late dinner and an overnight stay. I appreciated the effort. Kit lived thirty minutes away—a much longer commute in bad weather. And this new case demanded he be on duty by seven the next morning. However, both of us needed an evening together. With the Hollyberry Festival kicking off tomorrow, followed by the play, then the holidays, I doubted we'd see each other again until Christmas Eve.

"We've eaten half the loaf." Kit buttered another slice. "Did Natasha bake this, too?"

I swallowed a spoonful of soup before replying, "She did. I had no idea she could cook. I mean, the soup is impressive enough. But to actually bake Russian black bread from scratch! She deserved to be crowned Miss Russia for that alone."

The yapping of Dasha alerted us to her entrance into the kitchen, followed by her mistress. Natasha wore a fox-fur coat, one she rarely took out unless she was on her way to somewhere fancy.

"Where are you off to?" I asked.

"I have date." She placed a matching fur Cossack hat over her long wavy hair.

"It's after ten o'clock. Isn't this a little late?"

"Is Friday night. In Russia, we do not think about going out on date until much later."

"Who's your date?" I asked.

"Do we know him? What's his name?" Kit sounded like a cross between a concerned parent and a police detective.

I felt concerned, too. This was the first I'd heard of Natasha dating since she moved in.

"Alexei Fermonov. Is Russian, like me." She adjusted a dangly gold earring. "I meet him last month. He is architect who builds my condo. Alexei ask me out many times, but I pretend I am not interested. Woman should be hard to get. Like good apartment in Moscow."

I didn't remind her that she had married Cole Bowman six weeks after they met. I hoped we wouldn't have a repeat of that marital fiasco. Or the murder that followed.

"How are things going with Katrina?" I asked. "Are you satisfied with her suggestions?"

"*Da*. The feng shui will bring much good energy to my spa."

"And what about her spirit guides? Does she have messages from them? Messages for you?" If a single one of those messages sounded dicey, I'd pay a visit to Ms. May.

"I do not like the spirits of Katrina." Natasha scrunched up her nose, which made her look even prettier. Don't ask me how. "They bring messages from dead cousin Tatiana. I hate Tatiana! I tell Katrina her spirits must keep quiet. And that Tatiana is not to open mouth again or I will tell Russian witch to put curse on her."

"Natasha knows a Russian witch?" Kit asked in a whisper.

"I'm sure she does," I whispered back.

The doorbell rang. Dasha raced for the front door.

"Is Alexei," Natasha said. "He take me to dinner."

"Where?" Few places were open in Oriole Point past ten, even on Friday night.

"Alexei has chef come to new lake house he build in Saugatuck." She smiled as the doorbell rang again. "He cannot wait to see me."

When I got to my feet, she motioned me to sit down. "*Nyet.* You are not my *mamochka.* Stay. Enjoy dinner I make for you and Kit."

"Thank you again." He ladled another bowl of soup. "It tastes wonderful."

She pointed at the refrigerator. "I also bake *vatrushka* pie. Is greatest pie in world."

As Dasha's barks grew in intensity, Natasha swept out of the kitchen. I followed close behind and peeked around the corner. After she left, Dasha yapped a few more times, then chased Panther up the stairs. I was grateful Minnie was asleep in her covered cage.

When I returned to the kitchen, Kit looked up from his soup. "What's the verdict?"

"He looks like Daniel Craig. Very James Bond, but with Slavic eyebrows."

Kit laughed. "I have no idea what that means. I'm just happy to spend some alone time with you."

"Me too. The next week will be crazy busy." Although the bread and butter still called my name, I had consumed enough carbs and fat for one night. I cleared off my place at the kitchen island where Kit and I sat.

"You're leaving me to finish off the loaf *and* the soup?" He took a big bite of bread.

I kissed him on the forehead. "Natasha mentioned a Russian pie I need to leave room for."

While my carb and fat quota may have been met, I had few restrictions when it came to sugar. In that respect, I was as bad as Everett Hostetter with his crullers and gingerbread cookies.

"Today at the theater I had a conversation with Christine Madison, my old high school biology teacher." I rinsed off my bowl at the sink. "We were talking about Everett Hostetter and his nephew. She passed on something disturbing about Anthony."

"Disturbing how?"

"Her daughter is a TV reporter in LA. And she told Christine that Everett's nephew killed a man. But it turns out he was responsible for a man's death. He didn't actually kill him."

This took Kit's attention from the soup and bread. "What exactly did he do?"

I sat back down on the stool beside Kit. "After his trust fund ran out, Anthony formed a company called Hosborn with Justin Bornwick, an old college friend. They produced gaming consoles and devices. It became quite successful, attracting enough investors to allow them to expand from their hub in LA to Seattle and Portland. Then it fell apart."

"Why?"

"Investors suspected someone was cooking the books and brought suit against Anthony and Justin. Both men denied any wrongdoing, but investigators found a trail of financial malfeasance that led straight to Justin Bornwick."

"Where does the death come in?"

"Justin went to trial, where he accused Anthony of the crimes leveled against him: embezzlement, hiding assets, illegal tax shelters. He swore Anthony planted false evidence to make him look guilty. The jury didn't buy it and sentenced Bornwick to twenty years. The public humiliation and loss of freedom must have been too much for him. Justin committed suicide in his jail cell."

Both of us were quiet for a moment. "What a needless tragedy," Kit said finally. "If you don't want to be sent to prison, don't commit fraud."

"True. But Christine's daughter claims a number of business insiders at the time thought Anthony had been the real criminal. Clever enough to not only get away with the crime, but successfully put the blame on his business partner." I frowned. "A man he'd known since he was eighteen. His friend."

"Most criminals don't have friends," Kit said. "They have associates. If one of them decides to cheat or even kill the other, they look on it as a business transaction. Not a moral one. Also, if the jury found Justin Bornwick guilty, he very well might have been."

"Maybe. But what if Anthony framed his friend?"

"Then he got away with it. Nothing we can do about it now." Kit reached over and caressed my shoulder. "He's not the first greedy SOB to ruin lives over money. And he won't be the last."

Two copper pots that hung above us on the pot rack clanged together. We looked up as they continued to sway.

Kit's jaw dropped. "Is Mary doing that?" he asked in a stage whisper. I had told him about my resident kitchen ghost.

"Looks like she wants to remind us she's here." I reached up to stop the pots from swinging. "She might want to be part of the conversation, too."

"I confess I had a hard time believing you had a ghost that banged pots together. But now . . ." Kit regarded the pots above us with a mixture of amusement and astonishment.

"'There are more things in heaven and earth, Horatio, than are dreamt of in your philosophy.'"

Kit laughed. "Here I thought you'd only memorized *A Christmas Carol.*"

"Mom's an English lit professor. I better know my Shakespeare."

Kit grew serious. "Getting back to this Anthony Thorne, it's possible he is guilty of the crimes his friend paid for. However, it has nothing to do with us. Or Oriole Point."

True. Yet something nagged at me. First, Piper had passed on rumors of unethical conduct concerning Katrina May. Now I learn Everett's nephew might have been involved with fraud. Was everyone associated with Everett Hostetter dishonest? And did that include his daughter, Janelle Davenport? What about the old man himself? Had he been a criminal, too?

If Everett Hostetter did harbor dark secrets, this could explain why neither Anthony nor Janelle wanted a funeral or memorial service. Despite his seemingly natural death, I couldn't help but wonder if a secret had gotten him killed.

Chapter Eleven

I didn't understand why a woman who owned ten fur coats chose to wear my winter parka from Kohl's. Yet Natasha decided to don my only parka to clean off her car this morning. Since buying the black Audi last month, Natasha had treated it with as much loving care as she did Dasha.

"I have to brush the snow off my own car and leave for work!" I yelled from the porch.

She waved a snow broom at me. "I leave, too. Katrina meet me at spa to talk to construction workers. I give *obraztsy kraski* to everyone."

"Give them paint swatches while wearing one of your fur coats. I need my parka."

"I give back when done! Parka is best for working in snow. Is what they wear in gulag."

Stomping back into the house, I had a mind to reappear in her fox coat. But I had such an aversion to wearing animal fur, I couldn't bring myself to touch it. I wish now I'd taken Kit up on his offer to clean off my Berry Basket SUV. Then again, snow had fallen steadily since he'd left at six.

As I closed the door, I saw Natasha take long, slow sweeps with the snow broom. At this rate, she wouldn't be done for about an hour. And I needed my parka to wear at the Hollyberry Festival parade today.

I also had to meet Theo at the shop before we opened. In addition to his usual predawn baking, he and I had decided to whip up strawberry-peppermint donut holes as a special treat. After Gareth Holmes agreed to play Santa at The Berry Basket, I'd planned to give berry-flavored candy canes to the children. Then I ran across a delightful donut-hole recipe on Pinterest certain to delight the children even more. I couldn't wait to taste them.

Panther knocked off a bell from the blue artificial tree in the foyer. My fault for tempting him with bell ornaments. Minnie cried, "Merry Christmas!," in response, distracting Dasha from her kibble. Once the Yorkie launched into what promised to be a string of yaps, shivering in a thin jacket seemed a preferable activity. It was certain to be quieter.

I could feed the birds, too. The snow had sent even more flocks to my feeders. I'd been hard-pressed keeping them supplied with suet cakes, peanut hearts, cracked corn, and sunflower.

After I slipped on my winter boots, I put on my light quilted jacket. One that had been suitable earlier in the month before the lake-effect snow arrived. The last time I'd worn the jacket was the night I found Everett's dead body. It seemed another season ago rather than mere days.

At least no winds blew off the lake this morning. With the addition of my scarf and gloves, I hoped to finish filling the feeders before my fingers grew numb.

Indeed, the activity warmed me up, particularly the effort it took to plow through sixteen inches of fresh snow. I brought along a snow shovel to clear out a space beneath the feeders. The chipmunks were in hibernation, but my neighborhood still saw plenty of squirrels. Not that I was a big fan of squirrels. Squirrels often found ways to get into my feeders, where they cleaned out the entire supply in short order. But I didn't mind if they enjoyed the seeds that fell to the ground. After all, squirrels had to eat, too.

My arrival at the cluster of feeders on my front lawn startled sparrows, woodpeckers, and a flock of juncos. A large blue jay squawked at me from an adjacent fir.

"I'll be out of your way soon," I told the birds. A black squirrel chattered at me from beneath a holly bush. "You too."

After clearing a space beneath the feeders, I rummaged in my jacket pocket for a tissue. When I was done blowing my nose, I put it back in my pocket. But I felt something in there.

I reached in and pulled out a piece of gingerbread cookie. For a moment, I wondered where it had come from. Then I remembered I had cleaned up cookie fragments beneath the bench Everett died on. Because the weather turned cold the next day, I hadn't worn this jacket since that night.

The idea of carrying around a dead man's cookies made me queasy.

The squirrel chittered beneath the holly bush. On impulse I threw the cookie fragment on the ground. "Here's an appetizer until I get the feeders filled up."

During my trips to and from the shed, I took a moment to enjoy the snow falling softly around me. The lake had not yet frozen over, and a gentle surf could be heard beneath the bluff in front of my house. A pity the snowy mist hid much of the lake from view.

With each trip to the feeders, the birds came closer, losing their fear of me in anticipation of the banquet I was putting out.

On my final trek, the blue jay disregarded my presence to rip off pieces of suet cake. A chickadee briefly landed on my shoulder as I poured out oilers. And beneath the feeders, I counted six cardinals, ten dark-eyed juncos, three cedar waxwings . . . and a dead black squirrel.

"Natasha!" I yelled so loudly I probably shook some snow off the surrounding trees.

Much quicker than I expected, Natasha plowed her way through the snowdrifts to where I stood among the feeders. She grabbed my arm. "*Chto sluchilos? Vy udarilis?* Marlee, tell me!"

Although most of what she said was in Russian, I understood. As I understood the implications of what had just happened.

"Look." I pointed at the dead squirrel.

Natasha did as I asked. "What is problem?"

"The squirrel is dead."

"*Da.* In Russia, I once see dead otter outside my apartment. And I do not live near water."

"You don't understand. I killed it."

Her perfectly made-up eyes narrowed in my direction. "If you kill squirrel, you should not complain about beautiful fox coat. At least I do not kill fox."

"It was an accident. I didn't mean to kill him."

She shrugged. "I do not care if you run squirrel down with car. Russians do not like *burunduku.* My brother calls them rat with fluffy tail."

"Natasha, I gave him part of a cookie. One of the cookies Everett Hostetter ate the night he died."

"The old man in train museum?"

"Yes. And I forgot I put some of the cookies in my pocket. When I found them a few minutes ago, I gave part of the cookie to the squirrel. Now he's dead. You know what this means, don't you?"

"Do not feed squirrels."

"No! It means the cookies were poisoned. It means Everett Hostetter was murdered."

"Is winter." Natasha shot me a skeptical look. "I think *burunduku* die of cold."

"You're wrong. I have to go to the police station and give them the rest of the cookies in my pocket. The cookies should be tested." I bit back a sob at the sight of the dead animal. "And I better bring the squirrel. They should run tests on it, too."

She looked at me as if I were crazy. "How you bring dead squirrel to police station?"

"In a garbage bag. Or a shoe box. I could use this shovel to pick up his body while you hold open one of your shoe boxes—"

"*Nyet!* You will not touch boxes of my shoes." I had rarely heard Natasha be so emphatic. "Let dead squirrel alone."

"Maybe I should leave it here. His poor little body will freeze. That should preserve it for any tests. But let's make sure there are no more poisoned crumbs on the ground."

With an exaggerated sigh, Natasha helped pick up any remaining cookie fragments. Bad enough I had inadvertently killed the squirrel. I'd be inconsolable if one of the birds was poisoned.

"I've never killed an animal in my life," I wailed as Natasha and I headed back to the house. "I feel terrible."

"Is not so bad to kill squirrel," she said in a soothing voice. "My uncle Leonid once kill two men in alley for selling him bad vodka. This is after he break their arms with baseball bat."

When she put it like that, the death of a squirrel didn't sound so bad.

Chief Gene Hitchcock seemed even less impressed by my dead squirrel than Natasha. "Is this a joke?"

"Is no joke," Natasha said. "Marlee is upset she kill squirrel. I think squirrel die of cold, but she does not listen. Tell Marlee no one care if squirrel is dead."

"I care." Although I felt touched that Natasha wanted to accompany me to the police station, I suspected she wasn't going to make things better. "I fed the squirrel some of the cookies that Everett Hostetter ate the night he died. A few minutes later, the squirrel was dead."

"And you suspect the cookies were poisoned?"

I was frustrated he didn't seem more interested. "Of course. What other explanation could there be?"

Hitchcock looked over my shoulder as someone walked by his open office door. "Officer Davenport, will you come in here please?"

"I don't think we need Janelle to be part of this conversation," I muttered.

Too late. My least favorite law enforcement officer strolled in, her expression showing curiosity at the sight of Natasha and me seated before her boss.

"What do you need, Chief?" She took a position behind him, leaning against the wall.

"Marlee fed a cookie found in her jacket pocket to a squirrel. Now the squirrel is dead."

"Came here to confess, did she?" Janelle grinned. "That might reduce the charges from homicide to manslaughter."

"Very funny." I glared at her.

"What is this manslaughter?" Natasha looked confused. "Marlee did not kill man."

"And I did not intentionally kill the squirrel. But the cookies had something toxic in them. These were the same cookies Everett Hostetter ate before he died. So there's a high probability he was poisoned."

Janelle turned her full attention to Hitchcock. "What is she talking about? Why does she have Everett Hostetter's cookies?"

"Gillian and I found the body," I said. "While waiting for EMS to arrive, I picked up pieces of gingerbread cookies on the floor beneath the bench he sat on. There wasn't a trash can around, so I stuck them in my jacket pocket. I totally forgot they were in there until this morning, when I fed the cookie to the squirrel."

Natasha sighed. "Now squirrel is dead."

I stood up and carefully removed my quilted jacket. "I haven't touched what's left in my pocket. I didn't want to contaminate the evidence further."

Turning out the pocket, I gently shook the remaining cookie pieces and crumbs over the police chief's desk blotter.

"Sticking them in a plastic bag would have been preferable," Hitchcock grumbled. "And how do you know the cookies found beneath the bench were the same ones Hostetter had eaten? Assuming he ate any at all."

"The cookie crumbs around his mouth. And there was a bag on the floor with gingerbread cookies inside. He probably dropped one onto the floor when he lost consciousness."

"Where is this bag of cookies?" Janelle smirked. "Did you abscond with that, too?"

"I tried to hand it to Anthony, but he didn't want it. So Diane Cleverly took the bag. She said she was going to throw it away." I gasped. "I'd better make sure she did. What if she or someone else still had the bag and eats the cookies?"

Natasha frowned. "Maybe you did kill squirrel."

"Diane Cleverly is alive and well. At least she was a half hour ago. She and a friend arrived at the Sourdough Café as I was leaving." The police chief rummaged in a drawer, pulling out a plastic evidence bag. "But I will let her know there may be a problem with those cookies. And that she needs to bring them here if she hasn't already tossed them in the garbage."

Janelle straightened. "She's probably still there having breakfast. I'll run down to the café and talk with her."

"Don't bother. Give the café a call and have them send Diane over." Hitchcock carefully placed the cookie crumbs in the bag.

Janelle stepped out of the office, cell phone in hand.

"Then you believe me?" I asked.

"Why wouldn't I believe you? You have cookies in your possession the deceased may or may not have been eating. We'll look into it. But it's likely the squirrel died from natural causes. As the elderly Everett Hostetter did."

"We don't know that," I protested. "No autopsy was performed."

"There wasn't any reason for one, given his age and the circumstances."

"He was rich," I stated. "Hostetter might have been killed for his money."

"Happens all the time in Russia," Natasha added.

"I wasn't aware you were well acquainted with Everett. Sorry his death has upset you."

"I didn't know him at all. And I'm sorry he died. But I accidentally killed a squirrel!"

Natasha patted my shoulder. "Do not talk about squirrel. It make Marlee cry."

Janelle came back into the office. "I spoke to the hostess at the café. She told Diane to come to the station as soon as she's done with breakfast."

"Good," I said. "And you will run tests on the cookies?"

The chief nodded. "Yes. But as you probably heard from Kit, the county has a triple homicide on our hands. Every law enforcement branch has been called in. And the bad weather has caused havoc on the roads. Every state trooper and sheriff's car is out there helping motorists."

Natasha sighed. "No one here know how to drive in snow. In Russia, we drive through blizzard all the time. We do not even notice."

"Maybe you should go back to Russia," Janelle said in a sharp voice.

"*Nyet.* I am American now."

Although I knew Natasha was proud of her American citizenship, she looked like a character from *Doctor Zhivago.* She wore yet another fur Cossack hat and had exchanged my parka for her favorite brown sable coat. She was lucky no one from PETA had gotten close to her yet.

"And there's the Hollyberry Festival this weekend," Hitchcock continued. "At least two officers are needed to keep an eye on things. Also that stupid tree fell over again."

Mention of the Hollyberry Festival reminded me of all I had to do today. "Time for me to get to The Berry Basket. But I thought the police should know about the cookie and the squirrel."

Janelle snickered.

Anger flared up in me. "What's so funny? I'm worried Everett Hostetter may have been poisoned. Why aren't you? After all, he was your father."

She jumped back as if I had given her a vicious pinch. "That's none of your business."

"Officer Davenport is right," Hitchcock said in a reproving tone.

"Old dead man is father of policewoman?" Natasha got to her feet, pulling her plush fur about her. "I think you are worse than what Marlee tell me."

"And what is Marlee telling you?" Janelle barked.

"Please let me know what the test results are, Chief Hitchcock. Thank you." I grabbed Natasha by her furry arm and hauled her out of the office.

Natasha threw a scornful glance over her shoulder. "She is cold like *moroz*. Like frost. You are more unhappy about squirrel than she is about dead father."

I shushed Natasha as we made our way through the outer office, now bustling with law enforcement people, including the state police. That triple homicide had put everyone on alert.

Suzanne caught sight of me from her reception desk. "Are you here about the play?"

I stopped. "No. I had something possibly criminal I wanted to report."

She raised an eyebrow at that. "I don't wish to hurt your feelings, Marlee, but what's criminal is your acting ability."

Chapter Twelve

For the second time that morning, a conversation touched on poisoned cookies.

"Do we have enough Christmas desserts for the weekend?" Theo asked as we finished glazing strawberry donut holes in the shop kitchen.

I glanced at the trays of pastries wrapped in plastic: blueberry-pie bars, lingonberry thumb prints, and white-chocolate cranberry cookies. "We have more than enough to see us through today and tomorrow."

"But it's called the Hollyberry Festival. We didn't bake any hollyberry cookies."

"We can't." I dunked another donut hole in strawberry glaze. "The berries are poisonous."

His large gray eyes grew wider. "There are holly bushes in my yard. I thought about using the berries to make cookie batter. Only I couldn't find any recipes for it."

I breathed a sigh of relief. "Thank goodness."

"What if I had put the berries in cookies?" He looked alarmed at the prospect. "I make up my own recipes sometimes. If I had, I could have killed someone!"

I gave him a reassuring smile. "The berries from a holly bush don't taste good. After one bite, a sensible person would spit it out. If anyone did eat the berries, they'd suffer from nausea, vomiting, diarrhea. The same with holly leaves."

"The leaves, too?"

I nodded toward the door leading into the shop. "Before I decorated the store with fresh boughs of holly, I removed the berries. If any had fallen off, I worried a child might pick one up and eat it. I did bring holly boughs into my house, but I placed them on a floating shelf. Somewhere Dasha and Panther can't reach. Holly leaves and berries can poison a small animal."

That dead squirrel flashed into my mind.

"I don't want to kill anything!" Theo cried.

He had suffered a head injury as a toddler, which led to developmental problems. And the thirty-seven-year-old seemed younger than his years. Despite that, Theo had made a successful, independent life for himself. He was also the best baker in the county.

"Don't worry. We won't bake any cookies with berries from a holly bush."

But he still looked worried. "Marlee, I see the birds eat them. Especially cedar waxwings and robins." Like me, Theo fed birds in his backyard. "Do they all die?"

"No. The digestive tract of a bird can handle hollyberries. In fact, the berries provide sustenance for fruit-eating birds who remain over the winter." I placed the last donut hole on a cookie sheet lined with wax paper.

Theo counted donut holes while I rinsed the bowl of strawberry glaze. "How about the squirrels? Will hollyberries poison them?"

His comment brought me up short. The black squirrel who met his demise this morning sat beneath a holly bush. Had he eaten berries from the holly bush before I tossed the cookie his way? Maybe the cookie wasn't poisoned. Maybe the poor squirrel died from toxic berries.

Still, I couldn't dismiss the fact that both Everett Hostetter and a squirrel passed away after sampling the gingerbread cookies. I wished I knew where those cookies had come from. But no clues had been on the white paper bag.

Theo stifled a yawn.

"Go home," I told him. "You've been here for hours."

"But I want to stay for the Christmas parade."

"That's not until two o'clock. Relax. Feed the birds. Take a nap. Then come back later."

"Are you sure?"

I smiled. "I'm sure. You've earned a break."

The door leading to the back parking lot opened. "It smells like Christmas in here," Andrew said.

I agreed. The combined aroma of sugar, butter, and white chocolate was nearly intoxicating.

"You're cutting it close," I said to Andrew, who shrugged out of his coat and scarf. "We open in five minutes."

"Blame Oscar. He went into Iron Chef mode and whipped up a four-course breakfast." Andrew burped.

"I couldn't leave until the whole culinary performance was complete."

I tossed him a Berry Basket chef apron. "I've already counted the money in the till. After we fill the pastry case, we'll open."

Andrew looked at the donut holes. "When do these go out?"

"Not until Gareth Holmes arrives this afternoon to play Santa. I'm giving away donut holes instead of candy canes."

"Love it. Get the kiddies hooked on deep fry at an early age."

"We didn't fry them," Theo said as he wiped the kitchen counter. "Marlee found a healthy donut recipe on Pinterest."

"Healthier," I corrected. "We baked the donut holes in mini-muffin pans. But they're still donuts. Not a kale salad."

Andrew popped one into his mouth.

"Let the glaze harden first," I told him.

"Delayed gratification is overrated." He reached for another one, but I pulled him away.

"Since you're working more hours at the florist shop than here, I don't need you eating the treats set aside for the children. Now grab some cookie trays."

"I have no choice." He picked up a tray of cookies. "Oscar has floral orders for two winter-themed weddings this week and three office parties. It's sent him into a poinsettia panic."

Because Andrew's boyfriend, Oscar Lucas, owned a florist shop in neighboring Saugatuck, Andrew split his work time between there and The Berry Basket. I was resigned to the fact that Oscar's flowers took precedence over my berries.

"Besides, Oscar gets stressed out when too many orders come in," Andrew added. "I provide a calming presence at the shop."

"Right now it would be helpful if you took your calm butt into my shop to unlock the door. It's officially Hollyberry Festival. Time to go into festival mode."

As Andrew walked past, he left behind the scent of roses.

"You smell like a float at the Rose Bowl parade." I sniffed again.

"I delivered two big floral arrangements before I came here. They're for a memorial service this evening."

Picking up two cookie trays, I walked behind him. "Who died?"

"You found his body."

"They're for Everett Hostetter?"

"Yeah. Oscar got a rush order for the flowers right before closing yesterday."

"But Diane Cleverly told me there wasn't going to be a memorial or a funeral. She was really upset about it."

"I guess she decided to take matters into her own hands." Andrew arranged the cookie trays in the case. "Diane ordered the flowers. White roses. Lots of them. I delivered them to the historical museum."

"The memorial service is being held at the museum?"

"Apparently."

"Why haven't I heard anything about it?"

He chuckled. "I'm guessing because you aren't a friend or relative of the deceased."

"True. Only I wonder who will show up for this thing, besides Diane."

"Who cares? If I were you, I wouldn't waste any time over the dearly departed Everett Hostetter. Not with all those lines you have to learn." Andrew gave me a stern look. "And don't come unprepared to the next rehearsal. Otherwise, my mom will make certain the next memorial service is yours."

The Hollyberry Festival weather gods smiled upon us. Or maybe they feared Piper's wrath if things didn't go perfectly. By eleven the snow came to a stop again. That made it easier for drivers en route to our downtown. And for pedestrians once they got here.

Piper had seen to it that their efforts would be rewarded. In addition to our usual holiday street decor and the giant tree in the village square, food trucks offering everything from elephant ears to nachos were parked along River Park. Our local pet photographer set up a tent on Iroquois Street where people could have Christmas photos taken with their animal companions. And Piper's carolers strolled up and down Lyall Street.

Thanks to Piper's ruthless guilt-inducing measures, everyone at The Berry Basket, including Theo, had volunteered to carol. Gillian and Andrew were on the list today. Theo, Dean, and I would be caroling tomorrow. Dean wasn't happy; he recorded his podcast on Sundays.

To encourage visitors to stay past the two o'clock parade, Piper also convinced every downtown shop to run special holiday sales. Piper had even rented a horse and carriage from a local stable. Along with a coach driver dressed as Santa.

Every so often I caught a glimpse of the horse-drawn white carriage, festooned with garlands, as it went past my shop window. No doubt visitors enjoyed the carriage tour of downtown. Although given how much snow had fallen, Piper should have substituted a sleigh.

I didn't have a lot of time to watch horse-drawn carriages though. From the moment Andrew hung our OPEN flag, he and I were kept busy wrapping purchases, while serving hot tea, coffee, and pastries. Despite the cold temps, a number of customers wanted berry ice cream sundaes and cones, too.

One customer did remark about our lack of cookies decorated with holly leaves or berries. So Theo had been right to worry about not having holly-themed pastries. During a rare free moment, I googled hollyberry cookies and came up with a recipe perfect for the festival. Naturally, it didn't call for hollyberries, or even baking. But it required a trip to the grocery store for cornflakes. Maybe I could whip up a few dozen cookies tonight after we closed. Except, when would I have time to learn my lines?

While I wrapped bottles of berry syrup in red and green tissue paper, my shopkeeper neighbor, Denise Redfern, opened the door. "Marlee, I wanted to remind you about your lanterns out front. I know you planned to keep them lit during the festival, even during the day."

I'd been so busy painting berries on the lanterns, I forgot to light them. "Thanks. I'll do that now."

She grinned. "You'll need to put candles in them first."

I turned to Andrew. "I forgot to buy votive candles."

"First, you forgot the lines in the play. Now the candles. What next?"

"Next, I'm sending you to the grocery store to pick up a package of candles." I placed the bottles of syrup in a handled bag. "I also want you to buy cornflakes."

"Would you like a dozen eggs, too?" Andrew gestured at the eight customers in the shop. "You might want to finish your grocery shopping after the festival."

I handed the bag to the customer with a wide smile and a "Happy holidays."

When she left, I replied, "I found a recipe for cookies shaped and molded to look like holly leaves. I might be able to make a batch after we close tonight. But I need cornflakes. And green food coloring."

"Have Theo do it. He is the baker, after all."

"He's worked overtime this past week because of the holidays. And Sunday is his day off. So I'll take charge of the cookies." I threw Andrew a sly smile. "Unless you volunteer while I study my lines."

At that moment, Diane Cleverly entered the shop. Given how she marched straight toward me with a serious expression, I doubted she came to purchase berry jam.

"Marlee, I'm glad you're here." She nodded at Andrew, who went to assist a customer by our berry-themed greeting cards.

"And I'm happy to see you. Did Chief Hitchcock tell you not to eat anything from that bag of ginger-bread cookies? The one I handed to you at the museum."

"I threw the bag away about ten minutes after you gave it to me. Not that I would have eaten from it." She shivered at the thought.

"That's a relief. I fed a squirrel one of those cookies today and it died. Chief Hitchcock has promised to have what's left of the cookies tested." I frowned. "Of course Officer Davenport thinks I'm crazy."

"The woman is insufferable. I'd prefer to have no contact with Janelle at all, but I had to speak with her today. To extend an invitation."

"About the memorial service at the museum?"

She looked surprised. "How did you know? Oh, Andrew told you. I forgot he delivered my flowers this morning. Yes, I wanted to inform Janelle about the service. I hoped if I did it in person, it might shame her into coming. Which it did. But she's not happy about it."

"Then you know about Janelle?"

"That she was Everett's daughter? I've known for a while now. Not that she acts like a daughter." Diane grimaced. "Then again, he wasn't Father of the Year either."

"When we spoke yesterday, you said there wouldn't be a funeral or memorial."

"There wouldn't have been." Her voice grew hard. "Had I not taken it upon myself to see that the decent thing was done. I spoke to Anthony, too."

"How did he take it?"

"He claims I've overstepped my bounds." She shrugged. "But he'll come. I thought it best to have the memorial service at the museum. Everett has been responsible for keeping our doors open for nearly a decade. And all of my employees and board members will be in attendance. I'm closing the museum early tonight for the service. I'd like it if you could come."

"Thank you for inviting me, but I have no business attending Everett Hostetter's memorial service. I never even spoke to him. To be honest, he seemed a cold, disagreeable man."

"Yet you're the only one trying to uncover the truth behind his death." She lowered her voice. "Janelle may think the whole thing about the cookies is a joke. But I find it alarming. And suspicious."

"I agree. Why would the squirrel die right after eating them unless they were poisoned? That's why I asked the police to test the cookie."

Diane sighed. "By the time the police actually test the cookie, it will be Easter. Except for Chief Hitchcock, the Oriole Point police officers are an unimpressive lot."

"A shame the sheriff's department and state police are dealing with a triple homicide. And it is possible Everett died of natural causes. After the events of this past year, I've become suspicious of every death. I may be overreacting."

She took a deep breath. "I'm not overreacting to his death. Everett may not have been a lovable person, but his passing should not be ignored. That's why I'd like you to attend the service tonight. Besides, I'd find your presence more comforting than that of Janelle and Anthony." Diane smirked. "And Katrina May. She was pleased to learn there would be a service. She insists on speaking. Of course."

I didn't understand Diane's disapproval. At least Katrina wanted to come to the memorial, unlike Everett's nephew and daughter. "Seems kind of her."

"*Kindness* is not a word I'd apply to Katrina May. But she's keeping a high profile until Everett's will is read."

More customers entered the shop. Andrew sent me a look asking for help. Before I bailed him out, I had to finish this conversation. "Why would Katrina care about Everett Hostetter's will? Unless she expects to be in it."

"Of course she expects to be named in the will. She and Everett were once married. I'm sure that marriage, short as it was, came with strings attached. And a detailed marriage contract."

"Do you know why he proposed to her? I mean, the difference in their ages."

"Maybe she got him to propose by telling him a few ancestral ghosts said he should. Everett was more superstitious than people realized. I wouldn't be surprised if she scared him into buying her a ring. But his fear of letting another human being get too close was no doubt even greater. Probably why they divorced so quickly. At least that's what I assume."

"Seems a big step to take for a man who had been a bachelor that long."

"I agree. As far as I know, Katrina and I are the only women Everett ever asked to marry him. Although I'm sure there were a number of ambitious ladies who tried their best to become Mrs. Hostetter. Not that they would have had a chance with Everett. He cared about money more than any gold digger ever could."

"Until Katrina. Maybe she genuinely cared about him."

Diane gave me a withering look. "I'm the only woman who ever had feelings for Everett. Me and his sister, Sarah. And I cared enough about Everett *and* myself to turn him down."

I took a moment to process this. "Have you ever wondered why Katrina moved to this side of the state at the same time he did?"

"I assume she was following the money. Which is why I wouldn't be surprised if Everett left her a chunk of his fortune." Diane sighed. "Maybe all of it."

I also thought it possible Katrina might have done more than simply follow the money. She might have killed Everett for it.

Chapter Thirteen

"That ancient man and Katrina May were married?" Tess asked in horror.

"I know. He was a half century older than her."

"And he had the personality of a block of cement." Tess shuddered, and it wasn't because of the cold temperature. "An old block of cement."

We exchanged looks of disapproval, expressions difficult to pull off in our reindeer-antler headpieces. I bought them to wear during the parade. Tess wasn't an antler kind of person, but I knew she'd be a good sport and play along. If not, I might have brought up those dissection frogs I took the rap for.

Like most shopkeepers, Tess and I closed our store for the duration of the parade. Up and down the length of Lyall Street—now cleared of vehicles—stood several hundred people. Locals attended the parade because at least one family member took part. And visitors loved our floats featuring the Grinch, Santa's workshop, and Rudolph the Red-Nosed Reindeer. My old high school boyfriend Max Riordan had volunteered to play Santa on the Rudolph float, which is why I wore antlers.

The sound of horns signaled the start of the parade. The Oriole Point High School band, playing "Santa Claus Is Comin' to Town," began to march down the street. It would be the first of six high school bands from the county. Piper made certain there would be lots of music.

"Where's David?" I asked.

Tess sighed. "He's in the parade."

"Really? That's a first."

"Blame it on our trip to Disney World and his obsession with Chip 'n' Dale. When he bought the Chip costume, I never imagined he'd find so many opportunities to wear it."

I smiled. "He did make an impression at Halloween. No one could miss that enormous chipmunk head."

"Halloween is one thing. And I can accept Santa Chipmunk. But he puts on that costume a bit too often." She lowered her voice. "In circumstances I never would have dreamed of."

I giggled.

"It's not funny. An amorous giant chipmunk is an alarming sight."

That image made me bend over with laughter.

Tess elbowed me in the ribs. "Shhh. Everyone's staring. They probably can't figure out why you're hysterical about our marching band."

Someone grabbed my elbow.

"Ouch!" I pulled away from Piper's iron grip.

"Why are you laughing? Do you think the band sounds off? It's the trumpets, isn't it? Yes, I can hear the wrong notes. They're flat. I told the band director the brass section needed extra rehearsal." Piper raised her voice as the band drew near, horns and woodwinds blaring. "How mortifying if New Bethel's high school band plays better than ours."

I opened my mouth to explain why I was laughing, but she dashed off.

"I've heard New Bethel's band," I told Tess. "Our kids have nothing to worry about."

"Piper takes these festivals too much to heart." Tess said.

"Like our *Christmas Carol* director. Suzanne has gone full-blown Quentin Tarantino."

"Did you learn your lines yet?"

"Some of them."

"Marlee!"

"I know. But when am I going to find the time? And the last thing I need is to attend Everett Hostetter's memorial tonight. Only Diane really wants me there." I waved at Andrew and Dean, who watched the parade from the other side of the street. Suzanne stood beside them, gesticulating as she talked on her phone. I was sure her heated conversation involved the play.

"You can always say no."

"I did. But now that I know about Katrina and Everett, I'm curious as to how she interacts with Anthony and Janelle." I gave Tess a bright smile. "Why don't you come with me? It will be fun."

"No, it won't."

"Maybe *fun* isn't the right word to use for a memorial service. How about *interesting*?"

"How about I'd rather do almost anything else, even fend off the advances of a chipmunk." Tess laughed. "Speaking of chipmunks . . ."

Elves in green costumes and pointy shoes walked behind the band. A dozen volunteers outfitted as reindeer followed close behind. In their midst strode a chipmunk in a Santa suit. All of them handed out candy canes to the children along the parade route.

Next came the float devoted to the Rudolph the Red-Nosed Reindeer annual TV special. A sleigh pulled by life-size fake reindeer stood atop the platform, with Max Riordan's Santa waving from among a pile of toys. I found it a delightful inside joke that Danny Whitfield, our local dentist's son, played Hermey, the elf who wanted to pursue dentistry. And that Chuck, the rambunctious, bearded owner of the Sandy Shoals Saloon, strutted about the platform as Yukon Cornelius.

"Who's the Abominable Snow Monster?" I wondered as the shaggy, costumed figure walked past.

I didn't wonder long. Natasha pushed her way through the crowd to me.

"Is Uncle Wendall." She pointed at the white furry figure.

"Old Man Bowman is in the Abominable Snow Monster costume?" I took a second look.

Tess sent me an amused glance. "I always suspected he was Bigfoot."

Indeed. Old Man Bowman, one of our more colorful residents, spent most of his time searching for Bigfoot. Despite his eccentricity—or perhaps because of it—Wendall Bowman made a small fortune for himself decades ago with one of his inventions. This allowed him a lot of free time to hunt the mythic creature. He was also the uncle of Natasha's deceased husband, Cole Bowman. After that scoundrel died, Wendall took Natasha under his wing, and they viewed each other as family.

Right now I viewed his Abominable Snow Monster as perfect typecasting.

"He has best costume in parade," Natasha said proudly, then pushed through the crowd to follow him.

"I think she likes the costume because of all the fur," I said.

"The woman does love an animal pelt," Tess observed wryly.

"If I had a Christmas wish, it would be to convince her to buy fake fur."

The strains of "Jingle Bell Rock" drew my attention to the next marching band. Piper had put together a nice roster of parade participants. Some ideas were new, such as the Winter Queen and the dancing Santa Bears. My heart belonged to the colorful Grinch float, not least because Gillian had volunteered to play Cindy Lou Who.

But the biggest surprise on the Grinch float—even bigger than Old Man Bowman's surprise appearance—was Piper's decision to let her Great Dane Charlemagne appear as the Grinch's dog, Max. A pair of stick antlers tied to his head, the overgrown puppy I had dubbed Charlie calmly sat next to the Grinch.

Tess giggled. "How did Piper get her dog to keep those giant antlers on his head?"

"I'm betting a combination of his favorite biscuits and daily sessions with a trainer."

As the float went by, the children around me called out, "Max! Max!"

Charlemagne was officially the biggest hit of the parade. Deservedly so.

When I turned to look at the delighted children, I caught a glimpse of Anthony Thorne as he walked past. He paid no attention to the parade. In fact, he looked as if he was on the way to an appointment. But he was in enough of a festival mood to be munching on a snack.

To get a better look, I stepped out of the crowd. Whatever snack he munched on came from a white paper bag.

"Where are you going?" Tess joined me.

"I need to check something out."

Now that the parade had ended, a flood of people turned from the curb and thronged the sidewalk. I saw Anthony make a left at the next cross street.

"What are we checking out?" Tess asked.

"The bag Anthony Thorne is carrying looks like the same bag Everett's cookies were in."

We hurried along, not an easy thing to do with dozens of people going the opposite way. Most of them probably headed for the food trucks by the park. For a moment, Lyall Street had the bustling feel of Chicago's Mag Mile.

After we turned left at Iroquois Street, I spotted Anthony up ahead. "Where is he off to?"

"Maybe he parked his car on the next block," Tess

said. "And is that the town postmistress who's trying to get your attention?"

I looked toward the street where Jennifer Hamelin and her husband sat in the horse-drawn carriage. She appeared agitated. In contrast, the carriage driver looked bored to death as he waited for the parade viewers to finally clear Lyall Street.

I glanced back to see where Anthony went, but he had disappeared in the crowd.

"We may as well see what she wants," I said. "I'm guessing she wants to remind me about the play. Jennifer is playing Bob Cratchit's wife."

"She seems a bit astringent for the role. I don't think Jennifer has a maternal bone in her body. I can't see her mothering the Cratchit brood."

"I know. She'd give poor Tiny Tim self-esteem issues. Let's hope she's a good actress."

Tess and I walked over to the carriage.

"Merry Christmas." I gave the Hamelin couple a big smile, which wasn't returned. "Is there something you want to talk to me about?"

"I need to know if you've learned your lines for the play, Marlee," Jennifer demanded. "Dress rehearsal is in two days. With the first performance the following day."

I felt my stomach tighten up. Why had I let Andrew talk me into this? Because I once played Chava in high school? My arrogance had gotten the better of me this time. "I promise I'll have them memorized by then."

"Do you mean you still haven't learned all your lines?"

"I know most of them."

"Most of them?" Jennifer shook her head. "You're in only one scene."

"But it's a scene where my character does ninety percent of the talking."

Tess chuckled. "She's right. Jacob Marley is a chatty ghost."

"This isn't funny," Jennifer said. "There is no excuse for anyone in the play not to know their lines. If you haven't, you had no business wasting your time watching the parade."

I didn't know whether to be amused or irritated.

"What Marlee does is none of *your* business." Tess took the decision out of my hands.

"It's my business because the Green Willow Players have worked hard on this production." Jennifer ignored her husband, who attempted to get her to lower her voice. "And Marlee should not have agreed to take on a role as important as Jacob Marley. If we fail, the blame rests on her."

"Get over yourself," Tess muttered. "Silly twit."

I hoped Jennifer didn't hear that.

"Look, I promise I will be ready by dress rehearsal on Monday." If I had to, I'd write the lines on my arms.

Jennifer didn't look convinced. "Bad enough Everett died. Then Andrea got sick. People have started to talk. They're saying this year's production is jinxed. Cursed!"

Her husband sighed. "This is the first time Jen's performing in *A Christmas Carol*. She wants everything to go well."

"*A Christmas Carol* is the biggest event all year in Oriole Point," she declared.

Piper would take issue with that, especially since

she had nothing to do with any of the plays at the Calico Barn.

"We have a tradition to uphold," Jennifer continued. "Please take this seriously. Be on time for rehearsal. And, for Charles Dickens's sake, learn your lines!"

"Will do. I have forty-eight hours. I'll have it all memorized by Monday." At least I hoped so. "I also plan to have my costume cleaned tomorrow. So I should look and sound perfect for dress rehearsal."

A startled Jennifer stood up in the carriage.

"See you on Monday." I took Tess by the arm, eager to get away.

"Wait, Marlee!" Jennifer shouted. "You can't clean the costume. It's not allowed."

"Walk faster," Tess said.

I looked over my shoulder in time to see Jennifer step over her husband in an attempt to get out of the carriage. Was she going to chase me down?

"Jennifer, it's all right," I called over my shoulder. "Everything will be fine."

Or it would have been if she hadn't rushed to step down from the carriage. And fell.

Jennifer's scream stopped us in our tracks.

Tess and I raced over to where she now lay on the snowy sidewalk. The driver and her husband scrambled to join us.

"It hurts!" She pointed at her ankle. "It hurts so much!"

"Do you think you can stand up?" I asked.

"Are you crazy? I fell *and* I slipped on the ice."

Her husband knelt beside her. "We should sue the town for not keeping the sidewalks free of ice!"

The patch of ice they referred to lay over a yard away. And I'd seen the fall. Jennifer missed the last step of the carriage and fell to the ground. An unfortunate accident due to her being distracted by me. But I refused to take the blame for this.

The driver shook his head. "We need an ambulance. Her ankle might be broken."

Jennifer began to sob.

Tess and I exchanged nervous looks. "Do you think she's seriously injured?" Tess asked me.

"I have no idea. Only I don't want to be around when Suzanne finds out she may have lost another cast member." Even worse, I feared that Gillian had been right.

The play was cursed.

Chapter Fourteen

After the ambulance took a distraught Jennifer away, I tried to get back into a holly, jolly mood. I hoped she suffered from no more than a bruised ankle. Nothing that would prevent her from performing as Mrs. Cratchit on Tuesday. Although if an injured ankle served as an excuse to skip the performance, I'd keep that in mind if I didn't learn my lines.

Because a part-time clerk worked at Oriole Glass Studio today, Tess returned with me to The Berry Basket. Both of us wanted to see if Gareth Holmes made as good a Santa as we expected. Meanwhile David continued to parade about town as Santa Chipmunk.

Tess laughed as a family crowded around Chip for a group photo. "Next year I bet he convinces Piper to give him his own Chip 'n' Dale float."

"He'll need someone to play Dale. You two would make a cute chipmunk couple."

"Don't give him any ideas. Who knew a glassmaker

with spiked blond hair and a diamond stud in one ear could be transformed by a visit to Disney World."

"Look on the bright side," I said as we entered my shop. "If he'd gone to the Universal theme park, he might have become obsessed with Harry Potter."

"True. And I'd be living with Sirius Black."

"Merry Christmas! Ho, ho, ho!" greeted us.

Santa Claus sat on a chair by my corner Christmas tree. He was the spitting image of the classic 1881 Thomas Nast illustration: rotund, rosy-cheeked, white-bearded. His blue eyes even appeared to twinkle.

Andrew stood beside him. "Our bistro chairs seemed too small. So I took the desk chair from your office for Gareth to sit on. But I did cover it with the red felt blanket we had in the front window."

"It's comfortable, too." Gareth grinned.

"Looks good." I nodded with approval. "What do you think, Tess?"

"I like it. Only you're running out of space for customers to move about." She scanned the crowded shop. "Take a few snowmen off the floor, at least while Santa's here."

I loved the three-foot-tall stuffed snowmen—and women—placed about the shop. They all wore white scarves decorated with hollyberries. "People can walk around them."

"Save your breath," Andrew told Tess. "She won't remove a single Christmas decoration. Be glad she can't find the life-size wooden reindeer we had in here last year. I tripped and was almost impaled on his antlers."

"Somehow the deer vanished after I put him in storage." I shot Andrew a suspicious glance.

"It's a holiday mystery." Andrew avoided my gaze as he placed a tray of strawberry donut holes on the table beside Santa.

Behind me I heard children come into the shop, no doubt to see Santa. A sandwich board out front advertised his appearance.

"Merry Christmas, children." Santa waved at them. "Come say hi to Santa."

The children ran over to Gareth, who opened his arms wide. Their dad pulled out his phone for a photo.

I took four of the donut holes as Tess and I walked past. We munched on them behind the counter, both of us agreeing they were delicious. In the next hour, more families with children came in. As I hoped, the kids spoke with Santa and their parents shopped.

While Tess helped me wrap purchases, she observed, "Good idea to have Santa here during the festival."

"Even better with someone who looks like Gareth."

"I should get back to my own shop." Tess glanced up at the clock. "Our glass-blowing session starts at six, and I need to set things up."

Every Hollyberry Festival, Oriole Glass Studio took requests from customers for blown-glass ornaments. And then blew the glass in front of their captivated audience. It was their most popular event all year and a great chance for visitors to see how talented Tess and David were.

"You'll have a big turnout. Piper did a good job drumming up interest in the festival. We should have the food trucks every year. And the carolers are a nice touch. Even if she did strong-arm every shop-keeper and their employees to volunteer."

Although I had Christmas music piped through the store speakers, in between songs I sometimes caught a snatch from the carolers as they strolled past the store. Just now I heard them launch into "The Twelve Days of Christmas," one of my favorites.

Before the first chorus of "partridge in a pear tree" ended, a grim Suzanne Cabot marched into the shop. Dean followed close behind; he looked resigned to his fate.

"This is terrible," she cried. "Jennifer Hamelin won't be able to perform in the play!"

"Mom, keep it down," Dean said.

"Don't you realize the entire play is in jeopardy? All because of you, Marlee!" Suzanne pointed an accusing finger at me, a gesture used by the Ghost of Christmas Future when he pointed to Ebenezer's grave.

"Me?"

"She fell because you upset her."

"I am not responsible for Jennifer's emotional state."

"It was an accident," Tess said. "Jennifer rushed to get out of the carriage and fell."

"That is not how she tells it," Suzanne intoned in a dramatic voice.

"Then our postmistress is lying," I shot back. "Or she hit her head when she fell. She might have a concussion."

"Too bad it didn't knock some sense into her," Tess commented.

Andrew nodded at the children. "Why doesn't everyone discuss this somewhere else?"

"Come on, Mom." Dean steered his mother to the back of the shop and into our kitchen.

I didn't blame Andrew for not joining us.

Once we reassembled in the kitchen, I tried to take control of this meeting. "Tess and I were minding our own business when Jennifer called for us to come over to her. She and Ron were in that horse-drawn carriage Piper hired for visitors."

"I know where she was." Suzanne made a beeline for a plastic-wrapped tray of extra pastries on the counter. She removed a piece of cranberry white-chocolate pistachio bark. "I'm also aware she's worried you don't know your lines. We all are."

"Who is 'we'?" I asked.

"Everyone connected to the play." She took a big bite of the bark, spraying crumbs over her coat's faux-fur collar.

"The theater group should chill out," Tess said. "This isn't a Broadway production."

"To us, it is. And Marlee has a crucial role in the play. She needs to know her lines. *All* of them."

"I know most of them."

Suzanne gave me a doubtful look. Since she favored heavy eyeliner, it had an unnerving effect. "Then let's run through your scene. Right here. Right now."

"Okay. Maybe I don't know most of them. But I will. I promise."

Tess, loyal as ever, announced, "I'll run lines with Marlee tomorrow after work. She'll be fine. After all, both of us were spelling bee champs when we were kids."

Tess and I met in fifth grade when we tied for first place in a regional spelling bee.

"Why should I care if you can spell?" Suzanne reached for another piece of bark.

"Because to do well in a spelling contest requires the memorization of a huge vocabulary list." I winked at Tess. "We became philomaths."

"You might say we developed logolepsy." Tess giggled.

"Now they're going to show off all the words they know," Dean said to his mom.

"Some of them better include the lines in *A Christmas Carol*." Suzanne turned her attention to Tess. "So you have a good memory?"

"David says it's too good."

"How would you like to be in the play?"

Tess and I both exclaimed, "What?"

"Don't waste your breath," Tess said. "I refuse to take over the role of Jacob Marley."

"No." Suzanne frowned. "At this late date, we're stuck with Marlee in the role."

"I'm standing right here. If you want to insult me, wait until I leave the room."

Suzanne ignored me. "But we do need someone to step into the role of Mrs. Cratchit."

"Don't count Jennifer out just yet," I protested.

"Oh, she's out. I got a call from her husband. She broke her fibula."

"We weren't sure where the fibula was," Dean added. "I googled it. The fibula's here." He touched the front of his leg between the knee and ankle.

"Luckily, the fibula is not a weight-bearing bone," Suzanne informed us.

"Then what's the problem?" Tess looked puzzled.

"Because when she fell, the ligaments tore in her ankle."

That didn't sound good.

"She needs a pin surgically inserted," Dean said. "And Mom needs a new Mrs. Cratchit."

Suzanne placed a hand on Tess's shoulder. "You, my dear, would be perfect."

"I would not."

"A minute ago you bragged about your good memory."

"It's not a photographic memory." Tess looked at me for help.

"Leave Tess alone. And it's unfair to throw this at her so close to opening night."

Suzanne waved her hand. "Due to the circumstances, I'll let her improvise lines. All she has to do is sound maternal."

My mouth fell open. "Why can't I improvise?"

"Because Jacob Marley is too important a character. You must recite the lines from Dickens exactly as written."

Tess must have seen how unhappy this whole situation made me. "All right. I'll do it. Marlee may feel better if she's not the only performer who's unprepared. Only I reserve the right to say anything I like as Mrs. Cratchit."

Suzanne smiled in obvious relief. "Thank you. Just don't go too off script."

Dean laughed. "She means, don't ask Bob for a divorce. Or order pizza for the Cratchit Christmas dinner."

With that settled, Suzanne walked over to me. "As

for you, I have one more rule. Do not clean your costume."

"How do you know about that?"

"Jennifer's husband," Dean said. "He told Mom that Jennifer fell after she heard you planned to clean your costume. By the way, I don't blame you, Marlee. I wouldn't touch those costumes with a hazmat suit."

"Don't exaggerate," Suzanne said. "We clean the costumes every few years."

Her announcement made my skin crawl. "Years? That's worse than I thought."

"I may wear David's Chip costume," Tess said.

"This is not up for debate. The costumes are too delicate. No one cleans them until the board of the Green Willow Players all agree." Suzanne looked at me. "By the way, Everett Hostetter had no problem with that rule. In fact, he insisted no one was to touch his costume. Ever. Not even the chains."

"He might have disagreed if someone else had worn it for years." I confessed to being a neat freak, which included a phobia about cleanliness. No matter what Suzanne ordered, I planned to toss the costume into my washing machine.

"Now I need to get to the hospital." Suzanne grabbed another piece of bark. I guessed she needed a sugar boost to get her through the hospital visit with Jennifer. I didn't blame her. "I'll see both of you Monday night. And I'll have one of my sons drop off a script tonight at your studio, Tess."

"You told me I could improvise."

"And you can." She shot Tess a hopeful look. "But you might surprise yourself by picking up the lines quickly."

"Unlike me," I said before anyone else could.

"Exactly," Suzanne agreed. "Also a friendly word of advice the next time you go looking for a Santa. Don't ask Gareth Holmes."

Dean looked as puzzled as me. "What do you have against the duck decoy guy?"

"He seems nice," I said. "And a doppelgänger for Santa."

"All I know is what I hear at the police station."

Sometimes I wondered if Suzanne did more than answer phones there. I wouldn't be surprised if she also listened in on calls.

"What did you hear about Gareth?" Tess asked.

"I heard he is not to be trusted. And that his career as an attorney was shady at best."

"Who told you this?"

"Marlee, I don't like to carry tales."

Her son snorted.

"Let's just say Officer Davenport has cautioned me about Gareth."

I rolled my eyes. "The last person whose opinion I value is Janelle."

"Chief Hitchcock and I do not agree. Let's go, Dean."

"Why am I going?"

"Because I am much too upset to drive to the hospital." Suzanne put a hand over her chest. "This latest news about Jennifer may send me into another panic attack. I shouldn't be alone."

Muttering under his breath, Dean led his mother away.

I looked at Tess after they left. "Thanks for volunteering to be in the play. I need the moral support."

"My final payment to you for taking the blame about the dissection frogs in high school."

"I promise to never use those frogs as leverage again." I sighed. "And let's try not to screw up this year's *A Christmas Carol.*"

Tess grinned. "If we do, we can blame it on the curse. By the way, what do you think Janelle knows about Gareth Holmes? Do you think she's making stuff up about him?"

"Who knows? But for nine years, she never told anyone that Everett Hostetter was her father. I can't help but wonder what else she's hiding."

Chapter Fifteen

I decided to treat Santa to dinner. For three hours, Gareth held court in my shop as children recited their wish lists and tugged his beard. Even groups of giggling teens wanted to sit on Santa's lap for Instagram moments. The presence of a jovial Santa did what I had hoped: attract even more customers than usual. The least I could do was feed him.

At six o'clock Gillian arrived to relieve Andrew and me. Due to the festival activities, most downtown stores planned to stay open until nine tonight.

With a grateful smile, I went over to where Gareth presided from his makeshift throne. "You were fantastic. Not even the actor in *Miracle on Thirty-Fourth Street* made a better Saint Nick."

"My pleasure. Sorry to say, I neglected my own kids when they were growing up. Always chose work over family, even at Christmas. This was a real treat. It did my heart good."

"Please let me pay you. And take you to dinner."

"Santa does not accept payment, Marlee." With a

grunt, Gareth got to his feet. "But I will take you up on your offer of dinner." His eyes did their customary twinkle. I wondered how he did that.

"Anywhere you like. San Sebastian?"

"Much too fancy for Santa. Let's go to Sandy Shoals. That's my favorite."

I rarely ate at the Sandy Shoals Saloon, a popular hangout for residents who worked at the marina. However, it had a reputation for great fish-and-chips. And two-fisted drinkers.

"Sounds fine. Do you want to stop by your shop to change clothes?"

"Nah. I'll stay Santa awhile longer. In honor of the Hollyberry Festival."

"Then I'll keep my antlers on." I straightened my reindeer headpiece.

Andrew hurried past in his coat and hat.

"Hey, Andrew, how about joining Gareth and me for dinner?" I asked.

"Thanks, but Oscar and I have a Christmas party to attend in South Haven."

Katrina May brushed by Andrew as he left. "Marlee, have you seen Natasha?" She came to an abrupt halt. "Gareth? What are you doing here?"

Gareth held his arms out. "What does it look like?"

"He played Santa in the store," I explained. "Gareth was a big hit with the kids."

She lifted an eyebrow at that. "Seems out of character for him."

"Ho, ho, ho." Gareth's grin widened. "You only say that because you're afraid you'll find coal in your Christmas stocking this year."

Her expression grew hard. "You would know."

"Yes. I would." Gareth's smile vanished.

"I think Natasha had a date with that Alexei fellow," I said, trying to cut the tension. "The Russian architect. She mentioned they had a reservation at Bode's in Saugatuck."

Katrina threw a last hostile look at Gareth before turning to me. "When you see Natasha, tell her I have the estimated costs for the lobby decor."

She yanked open the shop door, but paused. "Are you coming to Everett's memorial?"

"Probably. Diane asked me to be there."

"Not you, Marlee." She gestured at Gareth. "I was asking Santa."

He shrugged. "I might show up. Then again, I might not."

"Keeping everyone guessing. As always." Katrina shook her head. "Next year, I'd find another Santa, Marlee. One who keeps his word."

"What was that all about?" I asked after she slammed the door behind her.

"Ms. May thinks the world should always listen to her. That's because she spends too much time talking to ghosts. Or pretends to." He chuckled. "But I'm not pretending when I say I'm starving. Or have you reconsidered your dinner offer?"

"A deal's a deal. Let's go." Only I did hope I could get Gareth to reconsider his earlier refusal to spill any secrets about Everett.

From the rowdy reception Gareth received when we entered the Sandy Shoals Saloon, I gathered he was quite the regular. Chuck, the owner, gave him a shout-out, with several guys at the bar doing the same. It was like walking into the *Cheers* bar with Norm.

Chuck still wore his Yukon Cornelius costume. The people in Oriole Point did love a costume. Sometimes it felt as if it were always Halloween here. Even at Christmastime.

Gareth nodded at a booth in the back, filled with two boisterous couples. "That's where I normally sit. Not tonight though."

I looked around the crowded, noisy bar. "The table by the front window is available."

"Perfect." He led me over. "This gives us a ringside seat."

As soon as we sat down, Denise Redfern strolled by outside. She looked surprised to see me at the Sandy Shoals with Santa. Gareth and I waved. She gave a cautious wave back. Since Gareth wore his Santa costume, most pedestrians noticed us, or rather they noticed Santa. They either smiled or did a double take.

After we gave our order, I sat back. "I never took you for a Sandy Shoals type of guy. It seems too blue-collar for an attorney. Especially one accustomed to working for CEOs."

He shrugged. "I wasn't always a high-priced attorney. Both my parents worked the assembly line in Flint. And I can relax here. Be myself. No one wants anything from me."

"I thought you were retired."

"Some things you never retire from." His Santa grin turned even merrier as our drinks arrived. Hot tea for me, and a boilermaker for Gareth.

I watched in amazement as he dropped the shot of

whiskey into his beer, then downed the contents in seconds. He raised his hand for another.

By the time our orders of fish-and-chips arrived, Gareth had slammed down three boilermakers. And ordered a fourth. I'd made enough small talk to be polite. Time to ask him pointed questions about Everett Hostetter. Considering how much alcohol he'd drunk, I'd better do it before he became incoherent.

"You and Katrina May didn't seem on friendly terms."

"She's used to be being the all-knowing one in the room. Passing on messages from the dead." He wiggled his fingers in a mocking gesture. "That's how she got Everett's attention."

"By passing on messages from the dead?"

"My boss also liked the way she looked." Gareth's grin turned lascivious.

"Everett didn't seem like a man who chased women."

"He was still a man. Especially if there were added benefits."

"I don't understand. Any more than I understand why he asked Katrina to marry him."

"Mainly a business arrangement. Katrina's readings can be remarkably accurate. Too bad she can't come up with the winning lottery numbers."

"I assumed there was a financial incentive for Katrina. But what did Everett get out of it? Aside from the obvious."

He chuckled. "There's nothing obvious about why he married her. But he regretted it. Katrina regrets not asking for a bigger divorce settlement. And it's hard for a person who claims to be all knowing to now find herself in the dark. She's angry."

"Why?"

"Because I know more than she does." He leaned over the table. The alcohol on his breath made me reel back. "You see, I know what's in Everett's will. I drew it up for him. And it looks like none of those spirits she talks to have figured out the details of the will."

"What are the details?"

Gareth hiccuped. "That's a secret."

"Everett's dead. Don't his beneficiaries have a right to know?"

"Who are his beneficiaries, according to the will? They have no idea. But I do."

"When will they find out?" I asked.

"When I file it with the probate court. I'm taking my own sweet time about it."

"Anthony and Everett lived together. His uncle must have kept a copy of the will in their house. All Anthony has to do is pull it out and read it."

"Everett didn't keep his will at the house. And I have the only other copy." His fourth boilermaker arrived. He quickly reached for it.

"Why don't you get some food in your stomach before drinking again," I suggested.

I breathed a sigh of relief when he grabbed a piece of fried fish from the plastic basket.

"Since Anthony is his nephew and Janelle his daughter—"

"Illegitimate daughter," Gareth broke in.

"That doesn't matter. Janelle is Everett's child. It

would be only fair for Janelle and Anthony to be named his heirs."

"Who said Everett was fair?" He chuckled. "The man didn't even draw up a will until this past year. As if death would somehow pass him by. Well, Everett is dead and I'm in charge. And I plan to keep everyone guessing."

I understood why Janelle and Katrina didn't like Gareth. He enjoyed playing games. "I don't blame people for wanting to know the contents. After all, he was wealthy."

"Not as wealthy as he once was," Gareth said with a mouthful of fish. "That's why he kept selling off his companies. But he still was rich enough to rule the roost." Gareth threw his head back and yelled, "Cock-a-doodle-doo!"

This promised to be a long dinner.

"It's sadistic not to let everyone know what's in the will." With my own stomach growling, I took a big bite of the piping hot fish.

"Don't waste your time worrying about the vultures."

"Janelle and Anthony?"

"Don't forget Katrina. They believe they'll be compensated for their mighty efforts."

"Were they?"

"Maybe." He dropped another shot of whiskey into his latest beer. I hoped he'd be able to walk out of here on his own two feet. Otherwise, I'd need a sleigh and eight reindeer.

"What mighty efforts?"

Gareth took a long swig of alcohol. "They had to

promise to be good little girls and boys. Not an easy thing for that unholy trio to pull off. But money is a wonderful motivator."

As I suspected, it was no accident that everyone ended up in Oriole Point nine years ago. "Then Everett asked the three of them to move to Oriole Point."

"When Everett Hostetter wanted something, he never asked. He demanded. He took." Gareth paused. "He threatened."

"Did he threaten them?"

Gareth pointed at me with a greasy finger. "You're a sharp little cookie."

"If Everett threatened all three of his possible heirs, he could only do that if they'd done something bad in the past."

He closed his eyes. "Listen. It's my favorite Christmas song."

Michael Bublé's version of "I'll Be Home for Christmas" boomed over the bar's speakers. Gareth began to sing along with Michael at the top of his lungs.

Given Gareth's inebriation, I thought it best to eat dinner and let him finish the song. I kept a cautious eye on him as he swayed back and forth. A few times he almost toppled over.

When the song ended, Gareth held the final note even longer than Michael, eliciting a wave of cheers and applause from the bar and booths. From behind the bar, Chuck yelled, "That deserves a round on me!"

I frowned when Chuck brought Gareth's fifth drink. "I think Gareth has had enough."

"He'll be fine." Chuck leaned down. "Don't worry. I always cut him off after six."

"Six! You let him drink six boilermakers in a row!"

But Chuck went off to greet a new group coming through the door.

"Don't worry, Marlee." Gareth patted my hand. "I hardly ever pass out."

"Please stop drinking," I begged as he dropped the whiskey and the shot glass into the latest boiler-maker. "And don't put the glass in your drink. It's not sanitary."

Gareth shook his head and laughed. "You're so cute."

Since I couldn't dissuade Gareth, I decided I might as well try to get more information from him. Before he died from alcohol poisoning. "Okay. So all three of them have a shady past. I know Anthony framed his friend and business partner, who later killed himself in prison."

Gareth squirted half a plastic bottle of ketchup on his fries. "Never liked Anthony. Lazy. Entitled. A real trust-fund baby. A shame. His daddy was a brilliant surgeon. Nice guy, too."

"Did his father set up the trust fund for him?"

"Dr. Thorne didn't have that kind of money. No, Grandma Hostetter took a fancy to Anthony when he was an obnoxious toddler. She created a trust fund for the brat. Which he couldn't touch until he was twenty-five." Gareth's eyes brightened as "Jingle Bell Rock" boomed from the speakers. "I love this song, too!"

Before he could start singing again, I asked, "What

happened to Anthony after he got his hands on the trust fund?"

"He blew it all on women, cars, fancy houses. He threw parties that cost a fortune. Then there were bad investments, bogus real estate properties. When the trust fund ran out, he went to old Uncle Everett, asking for a job in the family business. Everett turned him down flat."

Hard to blame Everett. Anthony didn't sound like he'd be a desirable employee.

Gareth belched. "Lucky for Anthony that his college buddy Justin had money. The two of them started up that company in California. The one Anthony proceeded to loot."

"Assuming I've got the time line right, Anthony moved to Oriole Point a few months after his business partner killed himself." I took a sip of tea.

"Yeah." Gareth gave me a bleary gaze. "Anthony and Everett moved here together."

"Since Anthony's company went bust, he obviously needed money again. A rich uncle probably seemed like the best option, even though Everett had turned him down before."

"Anthony had no choice. After the trial, no bank or investor would come near him."

"Why didn't Anthony go to his mother for help? The other day you said she and Everett had controlling shares in the family company. So she had access to the Hostetter money."

"Sarah had given her son money over the years, all of which he squandered. But after his friend's suicide, she refused to give him another penny. Sarah knew Anthony well enough to realize he engineered Justin's downfall."

Gareth swigged down half of his latest boilermaker. With his nose reddening after each drink, and his fur-trimmed cap askew, Santa looked blotto.

"I think it's time to cut you off." I moved his half-empty glass away from him.

He yanked it back. "No way, José. You promised to buy Santa dinner. That includes drinks." Gareth chugged the rest of his beer and whiskey, then held it aloft. "One more!"

"Oh, Lord," I murmured as Gareth reached for another piece of fish.

"Did the Thornes have other children besides Anthony?" I asked.

"Anthony was their one and only. They did what they could to curb his worst tendencies. But Granny's trust fund let him be as reckless as he wanted. Good thing his father died before the scandal with Justin. Anthony broke his mama's heart after he drove his friend to suicide." Gareth shook his head. "She cut him out of her life. Completely."

"Which explains why he came to Oriole Point and danced to his uncle's tune."

"Oh, Everett Hostetter made certain Anthony had no recourse but him. He even convinced Sarah to remove Anthony from her will. Everett told Sarah if she gave her son any financial help—now or after she died—it would ruin her son completely. She believed him."

"Did Anthony know his uncle got him disinherited?"

"Everett told him. Part of his plan, you see." He giggled. "When Everett dangled the prospect of being named in *his* will, Anthony had no other options."

"Then the price for being his possible heir was that Anthony had to clean up his act."

Gareth slammed his hand on the table. "Bingo!"

Chuck brought over a sixth boilermaker.

"Who is Janelle's mother?" I asked after Chuck left.

Gareth hiccuped. "She died years ago. Car accident in Green Bay. Alcohol-related."

I looked at all the empty glasses on the table. Thank heaven Gareth didn't have to drive home. "How did she and Everett meet?" I thought about the age difference between Everett and Katrina. "She must have been quite a bit younger than him."

Pointing at the wall speaker, he belted out, " 'Jingle bell time is a swell time'!"

As the verse ended, I asked again, "Who was Janelle's mother?"

Gareth looked puzzled for a moment, as though he'd forgotten where we were. "Candice Walker. A secretary for Hostetter Inc. in Wisconsin. Although we call them admin assistants now." He seemed to find that funny.

"And she and Everett had a relationship."

He snorted. "Everett didn't have relationships. Candice was an attractive young woman who worked for him. He also liked brunettes. Women who reminded him of Diane Cleverly." Gareth wagged a finger at me. "Everett would have found you most appealing."

I cringed at the thought. "How long were Everett and Candice involved?"

"Not long. There were other female employees he demanded sexual favors from. They didn't have much choice if they wanted to keep their positions at the company. When the women became troublesome, Everett fired them. Or paid them to keep quiet." Gareth burped once more. "I know because I paid them off."

I was starting to lose my appetite.

"Sometimes I had to threaten them. Scare them so they wouldn't make trouble. And don't look so disapproving, Marlee Barley. Things were different back then."

"Janelle's in her midthirties. It's not like we're talking about medieval England."

"But this was long before that You Too movement."

"Me Too," I corrected him.

He took another gulp from his boilermaker. "Whatever. Candice got pregnant. Tried to get as much money out of the situation as possible. Everett fired her. He asked me to handle it."

I was glad now that I'd never become friends with Gareth. He made my skin crawl. "Was it a sense of guilt that made Everett ask Janelle to move here?"

He laughed. "You're funny, Marlee."

"I wasn't trying to be."

"Everett brought her to Oriole Point because Janelle had been naughty. Like Anthony." Gareth launched into his rendition of "Santa Claus Is Comin' to Town." All three verses and the chorus.

"Can we get back to our conversation?" I asked when he finished.

He looked at me as if seeing me for the first time. "What conversation?"

"You said Janelle Davenport had been naughty. But Janelle is a police officer. As far as I know, she's been one for many years. Here and in Wisconsin."

"True." He tried to prop his elbow on the table, but was too unsteady to pull it off. "But she was a bad cop. Crooked. Took bribes. Stole contraband confiscated from crime scenes. Helped send innocent people to prison. All with the help of fellow bad apples in the department. Right before she came here, Internal Affairs investigated her. Everett made sure the evidence against her went away. When you're rich, you can do that."

I found this troubling in the extreme. "Does Chief Hitchcock know about her past?"

Gareth tipped back his glass and finished it off. "No reason he should. Janelle has kept her nose clean since joining the Oriole Point police force."

At that moment, Janelle and Officer Bruno Wycoff walked past the Sandy Shoals Saloon. Both were in uniform. While Bruno grinned at the sight of Santa and me kicking it back at the bar, Janelle did not look amused. I was grateful neither officer came inside to confront us.

"What about Katrina?" I asked after they moved on.

Gareth's eyes were now at half-mast. "Who's Katrina?"

I wanted to hang my head in frustration. "Katrina May."

He carefully placed both elbows on the table. "Are there two of you? I see two Marlees."

"I'm not surprised. Gareth, what did Katrina do to deserve a place in Everett's will? Was it because they were married?"

"More than that. She was his accomplint. I mean, his accomplish. His accompent."

"Do you mean his accomplice?"

"See! You already knew."

"His accomplice in what?"

When he bent forward, his long beard fell into his fish basket. "In scaring his sister."

"Why did they want to scare her?"

"Why else? Money. And they did a good job." Gareth swayed back and forth, his eyes fluttering. "Too good."

"What do you mean?"

"I thought it was obvious, Barney."

"Marlee. And what's obvious?"

"That Everett and Katrina scared her to death."

I gasped. "They killed his sister?"

Gareth opened his mouth wide, but it was only to yell, "Ho, ho, ho!"

Then he fell face forward into his basket of fish and chips.

If I wanted more information, I'd have to wait until Santa sobered up.

Chapter Sixteen

After several regulars from the Sandy Shoals Saloon offered to take a drunken Gareth back to his house, I gave a stern lecture to Chuck about overserving his customers. I almost threatened to report him to the police, but I didn't want to interact with Janelle. At least not until I discovered the truth about Gareth's allegations.

I also doubted I'd be welcome at the bar again.

My dinner left me little time to get ready for Everett's memorial. I sped home to change out of my black jeans and candy cane sweater. On the way to the museum, I called Kit, but it went to voice mail. I debated whether to leave a long message, but thought better of it. A triple homicide outweighed the allegations of a drunken woodcarver who moonlighted as Santa.

Because Diane had closed the museum earlier, I knocked on the door. While waiting for someone to let me in, I looked at the endless snowdrifts on the museum grounds. Enough snow had fallen to ensure a lavishly white Christmas. With more snow predicted for later tonight.

The wide door opened to reveal Diane Cleverly. Dressed in black, she looked pale and wan, like a Victorian widow. Even her jewelry was black. At least she stopped short of draping a black veil over her upswept white hair. Her grief must be even greater than I thought.

"No need to knock," she said. "I left the door unlocked."

"Hi, Diane. I hope I'm not late."

"Two board members haven't arrived yet. They called to say they're on the way."

She ushered me inside. The dimly lit main floor threw shadows on the toy train displays.

"Where are you holding the memorial?"

"Second-floor meeting room. Everyone is here, aside from the rest of the board. Oh, and Gareth Holmes."

We headed up the stairs. "Gareth isn't coming." I told her.

Diane stopped. "He was Everett's attorney for decades. Of course he'll be here."

"We had dinner earlier. I'm afraid he had too much to drink."

She frowned. "I suspect it was on purpose. Too many people in Everett's life have a guilty conscience. But it shouldn't prevent them from honoring his memory."

Because I knew she was the only person who genuinely mourned his passing, I didn't mention that Everett didn't seem to be worth remembering. Which made the whole memorial service an uncomfortable prospect. And hypocritical of me.

"Everett seems to have meant a great deal to you. Why didn't you marry him?"

"I caught glimpses of the man he might have been. But he was in his forties when I met him. And the cold, indifferent mask he hid behind was becoming impenetrable." She sighed. "It was too late. Everett was not a man who believed in happiness."

"You might have been able to change him. After all, he proposed to you."

"Not out of love. He wasn't capable of love. But Everett did like and trust me. Something very rare for him. The proposal was a way to stop me from leaving. Instead, it convinced me to look for another job. Also I didn't love Everett. Instead, I felt pity for him. Which is why I've insisted the man have a memorial service." She took a deep breath. "He was my friend."

That prompted us to continue our way to the second floor, where the assistant curator took Diane aside. As I entered the meeting room, the scent of roses overwhelmed me. When I saw the white roses placed behind the podium, I wondered how Andrew had delivered the floral arrangements by himself; they were as oversized as Piper's Christmas tree.

As for attendees, I recognized the employees of the historical museum, along with most of the volunteers. Various board members mingled by the coffee urn. What Gareth had dubbed "the unholy trio" stood in the corner, deep in conversation.

Janelle noticed me first. Was she really a dishonest

cop? If so, that made her dangerous. At least she had changed out of her uniform. Although her dark brown tunic top and pants gave off a paramilitary vibe.

Her unfriendly stare caused Katrina and Anthony to turn around. Anthony glowered, but Katrina walked over to me. Garbed in a plum cashmere wrap dress and matching suede knee-high boots, Katrina was the best-dressed person in the room. The sparkle from her crescent earrings led me to suspect the gems were real diamonds. Along with the tennis bracelet on her right wrist. I wondered if these were jewels she'd gotten from manipulating a client.

"Marlee, how kind of you to attend Everett's service."

"I told you earlier I planned to come."

"Yes. As a favor to Diane. Naturally, I look on it as a favor to me as well."

"Because you and Everett were once husband and wife?"

"Of course. I'm still recovering from the shock of his death."

This seemed an extreme statement. "I assumed your spirit guides would have given you a heads-up. And he was almost a hundred years old. How shocked could you be?"

Irritation flickered across her face. "As shocked as you were about a dead squirrel."

I wondered how she knew about the squirrel until I remembered Natasha had plans to meet Katrina that morning. A meeting delayed due to our visit to the police.

"It seems Natasha told you about the squirrel."

"She did. I feel you've become too affected by finding Everett's body. You must release your energy from his. It will only bring you harm."

"Why should Everett's energy harm me?" I asked.

"Energy is powerful, especially that of the recently deceased." Her pageant smile returned. "That's why I returned to your house with Natasha and disposed of the squirrel."

"What?" I narrowed my eyes at her. "You had no right to do that."

"I'm a sensitive. I had a responsibility to remove a dead animal that caused you such unnecessary concern."

"What if the police want to test the squirrel to see it if died from poison?" I fought an impulse to grab her by the shoulders and shake her.

"Be reasonable. The police aren't interested in a dead squirrel. Now that the squirrel is gone, it should no longer interest you either."

"I'm surprised the squirrel interested *you*. Unless you think it's wise to destroy evidence."

"Evidence?" She shook her head. "Don't be ridiculous. I stopped you from becoming obsessed about the squirrel's death. And Everett's."

"My obsessions are none of your concern. And Natasha should not have let you dispose of anything on my property. I'll speak to her about that. As I'm speaking to you now."

"Is that a warning?"

"You're the psychic. What does your sixth sense tell you?"

"I sense you are making things difficult for yourself. Possibly even dangerous."

"Is that a warning?" I repeated her own question. She shrugged.

"By the way, how did Everett's sister take the news of your marriage? It must have come as a great surprise to learn her elderly brother had at last taken a bride. A child bride, too."

Katrina looked at me for a long moment. I didn't want to be the first to blink, but couldn't help it. She had the gaze of a cheerful Medusa. "Due to the age difference, Sarah was shocked at first. But she came to trust me. And I did my best to help her."

"With feng shui and messages from the dead? Did you organize her closets, too?"

Several people noisily entered the room. The service would start any moment.

"Now you sound like Piper. And I thought we were becoming friends. I see I was wrong. All because of a silly squirrel. I was right to get rid of it."

I watched as Katrina returned to Janelle and Anthony, where they huddled once more. Were the three of them allies? Maybe even friends?

Diane marched to the podium at the front of the room. Everyone took a seat on one of the folding chairs that had been set up. The assistant curator lit the many candles placed about the meeting room. Once another museum employee shut off the lights, a nondescript meeting room became a place of shadow and mystery.

I sat in the last row, mercifully empty. As Diane led us in a prayer, I regretted coming here. I didn't know Everett. What I had learned about him gave me no reason to like the man.

Despite my parka, I shivered from the chill. It was

almost as cold up here as in the Calico Barn basement. I should also have worn a much thicker turtleneck sweater. And I regretted changing into my favorite pewter-gray skirt. It left my knees exposed.

As Diane read Psalm 25, I went over Gareth's drunken revelations. The cold, avaricious Everett apparently had a change of heart nine years ago when his sister died. A death he and Katrina may have caused.

I thought about the lines I had memorized from *A Christmas Carol.* Jacob Marley visited his miserly business partner to warn him how greed and selfishness resulted in a miserable, lonely life. Had Everett viewed himself as a modern-day Jacob Marley and forced Janelle, Anthony, and Katrina to change their lives? It explained why he felt an affinity for the role.

A tap on the shoulder made me jump. I swiveled about and met the suspicious gaze of Anthony Thorne.

"What are you doing here?" he hissed.

"At the moment, I'm trying to listen to Diane pay tribute to your uncle."

"He doesn't deserve any tributes and you know it."

Deciding to ignore him, I faced forward as Diane read from a book of poetry.

Anthony pulled out the chair beside me and sat down. Now I wished I hadn't sat in an empty row. I didn't enjoy being this close to Anthony. Now that I was, I realized he and Janelle shared a family resemblance. The cousins had wide mouths, thin lips, and alarming overbites.

"I heard you had dinner with the family lawyer tonight," he whispered.

"What's it to you?"

"The next time you get together, remind him that the three of us won't wait forever to see what my uncle's will says. And not just us." He pointed at Diane. "She wants to know, too."

"Maybe all of you should hire your own lawyer."

Attendees glanced over their shoulders at us.

"If Gareth has acted illegally by not filing the will," I continued in a lower voice, "then take the necessary steps to force him to."

"Oh, we plan to force his hand. Gareth doesn't have my uncle to protect him any longer."

This didn't sound as if they were considering legal action. "I don't know Gareth well. But it seems like he's just playing a game."

"A game?" Anthony barked, causing Diane to pause in her reading.

"Shhh. In my opinion, Gareth is gleeful about making everyone wait to learn what's in the will. I'm sure he'll eventually file it or do whatever he's supposed to do next." I gave Anthony a weary look. "And I wouldn't be too worried. Since you're Everett's nephew, I'm sure you're in his will."

"Really? Have you become a psychic, too?"

"There are enough psychics in this room. We don't need another." My throat felt scratchy, I was cold, and I regretted coming here rather than making those cornflake hollyberry cookies. I also wanted to kick myself for not stopping at the Calico Barn to pick up my costume. I was running out of time to have it cleaned.

"We don't need outsiders interfering in family business," he whispered in my ear.

"I agree. Now leave me alone. And tell Moe and Larry up there to do the same."

He stood up, causing the chair to scrape loudly. Everyone looked over at us again. In another moment, I expected us to be asked to leave. After he walked away, I wondered if Everett had left the bulk of his fortune to Diane, and none to the "unholy trio." It would serve them right if he had.

Diane sat down and a board member took her place at the podium. When he began to read a lengthy passage from C. S. Lewis, I decided to sneak out. My attendance felt unnecessary. And it was still early enough to make those cookies, especially since I might have a hard time sleeping tonight if my sore throat got worse. I had to nip this in the bud. Suzanne would kill me if I backed out because of illness. And Gillian would never stop attributing it to the curse.

After I crept back down to the main floor, my glance fell on the bench where Everett had died. Lost in the shadows, it looked forbidding.

I wondered if Katrina sensed the presence of spirits here. At the moment, I felt as if I did. It wouldn't take much to imagine the ghost of Everett Hostetter slumped over on that bench, determined to bring his killer to justice. Thank goodness, it wasn't my responsibility to do that.

Even so, I'd done my best to find out what really happened to him. It irritated me that Katrina got rid of the squirrel. At least I'd handed over the rest of the evidence to the police. I'd also pass on the information Gareth gave me about Janelle and Katrina to Kit. But I wouldn't blame him for taking Gareth's drunken ramblings with a grain of salt.

I heard a creak in the rear of the museum, followed by the tinkle of glass.

Because the museum formerly housed an 1896 inn, I knew there was a kitchen in the back. A kitchen the museum used to make coffee, tea, and various foods for events. No one had come downstairs since I left the service. I could hear the drone of voices overhead. If it was a ghost, it was a noisy one.

However, I should check out the kitchen to make certain a toy train burglar hadn't snuck in. The remaining rooms downstairs had no illumination whatsoever, and I bumped into more than one display table of trains. At least when I reached the back of the house, light from the kitchen made the rest of my progress easier.

I entered the farmhouse-style kitchen to see Odette Henderson poking about in one of the cupboards. Odette owned Lakeshore Holiday, a downtown store specializing in seasonal decor.

"Hi, Odette."

She smiled. "Hey, Marlee." Odette not only physically resembled Oprah, she possessed her orotund voice. "I thought I heard someone bumping their way in the dark."

"Diane should turn on a few lights when the museum is closed. What are you doing down here?"

"I'm a board member. We were ordered to show up for the memorial. This whole thing was so last-minute, too. None of us needs an extra thing on our plates during Christmas week."

"Ain't that the truth. And I still have to make cookies for the store tonight."

"Why are you here?"

"Diane asked me." I wondered if I should elaborate. "And I agreed with her that Everett's death is a little suspicious."

"Is it?" Odette rummaged about in the cupboard. "I've been expecting him to kick off for years now. At last. Here's what I'm looking for."

She held up a large plastic bag of hard candies.

"Is the candy that good?"

"I have a sore throat and forgot to bring lozenges." She unwrapped a candy and popped it in her mouth.

"Must be something going around. My throat started to feel scratchy about an hour ago."

She held out the bag and I took one. Odette was right. As soon as the butterscotch flavor hit my throat, it felt better. "Thanks. I love butterscotch."

"Diane has an entire cupboard filled with hard candy. She puts them out in bowls for visitors." Odette took a small white paper bag from an upper shelf. "Take some for the road."

She poured a couple dozen candies into a bag and handed it to me.

I stared at the bag. "When I found Everett's body in the museum, he'd been eating a gingerbread cookie. A cookie placed in a paper bag exactly like this."

"The museum keeps bags here for special events, like the opening of the train exhibit. The board always budgets for snacks, and that includes small bags and napkins."

"I don't remember gingerbread cookies being offered during the exhibit opening."

"That's because there weren't any." She pointed at a piece of paper taped to another cupboard door. "Here's a list of the sweets laid out last Wednesday. No gingerbread cookies. In fact, I don't think I've seen gingerbread cookies offered at the museum since the gingerbread-house exhibit five years ago."

"I didn't know the museum kept bags like this."

Odette shrugged. "Half the food shops in town have white paper bags like these. Along with the food-vendor trucks for this weekend's festival."

"But where did the gingerbread cookies come from if the museum didn't lay them out?"

"Visitors bring all sorts of things into the museum they shouldn't. Just like they do in our shops. Last week, a customer came into Lakeshore Holiday eating a cheeseburger from the diner." She put the bags and candy back in the cupboard.

"What did you think of Everett Hostetter?"

"Not much. As a board member, he attended meetings and always sat next to Diane, making notes. Believe me, nothing happened in this museum without his approval and input. And everyone jumped to do his bidding."

"But you didn't like him."

"Did anyone, aside from Diane?" Odette raised a skeptical eyebrow at me.

"He probably thought it didn't matter. Not with all the money he had."

Odette leaned against the counter. "Then it's a good thing he died when he did. Before he was no longer the richest man in the room."

"What do you mean?"

"I forget most people don't follow business news and the stock market as avidly as I do." Before she retired, Odette had written a business column for a newspaper in Chicago.

"Everett sold his companies," I said. "It shouldn't matter what the stock market does."

"It's more complicated than that. After the last buyout, the majority of Everett's wealth lay in company shares. That was an integral part of the buyout agreement. And the company has been in steep decline the past two years for all sorts of reasons: competition from China, tariffs, upper-management conflict."

"You're saying his fortune was diminishing?"

"Rapidly. The company is in major financial trouble. Whoever his heirs are should count themselves lucky. In a year or two, they might have inherited next to nothing."

My mouth fell open. "I had no idea."

"No reason you should. Unless you're a business junkie like me."

"So Everett's death is good news for whoever is his primary beneficiary in the will."

"Extremely good news. Whoever inherits will come into a fortune. And I'm assuming that person is his nephew. Who else would it be?"

It appeared Odette didn't know about Janelle's or Katrina's connection to Everett. "He and Diane were friends. It's possible he left money for the museum."

"Oh, I would be shocked if the museum didn't get a financial bequest. I only wonder how much." Odette chuckled. "Funnily enough, I discussed this very thing with Diane after our last board meeting. After Everett had left, of course. Told her the gravy train the museum had been riding on might come to a halt sometime soon. As you can imagine, that made her anxious."

"I'm sure it did," I murmured.

Odette shrugged. "I thought it might be a good thing. Force the board to reach out to other wealthy donors in the area. It's never wise to put all your financial eggs in one basket. And in Everett's case, a most unfriendly basket. Now it all depends on the will."

"Gareth Holmes mentioned the will to me. Only he and Everett knew the contents. But Gareth didn't file the will. He's still got it somewhere. And I have no idea how long he plans to keep it to himself. He also said Everett hid his copy of the will."

"That doesn't surprise me. Amusing, in a sardonic way."

"His likely heirs aren't amused," I remarked.

"No doubt. They're probably on the hunt for the will."

"The strange thing is, I have a pretty good idea where the will might be."

"If you do, let Diane know. She won't rest until the museum's financial future is secured."

I held up my hand. "Shhh. I heard something."

"It's the building. The floors creak like clockwork. Although I wouldn't be surprised if Diane sent someone to look for me." Odette smoothed her blazer. "Are you coming?"

"No. I attended as much of the memorial as I care to."

"I hear you." Odette gave me a wink, then hurried out.

I was glad I left the service early. How else would I have learned that the museum stocked the same bags Everett's cookies had been in. More important, Odette answered a question that had nagged at me. Why would anyone murder a ninety-five-year-old man?

Now I understood. In a year, there would be far less money to inherit. The murderer had to act quickly. But which of the unholy trio had done it?

Since seeing the white paper bags in the museum cupboard, I knew I should include the grieving Diane Cleverly among them. After all, the museum's financial future might have been in jeopardy if its main benefactor had lived one more year. But I couldn't imagine Diane murdering anyone. Least of all a man she regarded with friendship and pity.

An even bigger question concerned the will. Gareth hinted that only he and Everett knew what was in it. And where the copies were. One copy lay in Gareth's possession. Everett must have the other, except Gareth told me that Everett did not keep it at his house.

It wasn't yet eight o'clock. I knew the technical crew had been working late at the Calico Barn, getting the play ready for Tuesday's opening. Why not stop by the theater barn on my way home? I could pick up my costume, which I planned to throw in the washing machine. While there, I'd search the dressing room Everett had kept locked for the past few years.

Because I'd bet all the plum puddings in the world that Everett hid his will in there.

Chapter Seventeen

I found the drive to Calico Barn both scenic and daunting. The latest storm had dumped even more snow on the numerous evergreens lining Blue Star Highway. And snow was falling again. I felt as if I were traveling through a white tunnel of trees. A tunnel that lay on slippery roads.

My headlights did reveal snowplows had been through earlier, spraying their mixture of salt and sand. Whenever my SUV fishtailed, I silently thanked the road crews. I was also thankful I made it to the grocery store before it closed. A quick stop and I now had all the ingredients for hollyberry cookies inside my canvas tote bag. Now to find the time to make them.

When I made the turn onto Wolverine Lane, the brakes locked on the icy road. Although I had been driving slow, I needed to go even slower. As my windshield wipers swished back and forth, I finally spotted the big sign for Calico Barn through the falling snow. Given the hazardous conditions, I was glad there wasn't much else around, except for the horse farm across the street.

Fortunately, the white sign that trumpeted A CHRIST-MAS CAROL shed more than enough light to show me the way. As did the strings of Christmas lights on the shrubs beneath it. The lights were on a timer, and I smiled to see they were still on. They also showed the parking lot had been plowed.

I rolled to a stop by the wooden ramp that led to the front entrance. I saw only one other vehicle in the lot: a pickup truck. Given all the snow piled on top of it, the truck had been here a while. I guessed it belonged to Clyde Fenwick, who owned an ancient Dodge truck notorious for breaking down. Clyde had volunteered to run the sound system for the play. When his truck died again, a friend must have given him a ride home.

I noticed numerous footprints in the snow. Those crew members and volunteers who had worked here today probably left within the hour.

Disappointed, I nonetheless made my way to the barn. Since a big double barn door served as the entrance, it had no windows to peek through. I yanked on the brass door handle several times, then knocked. A shame I had only been given the key to Everett's dressing room, and not the theater barn, too.

Why had I not snuck my costume out of the theater earlier? I'd also missed my chance to search through the dressing room for that will. Tomorrow's schedule was packed with Hollyberry Festival activities, but maybe I could take a break and run back here while people were inside. And not only for the will. The idea of wearing clothes that hadn't been cleaned in years made my skin itch. Maybe I should burn the costume, rather than just wash it.

I suddenly recalled that the barn had side and back entrances. I once delivered berry pastries for a fund-raiser here. People in Oriole Point were notorious for leaving their homes and vehicles unlocked. Life in a small town gave one a false sense of security. I wouldn't be surprised if a volunteer had been careless and left one of the doors unlocked. It was worth a try.

Fortunately, someone had shoveled a path around the side of the barn. Which likely meant a path had also been cleared to the back entrance. Spotlights on the barn roof illuminated the shoveled path and white barn so well, I could see every plank of its wooden walls.

I made my way to the side entrance door, but had no luck getting inside. Of all the times for my fellow Oriole Point residents to be practical and lock every door. I no longer held out much hope that I'd be able to get in the back way, but soldiered on regardless.

The rear spotlights revealed the delivery door I had used in the past. When I pulled on the handle, I found it locked tight. The costume and the will would have to wait.

Before setting back, I stamped my feet to keep warm. Tall boots had been a good choice tonight. I couldn't say the same for my knee-length skirt. Cold air whipped about my bare legs. I made a note to add tights the next time I wore a skirt in freezing weather. A winter coat longer than a hip-length parka should be tacked onto my Christmas list, too.

I'd also spent too much energy concerned about Everett and his possible heirs. Time to devote my attention to hollyberry cookies. And I needed something besides butterscotch candy to alleviate my sore throat. Maybe I'd stop at the Chinese carryout on the way home for a pint of wonton soup. I pulled out my cell phone to call in a take-out order.

Just then, the exterior barn lights shut off. If not for the reflective snow on the ground, I'd be in pitch darkness.

The theater timer must have turned the lights off, including the sign out front. Good thing my phone was in my hand. Its flashlight would illuminate the shoveled path to the parking lot.

Before I could take a step, however, I heard a car drive up. On a silent winter night, the sound of wheels as they crunch on snow is unmistakable.

Maybe a member of the Green Willow Players forgot something in the theater. Or a friend drove Clyde back here to retrieve his truck.

I listened as the car crunched to a stop. A car door slammed shut.

If the visitor was connected to the theater company, they would see my SUV and be curious. Or it might be the police, making their rounds. Then again, maybe it wasn't.

This was silly. I was scaring myself for no reason. Should I call out to let the person know I was out back? I decided not to. Instead, my instincts warned me to keep quiet and listen.

But I didn't hear anything. Just fat, wet snowflakes slapping the ground around me. Wolverine Lane saw little traffic even at midday. At nine o'clock at night, cars were rare.

Only I couldn't stay here forever.

My head shot up as someone rattled the theater entrance door several times. This person didn't have a key either.

I crept along the barn wall and peeked around the corner. A figure now made its way along the same shoveled path I had come down. In the darkness, I could only make out a shape through the falling snow. I was no longer comfortable returning the way I had come. And I had no intention of staying here until this person found me.

Of course, this could all be perfectly harmless. Or not.

Trying to be as quiet as possible, I hurried to the other corner of the barn and began to plow my way through the snow. And *plow* was no exaggeration. No one had shoveled a path along this side of the barn.

Each step forward meant battling through a snow-drift. Wet snow coated my legs and slipped inside my boots. My feet became soaked in minutes.

As I pushed forward, I heard the side door of the barn rattle. Someone else wanted to get into the theater as much as I had.

Whoever continued along the shoveled path would soon reach the back entrance. Finding that locked as well, this person was certain to see my fresh footprints in the otherwise untouched snow. Faster, faster, faster, I told myself.

After stumbling twice in the deep snow, I reached the front parking lot. As I hurried past the snow-covered pickup, the unmistakable rattling of the back door reached me.

I flung myself in my SUV and locked the door. Turning on the motor would alert this latest visitor, who would probably return via the quicker, shoveled path. I had no plans to be here when that happened.

Even worse, whoever it was knew I was on the property. To get to the side of the barn meant some-one had walked right past my blue SUV, which had THE BERRY BASKEt emblazoned on both sides. My cover was blown.

I gunned the motor and sped for the driveway leading to Wolverine Lane. When I glanced over my shoulder, I spotted a vehicle in the lot that hadn't been here when I arrived. It was parked at the far-thest side of the lot, where the snow-laden branches of evergreens helped conceal it.

As much as I wanted to turn around and get a closer look, I thought caution the wiser move. If I didn't leave immediately, I feared I might be the next person taken down by the curse of this year's *A Christmas Carol* production. And I didn't want to do that to Suzanne.

Or myself.

Chapter Eighteen

"Trouble's headed our way," Dean announced as he hung the OPEN flag the next morning.

Busy counting the bills and coins in the cash drawer, I joked, "Did someone else drop out of the play?"

"Actually, Mrs. Fezziwig quit an hour ago. Mom called while I was having breakfast."

"The cast has become a blur to me. Who's playing Mrs. Fezziwig again?"

"Alice Bazil, the lady who runs Christian Neighbors at St. Veronica's."

Done with the money, I turned on the twinkling lights, then straightened my berry ornaments on the Christmas tree. "Maybe Suzanne should cut the character from the play. Have Mr. Fezziwig be a widower. I don't think Dickens would mind."

"My mother would. That's why she's stepping into the role. Mrs. Fezziwig has no lines in this stage version. All the actress has to do is dance around for the Fezziwig Christmas bash. Mom will love that. She and my dad took ballroom dance lessons." Dean gave a rueful chuckle. "I think that was one of the things that led to their divorce."

"Losing Mrs. Fezziwig hardly qualifies as trouble. Learning the rest of my lines does."

"That wasn't the trouble I referred to. As for your lines, what have you been doing all weekend?"

"Gee, I don't know. Waiting on customers, baking cookies for the shop, going to Everett's memorial service, prying information out of Gareth while he got drunk at dinner."

"That sounds promising." Dean adjusted the volume on the streaming service, now playing "Carol of the Bells." "Anything I can include in my blog?"

"Not unless you want to be sued by Santa. Don't forget he was a big-shot lawyer in his previous life. I only hope Gareth doesn't remember how indiscreet he was last night."

"I need details."

"So do I. What kind of trouble are we heading for?"

He jerked his thumb at the window, where snow continued to fall. "According to my phone app, west Michigan is in for a big bout of lake-effect snow. The Chicago area, too. If we get as much as predicted, we'll be buried in the stuff by Christmas Eve."

I perked up. "Yes! Let it snow."

This wasn't a normal reaction to lake-effect snow. Those of us raised along the Great Lakes were familiar with a phenomenon experienced early in winter before the surface of the lakes froze over. Cold air moved down from Canada and picked up moisture from the still-warm waters. This resulted in lots of snow, often more than three inches an hour for a long time. And by long time, I meant days—if not weeks.

Dean took a bite from the cornflake hollyberry cookies I made last night. They were delicious. I planned to add them to our holiday cookie list every year. I couldn't wait for Theo to taste them after he finished his caroling shift this morning.

"I understand why you want the snow to put a crimp in the play, but it might be a problem for your parents. They're supposed to drive up on Christmas Eve, aren't they?"

I frowned. "You're right. I forgot. Dad has a big breakfast event at his hotel that morning. He can't leave until noon. And Mom has a faculty Christmas dinner the night before." My father managed a prestigious boutique hotel in downtown Chicago, and my mother was a professor at Northwestern.

"Be careful what you wish for," Dean said. "Or you'll celebrate your thirty-first birthday *and* Christmas without Mom and Dad."

"I'd hate that. Especially since Aunt Vicki is spending the holidays in Arizona with her boyfriend Joe's family. The weather might play havoc for Kit's parents, too. They fly into Detroit today to visit relatives. Then they plan to rent a car to come here."

Dean glanced at the picture-perfect snowfall outside our window. "You might want to pray for rain. I'd add a prayer to help you memorize your lines."

"I'm doing my best. I downloaded an audio version of *A Christmas Carol.* I can listen to it with my earbuds while working."

He rolled his eyes. "Yeah, I'm sure that won't be distracting."

"I don't have much choice. Dress rehearsal is to-morrow night."

"Concentrate on the play, Marlee. Forget about Everett Hostetter and dead squirrels."

"Thanks for reminding me about the squirrel. I want to find out if the police sent the cookie fragments for testing."

Dean shook his head. "It's Christmas week. Why bother?"

"Aren't you curious as to what happened to Everett Hostetter? And the squirrel?"

"Why? I wasn't close to either of them."

"I know this sounds bad, but I feel much worse about the squirrel than Everett." I set up our coffee urn, choosing chocolate raspberry as our free selection for the day. "Since they both died after eating the cookies, I bet they were poisoned."

"If so, let the police handle it."

"I am. That's why I gave them the gingerbread cookies."

"What does Kit think?" Dean asked.

"I told him about the dead squirrel. But the whole thing sounds silly when you compare it to the triple homicide he's working on."

"The local news said it's connected to a ring of meth labs here in west Michigan."

"The sheriff's department is working around the clock. The state police, too. The death of a very old man and an unlucky squirrel aren't high on their list." As I walked past the pastry case, I gave an approving look at the green hollyberry cookies.

"You've done what you can, Marlee. Now give me a

quick rundown on what you learned from Gareth. I'm in the mood for gossip."

I told him about my conversation with Gareth at the Sandy Shoals Saloon. Then added what transpired at the memorial service afterward and my aborted attempt to get into the theater. But we had no time to discuss anything further because a wave of customers were upon us.

Despite the continuing snowfall, downtown was filled with people. Today's Hollyberry Festival events had a snowman building contest added to the hot-chestnut stands set up on Lyall Street, the street carolers, food trucks, and Piper's horse-drawn carriage rides. The most time-consuming activity promised to be the open-air Hollyberry Market at River Park. Over three dozen decorated booths had been set up, and Piper had arranged to have electric lines run out to those vendors who needed power. Since I was serving berry-flavored hot cocoa, I qualified.

I expected to freeze, even though Dean and I agreed to alternate shifts running The Berry Basket booth. At least my throat felt better. I'd been sucking on those hard candies Odette gave me. I also picked up an order of wonton soup on my way home last night.

"Looks like we inspired Garth to find his inner Santa," Dean said. "On the way here, I saw him walking down Lyall Street in the Santa suit."

"I figured he'd be in bed nursing a hangover."

"He might be willing to play Santa again in the shop."

Not that we needed Santa today. Everyone seemed

in a holiday mood, and sales passed a thousand dollars by one o'clock. So many gift packages of berry soaps and lotions flew out the door, I'd have to put together more baskets of bath products after we closed.

Due to the high volume of business, I barely had time to eat my egg salad sandwich at lunch. But I did play my Dickens audiobook whenever there was a lull.

Dean offered to man the outdoor booth for the first two hours. But eventually it was time for my turn. I had just zipped up my parka when Gillian came in.

"Right on time," I told her. "Did you have fun caroling?"

"I sounded flat compared to the group they assigned me to. Three of the singers were members of the Oriole Point Chorus. They were show-offs. Holding all the notes at the end."

"I'm sure you were great." I wound my scarf tight about my neck. "You only have to stay here for about five minutes. Long enough for me to get to River Park and send Dean back."

"No problem. I need to warm up before going out again. I'm meeting Mom for lunch at The Wiley Perch." She craned her neck past the shop's Christmas tree. "I see something new in the pastry case. And they look like holly leaves."

It seemed fitting that Theo arrived during Gillian's mention of pastries. He carried the songbook used by the festival carolers.

"How did the caroling go this morning?" I asked Theo.

"I liked it." he said with a solemn expression. "But they should have given us the songbook yesterday. Some of the carols I never heard before, like 'The Holly and the Ivy.' "

"That's why we had songbooks." Gillian made her way to the pastry case. "And you're supposed to give the books back when your group is done singing."

He tightened his grip on the green hardcover volume. "I asked if I could keep it. To help me learn all the songs. Was that wrong?"

"Don't worry about it," I told him. "Piper's committee has plenty of songbooks. Now that you're here, try a new Pinterest recipe I made last night. Hollyberry cookies made with cornflakes. I've already sold half the batch."

Gillian grabbed one from the case and took a bite. "Yum. Do you mind if I take a few with me? Mom's looking for new Christmas cookie recipes."

"Go ahead."

She pulled out a small white paper bag from her purse as Theo joined her.

"Where did you get that bag?" I asked Gillian.

"The police station. They're giving out bags of caramel corn this weekend." She grinned. "Along with a list of instructions about how to avoid home break-ins."

Theo put one of the hollyberry cookies on a napkin. "When we sang at the fire station, the firefighters handed out bags of popcorn. And a piece of paper telling people how to prevent Christmas tree fires. I have to read it tonight."

"It's all part of the festival. Our mayor's passing

out candy canes at city hall, accompanied by a reminder to register to vote." Gillian removed several
hollyberry cookies.

I watched her bag the cookies. "By the way, that
white bag matches the one which held Everett's gingerbread cookies."

"Really?"

"Yes. The historical museum keeps bags like that.
And during the parade yesterday I saw Anthony
Thorne eating something from a white paper bag, too."

Gillian shrugged. "Probably hot chestnuts. Street
vendors sell the nuts in these bags. I had some chestnuts yesterday. These bags are as common as the
plastic ones at the grocery store."

"This tastes good, Marlee." Theo held up his half-
eaten cookie. "And it has pretend holly on it, so no
one can be poisoned."

"The last thing I want is to poison my customers. I
only wish I knew where Everett got those gingerbread cookies."

Gillian's expression darkened. "Let's not talk
about Everett Hostetter. I want to stay in a Christmas
mood."

"We all need to stay in a Christmas mood," Theo
agreed. "This is a happy time."

"Well, I have happy news. I've memorized most of
my lines."

This didn't bring a smile to Gillian's face. "Marlee,
please quit the play. One person has died, with two
people sick or injured. And Alice Bazil dropped out
today."

"I heard."

"Is this the cursed play Marlee is in?" Theo asked.

"Yes, it is," Gillian said.

"The play is not cursed. Stop saying that, or no one will buy tickets."

"Did you hear Suzanne might lose Brandon Foy as well? He's the kid cast as Tiny Tim. His parents are nervous about all the bad luck connected with the play. And if Tiny Tim walks out this close to opening . . ."

"I like Tiny Tim," Theo murmured before finishing off his cookie.

"Suzanne will find a way for the show to go on, even if she has to turn it into a one-woman show."

"Let her," Gillian said. "As long as you're not that woman."

I stepped out of the way as two customers came in. They made a beeline for my wall of berry wreaths.

While they admired the wreaths, I turned back to Gillian and Theo. "I better get over to the park and relieve Dean. And don't be surprised if Santa shows up. It looks like Gareth is walking around town in the suit I bought."

"I saw Santa right before I met the carolers," Theo said. "He was eating breakfast at the Drop Anchor Diner. The spooky lady was with him. That woman helping Natasha with the spa."

"Gareth Holmes had breakfast with Katrina May?" I asked. "Are you sure?"

"It was them. But I don't like Katrina because she talks to ghosts." Theo looked a little fearful. "Maybe she doesn't like the ghosts either. She was crying."

"Crying? I wonder why."

Katrina May didn't strike me as someone who cried easily. If that woman had been brought to tears, she was deeply upset over something. Or she'd turned on the waterworks in hopes of getting information from Gareth Holmes about the will. Either way, Katrina's public breakdown seemed unexpected and disturbing.

I didn't possess Katrina's psychic gifts. But like Dean, I sensed trouble ahead.

Chapter Nineteen

After an hour at the open-air market, I had drunk three cups of hot cocoa, necessitating a trip to the public restroom. Because Dean took a two-hour shift, I offered to do the same. But our presence at the market seemed pointless. Snow fell steadily, making it difficult for visitors to plow through the drifts in the park. At least volunteers kept the sidewalks shoveled.

Also everyone was far more interested in the snowman contest, food-vendor trucks, and the ice-skating rink. Most of my business consisted of people eager for a cup of strawberry-flavored cocoa. Although I sold out of my berry glass ornaments in the first thirty minutes, few customers bought the berry jams, jellies, soaps, and candles we'd stocked the booth with. I didn't blame them. Shoppers could buy these products—and far more—while staying warm in my store four blocks away.

With visits to my booth few and far between, I spent the time listening to *A Christmas Carol* on my iPhone. By two thirty, I'd committed all my lines to memory. I had to restrain myself from giving a hoot of joy. Not that anyone would have heard me.

A brass band played "Deck the Halls" under the park gazebo, the park rang with the happy cries of children, and a noisy crowd skated at the nearby rink.

Listening to *A Christmas Carol* did keep me in a holiday mood. The only thing to dampen that was the sight of Officers Davenport and Wycoff on patrol. Every half hour, Janelle and Bruno made their unsmiling way through the park, no doubt hoping to find someone to charge with a minor infraction, such as using excessive force in a snowball fight.

Fortunately, Janelle ignored me. I loved Christmas and didn't want to waste any of the holiday interacting with her. I already regretted spending as much time as I had on Everett Hostetter. If only Gillian hadn't stumbled on the body. Otherwise, that squirrel might be alive.

I wondered if I was lucky to be breathing, too. Who was at the Calico Barn last night? Was the person looking for the will? If true, my big mouth was to blame. When talking to Odette, I mentioned that I thought I knew where Everett hid his will. Right after, I heard a noise.

Yes, it could have been the old building creaking. My house did all the time. But maybe it was a person creeping in the dark.

Did someone eavesdrop on our conversation? Katrina, Anthony, and Janelle had all been upstairs at the memorial service. What if one of them followed me to the kitchen and overheard my declaration? I couldn't forget about Diane. She might have left the memorial briefly to check on why I had left, or to see what had happened to Odette. Any of the possible beneficiaries to Everett's fortune could have been listening in the shadows—and followed me to the Calico Barn.

To stop obsessing about all this, I decided to wander about the market. A few holes on my Christmas gift list needed filling. And I could keep an eye on my own booth at the same time.

As I checked out a display of Christmas-themed jewelry, I spied Santa in the crowd. I guessed it was Gareth. When Anthony Thorne took him by the arm and spun him around, my guess was confirmed. I tried to watch them. But with too many booths close together and a bustling crowd, I only caught glimpses of the two men. They seemed to be in a heated conversation. If I could get closer without them seeing me . . .

"Marlee, I'm so glad to bump into you."

I took my attention from the two men and now focused on Diane Cleverly. "Hi, Diane. Enjoying the festival?"

"No. But the museum set up a booth by the gazebo. We brought Christmas items from our gift shop to sell. Before he died, Everett instructed us to have more of a visible presence at the town events."

"I guess what Everett wanted, he got."

Although I said this in a joking manner, she sighed. "Exactly."

"The night we found his body, you said Everett pushed himself. And pushed other people. What did you mean by that?"

She bit her lip. "Did I say that? I don't remember. But Everett was a stubborn man who believed he always knew best. Most of the time, he did. Although his methods for achieving his aims could be questionable."

"How so?"

"It doesn't matter. He's gone. And I wanted to thank you for attending the memorial service last night. You left before I could say goodbye."

I hoped she didn't realize how early I had left.

Diane waved toward Gareth and Anthony, still in the throes of an argument. "At least Anthony showed up for the memorial. But Gareth should be ashamed. He worked closely with Everett for decades. I intend to speak with him, but I need to let my anger cool."

"Looks like Anthony is angry as well."

"I'm not surprised. They never got along. And emotions are heightened because no one knows what's in Everett's will." She shook her head. "Except for Gareth. If he was as smart as he thinks he is, he'd make the details public."

"I agree."

We watched as Gareth and Anthony now took off in different directions.

She gave herself a shake. "I need to get back to the booth. But I wanted to let you know how much I appreciate your kindness and concern. After all, you barely knew Everett Hostetter."

I didn't add that I had learned an awful lot about him since his death.

After Diane left, I finished my tour of the Hollyberry Market, where I bought two pairs of fingerless gloves, a Father Frost nutcracker, a blue crystal star pendant, and a llama-wool scarf. I also kept warm by enjoying a mulled wine known as glühwein. A classic German-market drink, glühwein was sold along with the handmade mug it came in. So I had a red ceramic mug in the shape of a boot as well.

When I returned to my own booth, I found Santa waiting for me. Or rather, Gareth dressed in my Santa suit.

"I hope you don't mind." Gareth lifted his cup. "I've drunk some of your hot cocoa."

"Be my guest." Better for him to down cocoa rather than mulled wine or boilermakers. "I see you're Santa again."

"Some people posted photos of me as Santa in your shop on Facebook. After the mayor's wife saw them, she asked if I'd play Santa at the Hollyberry Festival today."

"Piper will make certain you're Santa for every Hollyberry Festival in the future."

"Then I'll have to borrow the Santa suit again. I hope you don't mind."

"It fits you so perfectly, I'm giving it to you."

"Why, thank you. What a sweet girl you are."

"Knowing Piper, she probably asked you to remain visible at all the festival events."

Gareth took a big sip of cocoa. "And she asked me to go into the shops to greet customers. I stopped by The Berry Basket about a half hour ago. Now I'm supposed to walk around the market stalls. And be on hand when Piper gives out the award for Best Snowman."

"What else? I hope she doesn't expect you to actually fly a sleigh overhead."

"I'm having fun. She did suggest I show up at the big tree for the closing carols."

"Suggest?" I laughed. "You ignore Piper's suggestions at your peril."

A band of carolers entered the park singing "Joy to the World."

"I hope you've taken the time to eat while on your Santa rounds."

"Don't worry. I never miss a meal. And I've had a snack in every store I visited."

He looked as he had during his Santa stint yesterday at the shop. Passing out from all those boilermakers hadn't left any lasting effect.

"How are you feeling? You drank so much last night, I was worried about you."

"To be honest, I don't remember much from our dinner. I might have had one too many. Christmas has been hard for me since my wife died." He sighed. "The guys at Sandy Shoals have become like family. They look out for me."

I didn't approve of Chuck giving Gareth so much alcohol, but they were all big boys. And not my responsibility.

"How was the memorial?" Gareth's smile turned boyish. "Did the vultures miss me?"

"Anthony said the three of them won't wait forever to learn the contents of the will."

This amused him. "He just got done badgering me about that very thing."

"Gareth, file the will and make it public."

"Let them squirm. They deserve it."

"That's a dangerous game to play." I lowered my

voice. "Don't you realize that one of them probably murdered Everett?"

"A ridiculous idea. They wouldn't have dared."

"I think you're wrong. My advice is to keep your distance from all of them, even Diane. Anyone who thinks they might benefit from Everett's death."

"Don't worry. I know these people. A lot of bark. No bite." Gareth pulled out a white bag from his capacious red pocket. "Look, Katrina even bought me a bag of hot chestnuts. I ran into her and the Russian beauty outside San Sebastian."

My eyes widened at the sight of the bag. "Did you eat any of the chestnuts? How do you feel? Stomach pains? Are you dizzy?"

He gave a hearty laugh worthy of the jolliest Santa. "I feel fine, Marlee."

For a former corporate attorney, Gareth now seemed as trusting as Santa. "Are you and Katrina bosom buddies now? Theo says he saw you having breakfast with her this morning at the Drop Anchor."

"Don't forget Katrina was Everett's wife. That made her a part of the Hostetter family. And I was the family lawyer, even after I retired." He grew serious. "We understand each other."

"Theo said Katrina was crying. Is she experiencing actual grief over Everett's death?"

Gareth looked off into the distance, but I didn't think his attention was on the skaters twirling on the rink. "Katrina is a sensitive woman. And not because she claims to be sensitive to energy and ghosts and all that. She's haunted by the past. Then again, who isn't?"

"Is she haunted by what she did to Sarah Thorne?

Last night you said Katrina and Everett scared her to death. Did you mean that literally?"

He looked startled. "I don't remember saying such a thing."

I gave him a knowing look. "You're talkative when drunk. And indiscreet. Let's not pretend you didn't reveal more than you intended. So what did Katrina do to Sarah?"

Several children yelled out a greeting to Santa. He gave a jolly wave and a "Ho, ho, ho."

"Did she scare Sarah into signing over her shares to Everett?" I asked after the children had moved on. "If so, how?"

Gareth looked uncomfortable. "Katrina told Sarah something that did frighten her. I don't know the details. And Katrina and Everett blamed themselves for her death."

"Is that why Katrina was upset this morning?"

He shrugged. "Even nasty people have occasional regrets."

"Did you tell her what was in the will?"

Gareth made a disbelieving face. "Why would I do that? Because she cried? No. Katrina deserves to suffer with the rest of them."

"People don't like to suffer. And if they know who's to blame for their suffering, there might be repercussions." I pointed at the bag of chestnuts. "At least promise me that you won't eat any more of them."

"If it makes you feel better, keep it." He handed the bag to me. "Chestnuts don't have the same appeal as Christmas cookies. And I'm sure to have a lot more cookies offered to me today."

With another "Ho, ho, ho," he went on his merry way. Leaving me with a half-eaten bag of chestnuts and a sense of foreboding.

Dean and I stamped our feet in an attempt to keep warm. Our instructions were to meet the carolers by the big Christmas tree in the village square. Either we got the time wrong, or the other seven people who volunteered for this gig bailed.

"How long should we wait?" Dean asked.

"I have no idea. And I'm freezing."

Dean shivered. "I know it's only six thirty. But it gets dark so early, it feels much later."

"Is that your mom?" I waved at a group of people leaving an art gallery a few stores down from where we stood. "Suzanne!"

She said something to her friends. They waited as she came over to us.

"Mom, for the love of Monet, please don't buy me a painting from the Ashley Art Gallery again. I hate everything in there. Even the font on their sign."

"You're so difficult to shop for. What choice have you left me? Unless you want me to buy you food again."

"No food!" He turned to me. "Last year, Mom ordered a gift box from Gilroy, California, garlic capital of the world. A crate packed with garlic-saturated food products. Parts of my apartment still smell like the kitchen at Olive Garden."

"Then be grateful for the art I buy. And aren't the two of you supposed to be caroling?"

"We may have been stood up. But I did want to let

you know that I've learned my lines." I smiled. "All of them."

She clasped her hands in a dramatic gesture and looked up at the heavens. "It's a true Christmas miracle!"

"Very funny. I also wanted to ask if anyone will be at the theater tonight. There's something I forgot in my dressing room."

"Nice try, Marlee. But no." She smirked. "You are not getting your hands on that costume. You intend to ruin it in your washing machine. Not going to happen on *my* watch."

"C'mon. It will be fine. I'll run it on the gentle cycle."

"Forget it." Wheeling around—not easy to do on our slippery sidewalks—Suzanne returned to her friends.

"Smooth, Marlee. So smooth." Dean shook his head.

"It was worth a try." I pulled off my gloves. "Let me text Piper to see where everyone is."

After a moment, he asked, "What does Her Majesty say?"

"She changed the meeting place. Everyone is waiting for us beneath the clock at city hall."

"A little advance word would have been nice. What's the reason for the change?"

"She decided the tree was too unstable." We looked over our shoulders at Oriole Point's giant Christmas tree. It towered over us, swaying in the winter wind. Half the ornaments had blown off or been broken during one of the times it fell. The remaining ornaments were now tied to the branches. I grimaced at the sight of the hopelessly tangled red-and-silver garland. At least most of the LED lights still worked.

"The tree's toppled over three times," I said. "The last time it nearly fell on the FedEx guy."

"Then why are we standing so close to it?" Dean offered me his arm.

But we'd only taken a few steps when a gust of wind almost knocked us over. Snow blinded us and we bent our heads.

"Are there hurricanes in Michigan?" he shouted.

Because the wind was so strong, we turned our backs to it. Just in time to see the giant Christmas tree fall again.

We exchanged puzzled looks. "Should we tell someone?" I asked.

"No. They'll figure it out soon enough." The blast of wind mercifully died down. "Besides, this time it fell where there's nothing but a park bench and the rose garden."

"Then let's go. The songbooks await."

Linked arm in arm once more, we set off for city hall. We had just reached the group when a scream rang out.

Everyone froze as the screams continued.

One of the carolers gestured in the direction we came from. "The tree fell again."

Dean and I looked at each other. "Maybe it did fall on someone," I said.

We ran as a group back to the tree. Over a dozen others already milled about the village square.

A woman pointed at the pile of snowy branches. "There's someone under the tree!"

A mob of us grabbed the branches and trunk to lift it.

"It's Santa!" someone yelled. "We need a doctor!"

As soon as the tree was lifted and placed off to the side, people clustered about the motionless figure of Santa Claus. It had to be Gareth.

Dean and I pushed through the crowd to kneel beside him.

"Is he okay?" Dean said.

I heard more than one person call EMS on their cell phone. Others reached for his pulse. But Gareth's half-open, unblinking eyes told me it was too late.

And why was a sprig of holly actually pinned to his chest?

"'Buried with a stake of holly through his heart,'" I murmured.

"What did you say?" Dean asked me.

I sat back, shaken. "I said Gareth Holmes was murdered."

Chapter Twenty

The crowd grew so quickly, I wondered if the whole thing had been posted on YouTube. Dean seemed stunned. I was pretty stunned myself. Someone shoved me out of the way before I could get a closer look at Gareth's body.

Janelle Davenport ripped open Santa's jacket and began to give him CPR. Officer Bruno Wycoff squatted beside her. He called for an ambulance on his phone.

"About ten people already called 911," I told them.

They ignored me. But no one could ignore Piper's distressed arrival.

"Move aside!" she ordered. "Let me through. What's going on?"

Someone shouted, "The Christmas tree fell on top of Santa Claus!"

A mother in the gathering picked up her toddler and hurried off. Smart move. This wasn't a Christmas memory I'd want my child to have.

Piper caught sight of Janelle giving CPR and gasped. "Gareth!"

"I'm afraid he's dead," I told Piper.

This caused a ripple through the crowd. I didn't understand the shocked reaction. It seemed evident to anyone paying attention.

"Impossible." Piper waved me aside. "He can't be dead!"

"I think he can," I said. "The question is why."

"A heart attack caused by the shock of being knocked over," Dean suggested.

Janelle shot Piper an accusing glance. "Sounds likely. After all, what amounted to a redwood fell on top of him."

Bruno examined the body. "Looks like he hit the ground hard when he fell. Cause of death might be a closed-head injury."

Indeed, the square had been kept cleared of snow for the festival. When Gareth fell, he landed on cement, much of it iced over.

I scanned the paved circle where the festival tree had been set up. It normally held a statue of Piper's ancestor Benjamin Lyall, who founded Oriole Point in 1830. But Piper had been so determined to make this the best Hollyberry Festival ever, she'd arranged for the statue to be temporarily relocated to the adjacent rose garden. It required a dozen men to move it. And to transport the Christmas tree.

In addition, a park bench stood within the circle. I estimated how far Gareth's body lay from the edge of the wrought-iron seat. He could have hit his head on the bench as he fell to the ground. My first thought was that Gareth had been murdered. However, his

death might be a tragic example of wrong place/
wrong time.

Piper grabbed my arm. "This is terrible!"

"I know. Gareth was so happy earlier today. It's
tragic."

"Yes, sad. Very sad. But what an appalling way to
end the festival. Santa dead under the town Christmas tree!" She yanked her beret off in frustration.
"No one will ever forget this."

Katrina May pushed to the front of the crowd.
Upon seeing Gareth, she covered her mouth with
her hands. I stepped back to allow her through.

She knelt beside the body. "I knew it. I felt something bad would happen."

"Let's everyone move back," Janelle ordered. "The
ambulance will be here soon."

"Please do as the officer says." Piper waved everyone in the opposite direction. "Just an unfortunate
accident. Please move along."

But more people joined the crowd, including Suzanne, Gillian, Theo, and a fur-clad Natasha. Street
lamps revealed everyone's alarmed expression. Except
for that of Anthony Thorne, who appeared exasperated.

He stepped around the huge branches of the tree
that now covered most of the paved circle. A stray ornament lay in his path and he kicked it aside. "What
the hell happened, Janelle?"

"What does it look like?" she said with a sneer.
"Gareth is dead."

"No way." Anthony squatted down beside Katrina.
"How did he die?"

Janelle snorted. "Look around, Einstein. A giant tree fell on top of him."

Dean cleared his throat, drawing their attention. "Marlee and I were here when it did."

Janelle shot to her feet. "I should have known people from the berry store would be involved. What were the two of you doing here?"

"Dean and I were supposed to meet the carolers at the tree," I explained, "but they changed the meeting place at the last moment."

"Good thing I did," Piper said. "The tree might have fallen on the carolers."

"I sensed death around him." Katrina laid a hand on Gareth's chest. "Poor man."

Anthony didn't even pretend to be shocked. Instead, he brushed snow off the dead man's white fur collar. I thought he should have been instructed to not touch the body, but Janelle had fixed her attention on Dean and me.

"Did either of you see Gareth before the tree fell on him?" Janelle asked.

Dean shook his head.

"I thought we were alone," I added. "There was a gust from the lake and the tree collapsed."

"And what did you do?"

Dean and I exchanged sheepish looks. "Nothing," I said. "We left to meet the others at city hall."

"Why didn't you report it?"

"Report what?" I gestured at the mountainous pile of evergreen before us. "This thing has fallen over at least once a day. We figured someone in authority would eventually notice."

"And who were we supposed to report it to?" Dean sounded exasperated.

"How about the police?" Janelle asked.

"Maybe the police should have kept a closer eye on things," Piper said. "I believe this is a case of vandalism."

"Don't try to place the blame on us," Janelle snarled.

"Piper, this wasn't vandalism," I said. "Winter gusts from the lake keep knocking the tree over. Count yourself lucky Gareth was the first person it fell on. Otherwise, the town might be in for a lawsuit."

Janelle's bellicose attention once more focused on Piper. "Oh, I think legal action is still in order. This tree was far too large for the space intended. And it was never installed correctly. Your negligence is to blame for this accident."

Piper's mouth fell open. "I beg your pardon. You have no right to—"

"I have every right," Janelle snapped. "If Mr. Holmes's relatives choose to sue the town, you will be at the center of it."

"Marlee, tell her I had nothing to do with this."

Although I didn't like Janelle, everyone had complained the stupid tree was too big. "The tree was a danger to the public." I pointed down at Gareth. "Obviously."

"I refuse to take the blame for this," Piper spluttered.

"No one is to blame." Katrina stood up, brushing snow off her coat. "My guides warned me that death was near. It was written. Nothing could have been done to prevent it."

Janelle rolled her eyes.

"None of us want to hear from you, Katrina," Anthony said.

"I want to hear what she has to say." Diane Cleverly squirmed through the curious crowd.

"Mind your own business, Cleverly," Anthony said. "Unless you want to pretend Gareth Holmes was in love with you, too."

"That's not fair," I began.

Diane held up her hand. "Let them babble, Marlee. I know how Everett felt about me. And I know exactly how he felt about them." She glanced down at the dead man. "Gareth knew, too."

"I tried to warn Gareth." Katrina sighed. "But he refused to listen."

She, Anthony, and Janelle exchanged a long look between them.

In the distance I heard sirens.

"What I want to know is, which one of you killed him?" Diane asked in a loud voice.

Dean started beside me, but the trio she directed her question at simply stared at her. If I'd been Diane, I would have taken a step back at such open hostility.

Chief Hitchcock now strode through the crowd. Even though he wasn't in uniform, everyone moved aside. Our six-foot-five police chief had that effect on people.

Bruno and Janelle snapped to attention as they told him what had happened. Katrina and Anthony moved closer to the police officers in a blatant attempt to listen in.

I leaned closer to Diane. "So you think Gareth's death is suspicious?"

"He knew too much. And he foolishly tried to keep his secret too long."

"You mean the contents of the will."

"Yes. Now he's taken his secret to the grave. As Everett did." Diane suddenly looked ten years older. "So much unhappiness and death, all due to greed, greed, greed. They've learned nothing."

"But the will might still be found," I said in a low voice. "There were two copies."

She shook her head. "It's possible one of them already found a copy. Only it didn't mention the right name as beneficiary, so it's been destroyed."

"Without a will, what happens to the estate?"

Dean had been listening closely. "Who's the closest blood relative?"

"Anthony Thorne." Diane virtually spat out his name.

"Don't forget Janelle is his daughter," I reminded her. "A daughter outweighs a nephew."

"As far as I know, Everett never publicly acknowledged her as his child. But I have no idea what her birth certificate says."

"A DNA test can confirm paternity," Dean said.

"Everett's dead, and his body cremated." I kept my eyes on Katrina, Janelle, and Anthony to make certain they weren't close enough to hear us. "How would paternity be proven?"

"Anthony," Diane said. "After all, he and Janelle are first cousins. But I doubt Anthony will be willing to provide a genetic sample."

I wondered if he could be forced to.

Chief Hitchcock had finished his discussion with his officers and went to inspect the body. "The ME will tell us if the blow to his head when he fell was the cause of death." he announced after he was done.

As the ambulance arrived, Dean turned to me. "Not the way I thought the Hollyberry Festival would end."

"It's what I feared," Diane murmured.

Piper paced back and forth as she spoke on her cell phone. I'd bet the call was to her attorney.

After Hitchcock conferred with the medical team, I held up my hand to get his attention. "Chief Hitchcock?"

He walked over, looking tired. "What is it, Marlee?"

"I spoke to Gareth earlier today. He'd been eating from a bag of chestnuts." I pulled out the crumpled bag I'd stuffed earlier in my parka pocket.

"You're not giving me another bag of food to test?"

Katrina heard this. "Are those the chestnuts I gave him? If so, both Natasha and I ate from it. No reason to be suspicious. Neither of us is lying dead on the sidewalk."

I ignored her. "I thought you should know. After all, the squirrel died after eating the cookies."

"Is she talking about that squirrel again?" Janelle shook her head.

"Let's put the dead squirrel to rest, shall we?" Hitchcock said.

"Have you gotten the results from the test?" I asked.

"Marlee, you gave me the cookie pieces only yesterday. I've sent them to the Department of Public Safety. It could be quite some time before the results come back. When I have them, I will let you know. Only I don't want to hear about the squirrel until then." He turned to leave.

"But it's not really about the squirrel. There's Everett's death."

Diane squeezed my arm. "Marlee's right. He may not have died from natural causes."

"Like the squirrel?" Janelle asked mockingly as Bruno chuckled.

"Chief Hitchcock, why is this shopkeeper still going on about my uncle's death?" Anthony said. "Uncle Everett was ninety-five!"

"We need to let Everett's soul find his peace," Katrina added.

"I can't listen to this any longer," Diane said, before hurrying away.

Chief Hitchcock took a deep breath, as though trying to control his temper. Not a good sign. He was a remarkably even-tempered man. "I am not interested in testing your bag of chestnuts. Now excuse me while I take care of the deceased."

He returned to the EMS team, now loading the body onto a stretcher.

"You're pathetic, Marlee," Janelle said. "Trying to insinuate yourself into every death in the county. You may want to see a therapist about that."

She left to join her boss. But Katrina continued to scowl at me.

"Did you really think I tried to poison Gareth?" Katrina snatched the bag from me. She popped a chestnut into her mouth and made a big show of chewing, then swallowing, the nut.

"I guess that's that," Dean murmured.

"Keep the rest." Katrina pushed the bag back into my hands. "If I die unexpectedly tonight, you'll have evidence to prove I was poisoned. Until then, happy holidays."

Dean turned to me after she left. "I'd think twice about giving the police another bag of food to be tested. Or the entire department will view you as a crank."

"Point taken. But there's another strange thing I noticed tonight. And it has nothing to do with food." I lowered my voice to a whisper. "When I first reached Gareth's body, I saw a sprig of holly pinned to his Santa jacket. Right over his heart."

"Seems Christmas appropriate," Dean whispered back. "Like a candy cane pin."

"No, this was a real sprig of holly."

"So?"

I sighed. "Never mind. It's *A Christmas Carol* thing."

"You may have spent too much time studying that play."

"At least it paid off. I know my lines. In fact, I suspect no one in the company knows the entire play as well as I do."

I also suspected the sprig of holly had been left there by the killer.

Chapter Twenty-one

An hour later, I got an early Christmas present. Kit called to let me know he'd be able to spend the night. But we'd be having even less privacy than usual.

After the Christmas tree debacle, Tess, David, Theo, Dean, Gillian, and Piper decided the night couldn't end without us parsing this latest death. Although I suspected Piper's real reason for attending was to escape from the negative attention now drawn to her giant tree.

When Kit arrived, he was met by a small gathering in the living room. Everyone munched on Christmas cookies I brought from the shop. Even Dasha had eaten a couple. Good thing Natasha hadn't come home yet; she'd recently put her Yorkie on a canine diet.

Kit scanned the room, now the picture of holiday cheer. Countless Christmas lights twinkled. The gas fireplace crackled. A fiber-optic Santa or angel dotted every table surface. My collection of nutcrackers marched along the fireplace mantel and any open wall space. Minnie warbled "Jingle Bells" from her perch, occasionally throwing in a refrain of "Ba-ba-ba ba-ba ba-ran." A contented Panther lay beneath the big white tree, playing with the manger scene.

Dean pointed at Kit's carry-on bag in the hallway. "It looks like you don't travel light."

I gave Kit a curious smile. "You already keep a lot of stuff here. What did you bring?"

Kit hugged me. "A change of clothes for my overnight trip."

Because my friends had already laid claim to the sofa and chairs, with Theo choosing the floor, Kit and I sat on the tartan loveseat. It was the closest to the fireplace and toasty warm. Something I knew Kit would appreciate after his drive from New Bethel.

"A work-related trip?" I asked.

"Nope. My parents arrived in Detroit this afternoon to visit Aunt Rose. Because of the snowstorm, they said the last hour of the flight was a real white knuckler. They intended to rent a car and drive to this side of the state to spend Christmas with my sister Ivy and me. But the snow is freaking them out."

I laughed. "They've lived in Texas too long."

"It freaks me out sometimes and I was born here," Dean said.

"Not surprised with that toy car you drive," Gillian said. "You need a four-wheel drive."

Dean owned an orange VW Beetle, which he loved with a passion.

"Well, I do have a four-wheel drive," Kit said, "and I'll leave early tomorrow morning for Rochester where my aunt lives." Rochester was a northern sub-urb of Detroit's. "But Aunt Rose wants to cook a big dinner for us, which means I won't bring Mom and Dad here until the next day. Naturally, they'll stay with my sister and Greg."

"Of course." I smiled. "I can't imagine they want to miss a second with the grandkids."

"Be careful," Tess warned. "Forecasts call for more snow, and driving conditions are already bad. By Tuesday, the roads may be impassable."

"I'll watch the radar." Kit looked at me. "How about your parents?"

"They drive up from Chicago on Wednesday. How-ever, they might not make it in time to catch our matinee. I don't care about that. But I do want them here for Christmas Eve."

"That's your birthday, too," Theo reminded me.

"Indeed it is. Because of the weather, I suggested they take the train. Dad refuses. He had a bad expe-rience on Amtrak years ago. The restroom door broke, locking him in for two hours." I shuddered. "Don't mention trains to him. Not even toy trains."

"What should I do?" Theo looked alarmed. "My dad doesn't want me to drive in the snowstorm. He bought me an Amtrak train ticket so I could go home for Christmas. And I have to ride two trains! What if I get locked in the bathroom?"

Theo often took things literally. I should have re-membered he was traveling by train to Champaign, Illinois. "You'll be fine," I told him. "My dad's experi-ence happened a long time ago. The trains have been updated since then."

Dean shot me a skeptical look from the club chair he lounged on.

"I'll try not to go to the bathroom," Theo said solemnly. "I won't drink anything."

Gillian leaned forward. "Theo, I promise you the bathroom doors on the train will work."

He didn't look convinced. I'd have a long talk with him about it tomorrow at the shop. I planned to go in early to help with the baking.

Kit looked around. "Aren't we missing some of the gang?"

"Natasha has another date with Alexei, the architect." I picked up the plate of cookies from the coffee table and offered it to Kit. He grabbed three. "I think it's getting serious. She mentioned they might spend Russian Christmas together. In Russia."

"Russians have their own Christmas?" Theo asked.

"The Russian Orthodox Church celebrates Christmas on January the seventh. And they call Santa Ded Moroz, or Grandfather Frost." I chuckled. "Since Natasha moved in, I've gotten a crash course in Russia 101."

"As for my absent brother," Dean said, "he and Oscar are attending yet another Christmas party. They're like Oriole County's version of Scott and Zelda Fitzgerald. I expect one of them to start jumping into fountains fully clothed."

Tess giggled. "Or write *The Great Gatsby*."

Theo looked confused, but didn't say anything.

Kit nodded toward Piper. She sat in the glider rocker, all her attention on the texts she was sending and receiving. "What's going on? Piper's never this quiet."

"Hollyberry homicide," Dean said in a mock-tragic tone. "Piper is worried she and the town are about to be sued big-time."

"No one will be sued." Piper did not look up from her phone. "Precautionary measures are underway to make certain of that. I've been texting Lionel and my attorney. We've come up with a few ideas on how to deflect this tragedy from Oriole Point. And me."

"There's been a homicide?" Kit tensed up.

"An accident," David said.

Theo sipped his apple cider before adding, "The Christmas tree killed Santa tonight."

"Wait. Someone tell me exactly what happened."

A bevy of voices rose up to answer Kit. All the noise inspired Minnie to imitate her favorite ring-tones, while Dasha turned her attention from cook-ies to attacking the laces on Theo's shoes.

When everyone finished giving their thumbnail accounts, Kit asked, "Did Chief Hitchcock indicate he thought the death was suspicious?"

Tess gestured at Dean and me. "Ask them. Those two were right in the thick of things."

"I was there, too," Piper said defensively. "And no one knows what caused the death."

"The police think Gareth died from the impact of the giant tree falling on him," I told Kit.

Piper glared at me.

"It was a very big tree," Theo announced in a solemn voice.

Kit shook his head. "I'm surprised the town ever got clearance to put up that thing."

"How *did* the town green-light it, Piper?" David asked with a sly grin.

"A miscommunication." Piper stood up. "Who knew the tree was so huge? And the installers are to blame for the whole fiasco. Which includes Gareth Holmes's death. My lawyer thinks we have a good case of negligence against Welker and Sons."

"You can't put the blame for Gareth's death on Billy Welker and his kids." Tess sounded appalled. "They're a little tree removal business. And they did you a favor by struggling to put up that tree every time it fell over."

"Shame on you, Piper," I said. "A major lawsuit will destroy their business."

Piper grabbed her Birkin from beside the rocker. "They should have thought of that before installing the tree incorrectly."

"You're to blame," Dean said. "You wanted the biggest tree in the county."

"We should blame the wind, too," Theo added. "Every time the tree fell over, it was because of the winds from the lake."

Piper shrugged. "Fine. Let the Holmes family sue Lake Michigan. I don't care as long as no one mentions *my* name in the lawsuit."

She stalked out of the room. When the front door slammed shut behind her, we all looked at each other for a long moment.

Minnie broke the silence: "You're to blame. You're to blame."

"If she throws the Welkers under the bus," Gillian said, "it will ruin them financially."

"Let's wait and see," I cautioned. "Gareth was estranged from his children. I don't even know where they live. They may have no interest in a lawsuit. Or even in their father's death."

"And if Piper does sue the Welkers," Tess said, "I'll ask my sister-in-law to defend them." Tess's brother was married to a high-powered attorney. "Elena has never lost a case. She'll make mincemeat of Piper."

"Why is Piper so mean?" Theo asked.

I sighed. "Despite what she says, Piper probably blames herself for what happened to Gareth. She feels guilty."

"But she blamed the men who put the tree up," Theo said.

"She's deflecting to make herself look less guilty. To be fair, Billy Welker and his sons should have refused to install it. Especially after it fell three times. Yet they hauled it back into place again and again. Technically, they're all guilty."

"I think Piper is the most guilty," Theo said with emphasis.

"Amen," Dean added.

I sat up as something occurred to me. "Hold on. They're all guilty. Every one of them. Guilty of greed, dishonesty, and selfishness."

"Even the tree men?" Theo looked uncertain.

"No, not them. I was referring to Everett Hostetter and the people he kept around him."

"Guilty about what?" Kit asked.

Restless, I got to my feet and began to pace. "Think about it. This greedy rich man fathers a child, only to turn his back on the mother and his baby. And that child became a police officer who cheated and lied, all for money."

Given Janelle's sour attitude toward life, I assumed Everett's neglect had left scars.

"Would Janelle have turned to a life of crime if Everett had been more generous?" I went on. "He was also miserly with his sister's son. When Anthony's trust fund ran out, Everett refused to give him a job. That led to Anthony starting his own company with his college friend."

"Which resulted in his friend's suicide." Kit wore a somber expression.

"Exactly. Everett also convinced Anthony's mother to disinherit her only child so Anthony would be dependent on him."

David shuddered. "They all sound repulsive."

"They are. Then Everett married a woman he used as a weapon against his sister, Sarah."

"Katrina May was a weapon?" Tess asked. "How?"

"Katrina passed on messages to Sarah from the spirit world, advising her on what to do. Everett wanted Katrina to persuade his sister to sign over all her shares in the family company to him. Which she did. Only somehow she scared her to death. Literally."

"The ghost lady killed her?" Theo looked outraged.

"In a manner of speaking, yes. If so, she and Everett share responsibility for her death. They're both guilty. And his sister's death was a life-changing epiphany."

"What's an epiphany?" Theo asked.

"A sudden realization," Tess answered. "Everett must have realized his insatiable greed led to his sister's death."

"That's when he moved to Oriole Point. He convinced the others to come here as well." I paused. "Or threatened them. Probably to keep an eye on everyone. Try to get them to straighten out their dishonest lives. And he let them think one of them would inherit."

Theo scooped up Dasha, who licked his face in delight. "My dad says people should be honest and kind. This way they can never get into trouble."

"Everett and the unholy trio were never honest or kind." I continued to pace. "Neither was his lawyer, no matter how great a Santa he made. Gareth's hands were plenty dirty."

"Then he should have washed them," Theo said sternly. "People need clean hands."

"As for Gareth," I said, "he and Everett were the only ones who knew the contents of the will. Knowledge that put him in danger."

Minnie muttered, "Who took the banana?"

"You need to bring us up to speed about this will, Marlee," Gillian said.

I quickly told them what I had learned.

"How could Gareth refuse to make Everett's will public?" Tess asked when I was done.

"He never filed it with the probate court. Only he and Everett had copies. Everett never even wrote a will until the past year. Which seems stupid, considering his age."

"Once a will is accepted for probate, beneficiaries would be notified within three months," Kit explained. "The will also becomes a matter of public record. If it hasn't been filed, I believe the state steps in to ascertain the distribution of assets. That's probably the time any possible heirs would make their personal appeals."

"But there is a will," I said. "Two copies. And I think I know where one of them is."

"Where is it?" Theo asked.

"Gareth had one copy. I have no idea where he put that. But I bet Everett's copy is in his dressing room at the Calico Barn. He kept the dressing room locked and had the only key. Which I now have."

"Is there somewhere a will could be hidden in the room?" Kit said.

I nodded. "I wanted to check it out last night. But by the time I got there, everyone had gone. And the theater was locked. Someone did show up while I was trying to get in the back door. I snuck out before they saw me. Whoever it was had to have seen my Berry Basket van in the parking lot. So they knew I was there."

Tess looked concerned. "You shouldn't have gone there alone."

"Call me the next time you go," Theo offered. "The barn is close to my cottage."

Kit frowned. "Marlee, why didn't you tell me all this?"

"You were busy with a triple homicide."

"I don't care if I'm chasing down Jack the Ripper. Your safety comes first."

Dean whistled. "Wow. You come before Jack the Ripper. This one's a keeper, Marlee."

"I know." I sat down beside Kit once more. "And I'll search the dressing room tomorrow. The entire cast and crew will be at the theater for dress rehearsal, even Tess. I'll be safe."

"I'll help you look," Tess said. "I'd love to know who Everett left all his money to."

Kit put his arm around me. "If you do find the will, call me immediately."

"I promise."

"And how is the triple-homicide case going?" David asked him.

"There was a big break in the case this weekend. We arrested two of the ringleaders of the meth ring. That's why I can take a couple days off. There's a good chance the two we arrested will give up some names. Only I'm more concerned about Gareth's death at the moment. After all, the last person to know the contents of Everett's will has been silenced."

"But the tree killed him," Dean said. "It was an accident."

"Or accidentally finished him off," I replied. "Gareth was probably sitting on the park bench when the tree knocked him to the ground. Only what if he was already dead?"

"Dead from what?" Tess asked.

The memory of Everett's gingerbread cookies flashed before me. "Poison."

"I have a feeling we're going to hear about that squirrel again," Dean warned.

"How would someone poison him?" Gillian wondered.

"Every time I saw Santa yesterday, he was eating something," Theo announced.

"I know he ate from a bag of hot chestnuts," I said. "One he got from Katrina."

"When he visited our studio, he brought cookies from Lakeshore Holiday." Tess thought a moment.

"Or maybe it was Gemini Rising. Every shop offered free food and drinks tonight."

"I bumped into him twice while I was caroling." Gillian shook her head. "Both times he had a cup or a bag of food in his hand."

"If he was poisoned, the killer had ample opportunities," Kit observed.

"There's something else. When they lifted the tree off him, Gareth was lying on his back. Pinned right over his heart was a sprig of real holly."

"Is this the *Christmas Carol* reference again?" Dean asked.

Tess snapped her fingers. "She's right. It's from something Ebenezer Scrooge says."

"I've memorized more than my own lines. I also know most of Scrooge's. Especially this one." I took a deep breath before reciting, "'If I could work my will, every idiot who goes about with 'Merry Christmas' on his lips, should be boiled with his own pudding, and buried with a stake of holly through his heart.'"

"Could be a dark joke left by the killer," David suggested.

I agreed. To kill Gareth while he was playing Father Christmas seemed deliberate.

"Maybe someone poisoned him with berries from the holly bush." Theo looked at me.

"They're not the berries I would choose," I said. "The taste is hard to mask."

"Is there any significance to holly, besides *A Christmas Carol*?" Kit asked.

I gazed at the crackling fire while I considered this question. "Nothing that makes sense in the context of a murder. The holly bush has symbolism for Christians. The sharp holly leaves represent the crown of thorns that Jesus wore. The red berries symbolize the blood Jesus shed. Only I don't think there's any way to view Gareth Holmes as a Christ figure."

"Not even close," Tess said.

"Holly plays a different role in Celtic mythology," I went on. "From summer until the winter solstice, a nature god called the Holly King reigns supreme. His weapon of choice is a holly bush, and he's pictured as covered with holly leaves and branches. Again, I don't see any connection to a lawyer too clever for his own good."

"Does the holly bush represent anything else?" Kit knew I was an expert on berries.

"The Celts viewed it as bad luck to cut down a holly bush, but removing its branches was allowed. And they believed the wood of a holly bush held magical properties. Most English horsewhips in the past were made of holly because it was thought holly could control horses."

"Could it?" Theo asked in wonder.

"Doubtful. But holly trees and bushes were also said to protect buildings from lightning strikes. We've since learned the spines on holly leaves may serve as tiny lightning conductors."

"Our Marlee is a fount of berry trivia." Dean grinned.

"Berries are fascinating. And beautiful." I pointed at a vase of holly branches on a floating shelf by the window, placed high enough so none of the animals could reach it. "I always bring holly inside during the holidays. It screams 'Christmas.'"

"So does your entire house." Dean eyed the snow globes on the bookshelf beside him.

"It's not just about Christmas. The Celts kept holly branches in their home for good luck, and to protect against evil spirits." I smiled. "Legend claims that if you have holly branches inside the home, it provides shelter for good fairies during the winter."

Theo's face lit up. "Fairies," he said in a dreamy voice.

"All very interesting." Kit nodded. "And I think you're right. The sprig of holly pinned to his jacket points to *A Christmas Carol*. When I get back, I'll have a long talk with Chief Hitchcock. Or have Greg talk to him tomorrow. Until then, let's keep these suspicions to ourselves." Kit turned to me. "And after you've had a look around the dressing room, please call a halt to the sleuthing."

"Gladly. I have a play to perform, gifts to finish wrapping, and Christmas to celebrate."

"Along with a birthday," Gillian added.

"That too." I stood up once more. "Since we've all skipped dinner and already had dessert, it's time we head to the kitchen. This is perfect weather for grilled-cheese sandwiches and tomato soup. Lucky for us, I went grocery shopping last night."

Dean jumped to his feet. "I'm in!"

"I'm starving for real food," Gillian cried.

Everyone stood up and stretched.

All this sudden movement set Dasha to barking, and Minnie into a refrain of "Jingle Bells." Panther climbed up the big velvet bag of wrapped Christmas presents by the white tree.

Kit and I followed the others into the kitchen. But

I couldn't resist a glance back at the holly branches in my vase.

I may not believe in fairies, the Holly King, or magical horsewhips. But I hoped holly had the power to protect me from evil spirits.

And murderers.

Chapter Twenty-two

My skin crawled even before I changed into my costume for dress rehearsal. The ghostly gray ensemble hung on the rack before me. At that moment I would have paid a hundred bucks for a washing machine to magically appear.

Tess, already in Mrs. Cratchit's mobcap, ankle-length skirt, and paisley shawl, gave me a sympathetic smile. "Be of good cheer and put the silly clothes on. Otherwise Suzanne will order the crew to forcibly dress you. And I'm only half-kidding."

With a resigned air, I pulled off my sweater and stepped out of my jeans.

Tess started to laugh. "What do you have on?"

"Thermal underwear. I need a layer of protection." I pulled a shower cap from my cross-body bag on the dressing table. "And this is going on over my hair. Heaven knows how many decades of use Marley's wig has seen. I'm not risking lice."

Trying to keep a straight face, Tess helped me step into the stovepipe pants. "Your waist is smaller than his, so I'll pin it. But you and old Everett apparently worked out at the same gym. The pant legs fit like a glove. What are you wearing for shoes? I can't imagine your feet were the same size as his."

"I found a pair of ugly gray flannel slippers in my closet. Never worn. I don't even remember which relative gave them to me. But they'll work fine for my Dickensian debut."

"Have you had time to search the dressing room for the will yet?" she asked quietly, even though the dressing room door was closed.

"No. Suzanne keeps barging in every two minutes. I think she's terrified I still don't know my lines. I'll sneak back during rehearsal. But the boxes and bookshelves might not be the only hiding place in here. We should look for pockets in the costume, too. Everett might have refused to clean his Jacob Marley getup because he hid the will in it somewhere."

"Good idea." Tess patted down my legs like a TSA inspector at airport security.

I explored the gray shirt and long frock coat. The coat pockets contained nothing but lint and a cellophane-wrapped peppermint candy. Next, I examined the interior for secret compartments. Nothing.

Tess wrinkled her nose.

"The costume stinks, doesn't it?" I said.

"Smells like a cross between mildew, sweat, and sour milk."

"Why *is* this costume so rancid?"

"We probably don't want to know." She held up her hand. "Wait one second."

As Tess dashed out of the room, I turned my attention to the white periwig. It slipped on easily over the shower cap, thank goodness. Although I looked repulsive, not frightening. Or maybe that was because of my expression.

A breathless Tess returned with a small spray bottle. "My Black Opium by Yves Saint Laurent should mask the stench."

"I wish you hadn't used the word *stench*."

She sprayed me generously from head to toe in what I knew was her favorite perfume. I made a note to buy her a bottle for Christmas.

Tess stood back and sniffed. "That's better."

I sniffed, too. "Although if anyone in the cast is allergic to perfume, this will send them into anaphylactic shock."

"Five minutes!" Suzanne yelled from outside my door.

The babble of voices from the actors in their dressing rooms rose to a nervous roar.

"You're not even made up yet." Tess pushed me down onto the chair before the dressing table. "Don't worry. I asked Suzanne about the makeup. The company buys new every year. Because there are so many ghosts in *A Christmas Carol*, they go through it quickly."

That made me feel better.

"Keep your eyes closed," Tess said as she covered my neck and face with white makeup.

When I saw myself in the mirror, I scared myself. "I look a fright. Literally."

She giggled. "And you haven't even put on the cloth to keep your dead jaws closed."

Once the white kerchief had been wrapped beneath my chin and knotted at the top of my head, I no longer resembled a thirtysomething young woman in twenty-first-century America. Instead, I was the Victorian image of a cantankerous old male ghost.

I smiled at my ghoulish reflection. "This play might turn into a lot of fun. Think how I'll scare everyone when I appear and rattle my chains."

Tess brought the chains over.

"Onstage!" Suzanne bellowed.

"Wrap them crisscross around my body," I instructed. "But leave enough chain for me to carry and rattle in one hand."

"This is a real chain," Tess observed. "It must feel heavy."

"It's not that bad. And the keys, padlocks, and cash boxes connected to the links make it look heavier than it is. Only I have to be careful not to get tangled up in anything."

Tess and I exchanged smiles of approval at the final result in the mirror.

I made jazz hands and cried, "It's showtime!"

Right before I locked the door, I grabbed my cross-body bag. Like any decent millennial, I refused to be away from my phone. Especially since I was getting updates from Kit and my parents about the weather and driving conditions. I was relieved that Kit had safely made the drive across the state earlier today. Now I only had his return trip to worry about.

Tess and I were the last to arrive in the upstairs auditorium. We took a seat in the fourth row, trying to be inconspicuous. Not an easy thing to do with my chains, keys, and padlocks clanging with every movement.

Andrew, who sat right in front of us, turned around. "I can't believe I wasn't there last night for all the drama. First, I miss Piper's Christmas tree killing Santa Claus. Then I learn there was a big party at your house afterward."

"You're not seriously upset you weren't there for a tragic death?" Tess shook her head.

"Why not? For your information, Oscar and I were stuck at the dullest Christmas party ever. They didn't even serve alcohol. Or decent chip dip."

I sighed. "You do love a good chip dip."

"Absolutely. And don't act like either of you were buddy-buddy with the duck decoy guy. Until this past week, we probably all said about six words to Gareth."

"He still died unexpectedly," Tess countered.

"Jeez, are you going to get upset about old Everett's death as well?"

"Calm down, you two," I chided. "The last thing we should fight about is anyone's untimely end. Death is sad. Whether we knew the person well or not. As for my big party, it was just a bunch of us talking and eating grilled-cheese sandwiches and cookies at my house."

"That's a party!" Andrew protested.

A half dozen actors said, "Shhhh!"

Andrew sniffed. "What's that odor? It smells like a wet dog fell into a vat of vanilla."

"Turn around," I said. "And take shallow breaths."

"Attention!" Suzanne now faced the actors in the theater seats. She wore her holly-green Mrs. Fezziwig party gown, along with a long-suffering expression. I hoped our upcoming performance didn't make her suffer even more.

"As all of you know, this is a dress rehearsal *and* a tech rehearsal. We will stop if one of you flubs a line, or if the wrong lighting cue goes off. Otherwise, we proceed to the end just as if there is a paying audience in the theater." This was followed by a weighty pause: "As there will be tomorrow night."

That sounded like a threat.

Before she stepped into the wings, Suzanne waved at the actor cast as the play's narrator.

He sat on the corner of the stage, waiting for the spotlight to find him. When it finally did, he recited the opening lines of Dickens's tale.

I leaned close to Tess. "Did you memorize your dialogue?"

"Mrs. Cratchit is easy to improvise for. I'm not worried."

"Again!" An angry Suzanne peeked around the curtain to glare at the narrator. "You skipped a line. This is unacceptable so close to opening!"

If I were Tess, I'd be worried. This must have given her pause as well. She reached for her script and began to thumb through the pages.

A half hour later, we still hadn't gotten to my scene, and Marley appeared near the beginning of the play. I lost count of the technical glitches. The sound crackled, accompanied by an occasional deafening hum. Bob Cratchit got his scarf caught on a nail and nearly choked himself. One of the businessmen soliciting donations from Scrooge tripped and knocked over the coal scuttle. Numerous times the spotlight fell on the narrator when he wasn't speaking, only to appear on the actors when they weren't. At one point the spotlight lingered on the theater exit door. Which I bet Suzanne wanted to escape through.

"Did someone blindfold the lighting guy?" I asked Tess, who gave an amused snort.

At least Andrew's performance went well. He looked dapper as Scrooge's good-natured nephew. I paid close attention to the exchange between him and his miserly uncle. It included the now prophetic lines about being buried with a stake of holly through one's heart.

My appearance was delayed when they couldn't find the video of Marley's ghost to project over Scrooge's door knocker. It gave me a funny feeling to know the visage used was of Everett as Marley. As I stood in the backstage shadows, I imagined Everett's ghost watching us. And not with approval.

Then I was on.

Miraculously, the spotlight fell on me as soon as I stood before Scrooge. I don't think Ed Wolfson had seen me earlier in the auditorium because his Ebenezer looked quite frightened by my appearance. That, or our local contractor was a helluva actor.

When Scrooge asked what I wanted with him, I boomed back, *"Much."*

Each line came easily. I heard the lines in my head right before I had to say them, as though an invisible audiobook prompted me.

My enthusiasm did bring things to a halt once. When I rattled my chain at Scrooge, I did it with a little too much force. Ebenezer/Ed jumped back to avoid being hit in the mouth with one of the chain's padlocks, causing him to spill his bowl of gruel.

"Not the costume!" Suzanne shrieked as crew members rushed onstage to clean the mess before it stained Scrooge's nightshirt.

"Sorry, I got carried away," I said.

When we resumed, I kept my chain rattling to a minimum. Even when extending my arms as I proclaimed, "I wear the chain I forged in life."

As our scene progressed, I suspected I might be stealing the scene from Ebenezer himself. By the time we got to my big finish, "I am here tonight to warn you, that you have yet a chance and hope of escaping my fate," I was on a roll.

Suzanne gave a nod of approval as I rattled my way off the stage. "Good job."

"You didn't think I had it in me, did you?" I smiled.

"No, I didn't." She wasn't joking.

"Since I don't appear in any more scenes, is it okay if I run downstairs for a moment?"

"There's a restroom in the lobby. No reason to go downstairs. Oh, wait. I do need something."

I tried not to grin with relief. Sneaking off to the basement would be a piece of cake. Especially since now I didn't have to sneak. "What do you want me to bring back?"

Suzanne sighed as the spotlight swept over part of the backstage area. "Let's do that lighting cue again!" She turned her attention back to me. "I need the other crutch for Tiny Tim. It seems Brandon has gone through a growth spurt during the rehearsal period. He says the crutch we've been using is too short for him. But we have a bigger one downstairs."

"I think I saw it by one of the prop trunks."

"Bring it up as soon as you can. Brandon appears in the second act."

That was welcome news. This rehearsal was crawling along. If it continued in this fashion, we had another five hours before we reached the end of the play.

More than enough time to search the dressing room for Everett's will.

When I got back to the dressing room, I pulled out the three metal boxes beneath the makeup table. I shook each of them and felt things shift around. Now there was the matter of those locks.

I attempted to break the locks with the tip of Tiny Tim's crutch, but only ended up shaving some wood off the crutch. I needed the key or keys. Maybe they were taped to something in the room.

After I examined the bottom of the chair and the makeup table, I looked behind the mirror. I stood on the chair and felt for a loose ceiling tile that might conceal a key. Next, I pulled out every book. I did discover that first edition of *A Christmas Carol.* An easy find. The red slipcover volume was covered in plastic. It took every bit of moral fortitude not to slip it into my parka so I could take it home with me later.

After replacing the book on the shelves, I returned my attention to the metal boxes. I tried the dressing-room key, but it was too large.

Maybe Everett didn't hide the key here at all. I sat down with a clank in the rocking chair.

The noise made me look at the long chain wrapped about my body. As Dickens had described, Jacob Marley's chain links held padlocks, cash boxes, ledgers, and keys. Lots of keys!

In an instant I had one of the boxes in my lap. I inserted one key after the other into the lock. The fifth one slid in perfectly. When the lock sprang open, I lifted back the lid. It held file folders, each marked with a printed label.

While the bulbs around the mirror were fine for applying makeup, they weren't so great for reading papers. But the adjacent bathroom had megawatt illumination.

I picked up all three metal boxes and took them into the white-tiled bathroom. Even though I'd locked my dressing-room door, I closed the bathroom door behind me as well. If anyone came looking for me or Hostetter's will, I wanted advance warning.

I sat cross-legged on the floor. Above I heard a hum of voices from the stage. I hoped Suzanne was so preoccupied with the play, she wouldn't notice I hadn't yet returned.

Pulling the opened box onto my lap, I rifled through the file folders. They contained letters, court documents, emails, bank transactions, tax statements. All pertaining to Anthony Thorne and the financial scandal at his company. The one he betrayed his friend over. Everett had amassed proof that his nephew was the guilty party. There was also evidence of credit card fraud by Anthony since his move to Oriole Point.

Mindful of the time, I put that box aside and tried the second box. I lucked out when the first key on my chain opened it. Inside were file folders containing proof that Janelle Davenport had given false testimony against witnesses, taken bribes, stolen evidence. I glanced at the third box. It must hold damning files against Katrina May.

I sat back, sweating profusely. It wasn't the space heater in my dressing room since I had turned it off. Maybe I was overheating because of what I'd stumbled upon. Proof that Janelle, Anthony, and Katrina had broken the law. Evidence that Everett Hostetter had used to compel all of them to move to Oriole Point.

I heard a noise outside the locked door of my dressing room. How long had I been down here? From the sound of pounding feet and music above me, I knew they had reached Mr. Fezziwig's party scene.

No time to look through the third box now. Instead, I locked up the other two boxes and stacked them in a corner of the bathroom. I had to get back upstairs.

But when I stood, I felt light-headed *and* overheated. In fact, the air seemed to shimmer around me. I took a deep breath. Although I smelled Black Opium first, there was something acrid as well. Smoke!

I opened the bathroom door to find my dressing room hazy with smoke. I raced for the outer door, only to yelp when my hand touched the doorknob. It was hot to the touch. Had a fire started in the basement?

Yanking off the kerchief wound about my head, I tied it over my nose and mouth. After I pulled my sleeve over my hand, I tried to open the dressing-room door again. Even through the fabric, the doorknob's fiery-hot metal made me cry out in pain.

Once I opened the door, I saw smoke and flames. The advice given by firefighters during school visits came back to me and I dropped to the floor. Terrified, I began to crawl out of the room only to bump into something hot to the touch. I panicked and retreated to the dressing room. Needing something to help clear my way, I grabbed Tiny Tim's crutch.

This time when I crawled through the basement, I used the crutch to sweep aside any object in my path. Visibility was nonexistent, as the thick smoke made my eyes water. I choked beneath the kerchief about my mouth. And the linoleum felt dangerously hot.

The strongest wave of heat came from my right. I spotted flames through the open door of the women's dressing room. Why didn't the smoke alarms go off? And was anyone else down here? If so, I couldn't do anything about it if I wanted to stay alive.

Keep crawling, I told myself. Keep crawling. Occasionally, the crutch I swung along the floor knocked something down. But it also helped clear a path to safety.

When I reached the stairs, I scrambled up the steps. I found myself using the crutch once more, this time as a support. I felt close to passing out. Behind me I heard a whooshing sound. I looked back as a sudden brightness illuminated the smoke. The fire had gotten bigger.

At last I came to the top of the stairs. Struggling

for air, I stumbled toward the back exit and flung open the door. The icy winter air felt like a balm. I tore off my kerchief and took huge gulps.

Then I raced back into the theater. I had no idea where the fire extinguisher was. Or the fire alarm. But I had to get everyone out of the building.

I ran onstage, waving my crutch in the air. As my chains clanged with a fury, I burst right through the actors dancing a jig. Young Ebenezer was knocked to the ground.

Suzanne, now dancing about as Mrs. Fezziwig, threw me an astonished look.

"Marlee, what's wrong?" Tess shouted from the audience.

"Fire! There's a fire in the basement!" I waved the crutch toward the front of the theater. "Everyone get out! Now!"

A chorus of cries rose up. Someone screamed. Half the actors hurried to get off the stage, the others stood stunned.

"A fire?" Suzanne shrieked. "Impossible. I'll go see." She started off to the basement.

I poked her with the crutch, pushing her back. "Don't be a fool! Get out! And someone call the fire department!"

Andrew grabbed his mother's arm. I sent him a grateful smile as he dragged his mother away.

"Don't run!" I shouted at the people racing up the aisles. My memory of a similar stampede at the October health fair still haunted me.

Smoke now found its way backstage. The smell of burning wood was everywhere.

"Evacuate the building!" I ordered the remaining actors, who seemed frozen in shock.

The air around us grew hazy with smoke, finally prompting their exit. I hurried after them. Tess waited for me in the theater aisle.

"How bad is it?" she asked.

"Bad." I grabbed my bag from the auditorium seat, then followed her out of the theater.

By the time we ran out to the front parking lot, flames were visible from the back of the barn. Suzanne and several Green Willow Players wept. Others spoke on their cell phones. All of us stood in the snow and watched in horror.

The fire department came quickly. In a small town, the alarm goes out not only to the local fire department, but to every volunteer brigade in the county. Within ten minutes, fire trucks had arrived from four different towns.

Tess and I hugged each other as the drama unfolded. Many others did the same. We all needed to stay close not simply from the trauma, but because we'd left our winter coats in the basement. All the actors shivered in their costumes.

"What happened down there?" Tess asked.

I described what I'd found in the boxes. And how I hadn't noticed the fire at first because I'd been in the bathroom trying to read as much as I could.

"The first clue was the heat. I started to sweat, which is next to impossible down there."

Tess frowned. "I blame those space heaters. And all of them were turned on."

I looked at the fiery blaze, recalling how only two nights ago I'd tried to find a way inside the locked theater. As had some other unknown person. "It might have been arson. The space heaters were simply a convenient method."

"No way. Who would want to burn the Calico Barn down?" Tess gasped. "It's the will, isn't it? Someone doesn't want anyone to find Everett's will."

"Maybe the person who heard me say I thought I knew where the will was." Tongues of flame shot through the barn roof. "The same person who followed me to the barn that night. I guess destroying the building seemed an effective way to get rid of it."

"Why wait for rehearsal night? Why not do it when the barn is empty?"

I thought of those space heaters carelessly left on. "Precisely so it doesn't look like arson. All the doors were open tonight, including the side and back ones. Anyone could have slipped inside during rehearsal."

"Will you tell the firefighters this?"

"They're trained to look for signs of arson. If it seems suspicious, they'll know." I sighed. "And I've given the authorities enough unsolicited opinions this week."

A firefighter handed Tess and me each a blanket. "You need to keep warm," he said, then left to give blankets to the others.

I wrapped the blanket around me. "I hope they pass out boots next. All I've got on my feet are flannel bed slippers. And they're soaked."

Theo appeared next to us. "I have extra boots in my car."

"What are you doing here?" I asked him.

"You know I live close by. When I heard the fire trucks, I wanted to see where the fire was. In case it started to come my way." Theo shook his head at the flames, smoke, and fire hoses shooting water into the snow-filled air. "Is the barn going to burn down?"

Tess frowned. "Probably."

I shivered again.

"I'll bring you those boots." Theo went off to where he'd parked his car.

"The kid brother I never had," I said with affection. "Even if he is older than me."

Tess swore under her breath. "I left my purse in the basement. I've got no wallet or phone. *Or* car keys."

I patted my cross-body bag, which I had the foresight to take as we hurried out of the auditorium. "I'll drive you home."

"Better if I call David on your phone and have him pick me up. If he hears the Calico Barn is on fire, he'll be terrified."

After I handed the phone to her, I walked over to an inconsolable Suzanne. Andrew held her. He looked as upset as his mother.

"Do you believe this?" he said in a shaky voice.

"At least you can't say you missed all the excitement this time."

He frowned. "It's not all it's cracked up to be."

"Suzanne, why didn't the smoke alarms go off downstairs?" I asked.

"We may have forgotten to replace the batteries." Her breast heaved with sobs. "And we never got around to repairing the sprinkler system upstairs. I can't keep track of everything!"

This sounded bad for the theater group, which

owned the barn. No insurance company would pay for damages in a case of such negligence.

"Those terrible space heaters are to blame," she cried. "But Everett insisted we keep them down there to heat the basement. Now look what he's done."

Andrew shook his head. "When all else fails, blame a dead man."

"This is the end of our production." Suzanne sobbed. "Even if we don't lose the entire barn, it's in no shape for a performance tomorrow night. And we worked so hard to make it the best *Christmas Carol* ever! Instead, we've had one terrible thing happen after the other."

"I guess this literally lends fuel to the fire about the play being cursed this year," I said as smoke billowed into the night sky.

Suzanne blew her nose. "Do you really believe the play was cursed?"

I gestured at the burning barn with the crutch I still held. "Ya think?"

"Look on the bright side, Mom," Andrew said. "This is one *Christmas Carol* production no one will forget. And we never even made it to opening night."

Chapter Twenty-three

My drive to work the next morning felt like a journey through the forest in *Frozen*, but without Elsa singing "Let It Go" beside me. The storm had stopped, leaving a world covered with another foot of snow. Quite beautiful, actually. Although close attention had to be paid to the hazardous conditions following such a heavy snowfall.

The storm system was now hitting the other side of the state, delaying Kit's return. A regretful Kit called to say he planned to get on the road early tomorrow. I reassured him that his safety and that of his parents came first. I also worried about my parents' drive up from Chicago tomorrow. The forecast warned of gale-force winds, which meant blowing snow on the freeways. I'd be anxious until my parents and Kit finally arrived.

Until then, I had lots to do. Gillian and I were working at The Berry Basket today, though I doubted we'd have many customers. Or any customers. That was fine. It gave me the opportunity to bake my parents' favorite Christmas cookies. And I'd be able to dart out during the workday to drop off gifts to those shopkeepers I considered friends.

I did make a detour to what was left of the Calico Barn. The parking lot was filled with emergency vehicles, including two fire trucks, a state police cruiser, and three sheriff's department cars.

Lots of civilians milled about, too. Gillian's newspaper editor dad, a dozen members of the Green Willow Players, and curious residents. I also couldn't miss the big hair and dramatic gestures of Suzanne Cabot. I made straight for her, happy to see she was conversing with State Trooper Greg Trejo, who happened to be Kit's brother-in-law.

I wasn't happy to see that little was left of the historic barn, now a heap of blackened wood and rubble.

Suzanne threw her arms around me. "It's worse than we thought, Marlee. The fire destroyed everything! We've lost our beautiful theater!"

I patted her on the back. "Have you spoken to the insurance company?"

"Any insurance money will depend on the cause of the fire," Greg said. "You'd better hope the fire department doesn't find evidence of negligence or arson."

This caused Suzanne to clutch me harder.

"Is there evidence of either?" I asked him.

"Those space heaters are a red flag. I don't know who approved that many heaters in such a small space, but someone will be called to account. And it won't be pleasant."

Suzanne sobbed. I shook my head at Greg, who

lacked Kit's people skills. It had taken me a while to discover the nice guy who existed beneath Greg's Mr. Spock exterior. And I thought it best to get Suzanne away from him before he made her feel even worse.

"Three of the actors look upset, Suzanne. Maybe you should reassure them."

She tried to get herself under control. "Yes. As director of the current production, it's my responsibility to keep it together. But there isn't a production any longer, is there? I can't believe it. Do you know we lost every set and prop for *A Christmas Carol*?"

"I'm so sorry." I had no intention of telling her that I took Tiny Tim's crutch home. After it helped to save my life, I viewed the prop as a good-luck charm.

"At least we still have the costumes. Thank goodness the fire happened during dress rehearsal. And I need you to bring your Jacob Marley costume to my house." She grabbed my hand. "Marlee, please tell me you still have the costume! You didn't throw it away! Or wash it!"

"No. I have it." When I got home last night, I stuffed the costume and chains in a garbage bag, then tossed the bag onto my front porch. The costume reeked of smoke and I refused to bring it into the house.

"Bring the costume to me as soon as you can," she repeated. "Or give it to one of my sons." She took a deep breath. "As God is my witness, the Green Willow Players will perform *A Christmas Carol* again."

Greg and I exchanged amused glances as she walked away. "That was her best Scarlett O'Hara," I told him. "All she needs is a fan and hoopskirt."

"Speaking of costumes, what are you wearing?" Greg shook his head. "You look like a character in an old movie."

"It's one of Natasha's fur coats. I think this one is raccoon. I'm mortified because I don't believe in fur. But my only winter parka went up in flames last night."

He smiled. "Kit was still buying gifts for you when I spoke to him last week. I may text him and suggest he add 'coat' to the list."

"I won't stop you." I spotted Officer Davenport and Chief Hitchcock in the crowd. "Greg, I need a favor. A law enforcement kind of favor."

His customary wary expression returned. "What sort of favor?"

"Among the remains of that barn are three metal boxes. They each contain evidence of wrongdoing by several people close to the recently deceased Everett Hostetter. Three people now trying to find his will." I lowered my voice. "Everett may have been murdered last week so someone could get their hands on his money. And two nights ago, Everett's attorney, the only other person who knew what the will said, conveniently died."

"Why were boxes of evidence kept in a theater?"

I explained about Everett, the play, his dressing room, and Gareth's drunken ramblings. I even mentioned the dead squirrel, but unlike the Oriole police, Greg grew even more serious.

"Have you told Kit about this?"

I nodded. "He knew a lot before he left for Detroit. And this morning, I let him know about the fire and what the boxes contained. But I have no idea if those metal boxes were fireproof. If I could hunt around in the rubble—"

"Absolutely not. Only the fire department and arson division are allowed past the yellow barrier tape."

"Does that include the Oriole Point police? Because I don't trust Janelle."

"The town police department is too small. They don't have an arson specialist. But the sheriff's department does." He nodded toward a man and a woman wearing sheriff department jackets, who spoke with a firefighter. "That's why Officers Pollard and Sykes are here. They'll be investigating this fire."

"Could you talk to them about this? Ask them to search for the boxes?"

He nodded. "Will do. None of us like the look of this fire."

"Last night, the firefighters spoke to everyone who was in the theater. Since I was the only one in the basement when the fire started, they questioned me for quite a while. I don't know how much help I was. When I came out of the bathroom, I saw nothing but smoke and flames."

"Most of the firefighters have already pegged this as arson. Only don't say anything until the department makes it public."

"I appreciate that you're willing to help me. I'm baking cookies today, and I'll put together a big box for your family. Not you, of course. I know you think cookies are unhealthy."

"No need to bribe me to do the right thing," he said gruffly, then flashed a grin. "But my wife and kids do love cookies. Now let me take Pollard and Sykes aside to explain all this."

I watched as Greg and the two arson specialists walked past the yellow tape to inspect the destroyed barn. Fingers crossed, they'd find the boxes. I prayed they didn't do it when Janelle was around.

With a last look at the charred site, I turned to go. As much as I hated to admit it, the fur coat was incredibly warm. I ran a hand over my furry sleeve. If only faux fur felt this wonderful.

Trying to avoid slippery patches, I kept my eyes on the ground as I made my way back to the van. With my head down, I didn't see Anthony Thorne until I was almost upon him.

"Returning to the scene of the crime?" he asked with a humorless smile.

I took a step back. "What does that mean?"

"I heard you replaced my uncle in the play. That means you were here last night when the barn burned down. The day before opening night is always dress rehearsal."

"You know an awful lot about the schedule of *A Christmas Carol.*"

He rolled his eyes. "I lived through nine years of the old man's obsession with that play. You're damn right I know the actors' schedule."

"Then you're probably happy the barn burned down."

"That I am. With Uncle Everett dead, my future attendance is no longer required here."

"Why are you here now?"

"Why are you?"

I gave him an exasperated look. "I asked you first."

"For starters, I wanted to make certain the theater was really gone. My uncle spent too much time and money on this ridiculous amateur troupe. Particularly that tiresome play."

"It might have been his way of showing the Christmas spirit."

Anthony snorted. "What did my uncle know of Christmas? He never gave a single person a gift for Christmas. Not even his own sister. He thought gifts were a waste of money. And his company Christmas bonuses were meager at best. I don't know why he didn't play Scrooge."

"And you're the soul of Christmas cheer?" I tried not to laugh.

"Yeah. Or at least I was. When I had money, I spread it around. Easy come, easy go. I once chartered a yacht in the Mediterranean and took two dozen employees for a Christmas party. I knew how to have a good time. Made sure my friends had a good time, too."

"Not all your friends were so lucky."

"Guess you've googled me. And talked to that gossipy excuse for a lawyer."

"Also now deceased."

He smiled. "Yes. Two things I can check off my Christmas list."

"You hated them that much?"

"*Hate* is a strong word. How about *disgust*? Or *weariness*?"

I gave him a searching look. "Weary of being on your best behavior?"

"Something I'd suggest you try to do. Because my behavior is none of your business."

"When I asked why you were here, you began by

saying 'for starters.' Why else did you come here this morning?"

He stared at what was left of the Calico Barn. "To make certain this is really over. I don't like loose ends. They're messy."

I waved in the direction of last night's fire. "So this was a loose end?"

"Yes, it was." A note of relief was evident in his voice. "But not anymore."

Anthony walked on, making his way to where Janelle and Hitchcock stood talking. I wondered how much Anthony wanted to tie up loose ends. And if he'd been willing to burn the barn to the ground to do it.

"Exactly how many cookies do you expect your parents to eat?" Gillian asked as I pulled my ninth cookie sheet from the shop kitchen oven.

"Some of these I'll put in tins and bring to neighbors and friends." I inhaled the aroma of this latest batch, the delicious smell of chocolate chips wafting over me. "Another dozen and I'll be done."

Gillian leaned against the sink. "Good thing it's been slow. Only two customers."

"And no sales. I'll close early. Why stay open if no one is shopping? In fact, you can go now. But I'll pay you for the whole day." I shot her a grin. "After all, it's Christmas."

"Thanks, boss." She untied her Berry Basket apron.

"My accountant does payroll tonight. So all electronic paychecks will be deposited tomorrow." I didn't add that I had included a hefty bonus for my employees. The Berry Basket had enjoyed a profitable year, and Gillian, Dean, Andrew, and Theo were a big part of that success. "Don't forget that I'm taking all my Berry Basket people out for a big holiday brunch next week. Theo should be back by then."

"I hope he made it to the train station okay. The only Amtrak train to Chicago leaves before dawn, and the roads were probably a mess."

"I'll text him later to see how he's doing." Using a nonstick spatula, I placed the warm cookies on cooling racks.

By the time, Gillian put on her coat, scarf, gloves, and boots, I had the final tray of cookies in the oven. Despite the lack of customers, I had enjoyed a productive day. I deserved the six cookies I'd already eaten.

"Don't forget your present," I said. "It's the big one wrapped in blue with a silver bow. Only don't open it until Christmas."

"Thanks! And this is your Christmas present." She handed me a thin box in glittery silver paper. From the shape, I'd guess it was jewelry. Gillian knew I had a weakness for bracelets. "As for your birthday present, I'll stop by your house tomorrow and deliver it myself. How else can I sing 'Happy Birthday' to you?"

"Exactly." I gave her a big hug. She held on to me longer than I expected.

When we finally separated, she said, "To be honest, I already got my Christmas gift from you. You're out of that play. I'm so relieved."

I chuckled. "I hope you didn't have a hand in burning the theater down."

"No. But it might have been an option if it hadn't. I told you the barn was unlucky."

After she left, I admitted to feeling relieved, too. Sometimes, bad luck hovered about certain people or places. This year's production of *A Christmas Carol* had seen far too much bad luck to dismiss it as coincidence.

I heard the back door to the kitchen open. "Did you forget something, Gillian?"

"It's not Gillian."

"Theo! What are you doing here?"

"I missed my train." He looked quite woebegone. "The trucks didn't plow my street this morning and I got stuck in the snow. It took me an hour to dig out and drive to Holland. Only it was too late. The train had left."

"What bad luck, Theo. Did you let your dad know?"

Theo nodded. "He bought me another ticket online. One I can use tomorrow. But it was my mistake. I should have gotten up earlier. What if I miss the train again tomorrow?"

"I'm sure lots of people missed their train in this weather. And your dad only has to drive to the Champaign/Urbana station to pick you up. No big deal."

"It was my mistake," he repeated. "I can't miss another train. I have my suitcase in the car, so I can spend the night in the station. I'll sleep on one of the benches."

I knew he was serious. Only there was no way I'd let him spend the night twenty miles away in a train station. "I have a better idea. Sleep over at my house. There are plenty of bedrooms. And I promise to drive you in plenty of time to catch the Pere Marquette train. We'll leave super early."

A huge grin creased his face. "Really? You'll make sure I get there on time?"

"Scouts honor." While I didn't relish the idea of getting up before dawn, I would not have been able to sleep knowing Theo sat shivering in the train station alone. "Natasha is at my house making dinner again. Something complicated and Russian. She'd love your help in the kitchen."

"I'd like that." Theo found Natasha confusing, funny, and fascinating. I suspect she felt the same way about him. The two got on remarkably well.

Theo looked at all the fresh-baked cookies. "You're baking. Do you want me to help?"

"Thanks, but I'm almost done. When the cookies cool, I'll box them and head on home." I gave him a gentle push toward the back door. "But you drive over there now. If you ask nicely, Natasha will put aside the electric kettle and make Russian tea in her samovar for you."

"The tea that has strawberry jam in it?"

"The very one."

No need to add another incentive. Theo was out the door in a flash, his boots leaving a trail of slush. Smiling at the prospect of another houseguest, I mopped up the floor. I had no sooner finished when the bells above my shop door tinkled. What do you know? An actual customer.

Except it wasn't a customer who waited in my shop.

"Katrina. I didn't expect to see you here today."

"Because of the weather, or because of the suspicious feelings now existing between us?"

"Both. You certainly weren't happy with me on Sunday."

"Yes. Being accused of giving Gareth poison chestnuts was insulting." She fixed her unblinking gaze on me. "And untrue."

"Since you sampled the chestnut, I do concede the cause of death lay somewhere else."

"I hope you allow the police to handle it from here."

I shrugged. "Depends on the police officer. I'd prefer Janelle Davenport stay out of it."

Today her dark hair was swept back into a tight ballerina bun, showcasing that elegant long neck. Somehow it made her seem more formidable. "You don't trust Janelle?"

"No. And I don't like her."

"My guides say she is to be pitied. Janelle wraps herself in bitterness as if it were a protective cloak. She cannot break free of the past. It has left her sour and unhappy. Hostile."

"Gareth said Janelle was a dishonest cop back in Wisconsin. And that Everett managed to get Internal Affairs to drop their investigation. Maybe some of that pity your spirit guides recommend should be extended to people she falsely accused and stole from."

"Justice is not their concern. Nor is it mine. But Everett didn't agree. He thought redemption was possible for everyone. Even Janelle."

"And Anthony? He seems to have led a pretty libertine life. One marked by self-indulgence and financial ruin. Capped off by the betrayal and death of his friend."

"Anthony is an immature soul interested only in self-preservation. He is incapable of feeling guilt. That is his tragedy."

"And what is yours? Perhaps you feel too much guilt. At least where Everett's sister is concerned."

She forced me to endure another of her Medusa stares. "I see Gareth has told you everything, Or as much as he knew. Because no one knows the whole story, except me."

I sat down at a bistro table, trying to appear casual in what felt like a tense situation. "I believe your psychic gifts are real, Katrina. The things you passed on from my grandmother were only known by her and me. However, that doesn't mean you're always accurate. Or even honest about your readings. At least not if money is involved."

She looked away. It felt as if a laser beam had shifted to the side. I also felt a blinding headache coming on.

"My gifts are a tool." She shrugged. "I won't pretend I haven't used them for my own advantage. When I was younger, I often manipulated clients for gain. Why not? They could afford it. But it wasn't until Sarah that I corrupted my gifts. Betrayed them."

"Everett wanted you to persuade Sarah to sign over her company shares to him, didn't he? No doubt in exchange for a payout. That's why he married you. Being his wife gave you an entrée into her home. A woman who had become a recluse."

"Sarah didn't have much family left. Only a worthless son and Everett. As Everett's wife, I was able to get her to trust me."

"Only I'm guessing your spirit guides did not think it wise for Sarah to hand over those shares to her brother. So you pretended they did. And she believed you."

Katrina rubbed her arms, as though she felt a sudden chill. "Greed is a terrible thing. It makes you dishonest and cruel. A shameful abuse of my gifts."

"But why did Sarah die? Gareth said you and Everett scared her to death."

"Insidious man. I'm glad he's dead. He made every situation worse."

"That doesn't answer my question."

She walked over, her high-heel boots making sharp clicks on the wooden floor. Although she wasn't tall, I felt intimidated when she stood over me.

"I simply passed on messages from the dead. Yes, the ones about those company shares were false. However, I did relay messages from her deceased husband that were true. Dr. Thorne wanted to let Sarah know she was about to join him soon. That her time was nearly up. She seemed by turns frightened and relieved. Whatever she actually felt, those messages had too great an effect on her. And she suddenly died."

"Mind over matter," I murmured, thinking of the victims of voodoo, who sickened as soon as they heard a curse had been put on them.

"Her death lay heavy on Everett's conscience. And mine." Katrina gave a great sigh. "Until then, I never let clients know they were about to die. It seemed pointless. Sarah's death is a result of my great error in doing so with her. If I hadn't gotten involved with Everett and his scheme, Sarah might still be alive."

"Since you and Everett were both guilty—"

"Everett far more than me," Katrina snapped. "I didn't know he had already convinced her to disinherit her only child. Everett was a master of manipulation. Ruthless and without feeling. And the Hostetter wealth blinded me for a time. But I haven't lied to a client since."

"How kind of you." I stood up and she took a step back. Enough with her spooky intimidations. "I hope you've been honest with Natasha. I'll be quite angry if I discover you've deceived her in any way."

"I told you that I haven't lied to a client since Sarah. It has taken a long time for my spirit guides to trust me again. I cannot breach that trust. Or my gifts might be taken from me."

Whether that was true or not, Katrina seemed to believe it. "Do you or your spirits know why Gareth died?"

"That's easy. Gareth's downfall was his arrogance. And look where it got him."

"Killed by a Christmas tree?"

She ignored my sardonic smile. "No longer able to wield the power left him by Everett. I warned him. I saw darkness gathering around him, as vividly as a thunderstorm on the horizon. But he wouldn't listen to me. Wouldn't do the rational thing and simply make the will public."

"Why do you even care? It's likely the money has been left to his daughter or his nephew. Maybe both

of them. Why do you think you're one of the beneficiaries? Yes, you were his wife. For all of five minutes.
It doesn't make sense."

"Because Everett made a promise to all three of us.
Come to Oriole Point where he could keep a watchful
eye on Anthony, Janelle, and me. Make certain we
didn't do anything dishonest or criminal." Her voice
grew bitter. "Being lumped in with Janelle and Anthony has been hard to stomach. My misbehavior
doesn't begin to compare to theirs."

"You did help kill his sister."

"Stop saying that! You sound like Gareth. And how
long do I have to atone for my sins? That's all very
well for Everett. He devoted his life to avarice. It was
only right that he try to make amends. But not
through us! We've been kept captive here for nine
years, all on the hope that when he died the Hostetter fortune would pass on to one of us."

"Only one?"

She nodded. "Whoever he judged to have made
the most honest life for themselves would inherit.
Now he's dead. And we need the will. That is why I'm
here."

"I don't have it."

Katrina gave me another of those spooky looks
that scared Theo so much. "But it's close to you. My
guides tell me that you know where it is."

"Your guides are lying to you."

"They never lie." She put her hands on my shoulders. "Also I don't need spirits to read a person. I
sense energy. And Everett's energy is somehow connected to you."

I banished the image of those metal boxes in case she could read minds. "I did replace him as Jacob Marley. You're probably picking up on that."

Katrina closed her eyes. "No. More than that. You have the will."

Irritated, I pulled out of her grasp. "If I do find it, I'll let everyone know."

"You may not be able to. Death is coming for you. Fast. As it did for Gareth."

I refused to show how this upset me. "I thought you didn't lie to clients any longer. Or tell them death was imminent."

"I've made an exception in your case, in hopes of preventing another tragedy." She frowned. "I can see you don't believe me. That shows you're as arrogant as Gareth was."

The image of Gareth's dead body in the village square flashed in my head. "If you're so all-seeing, how come you don't know? Ask your spirits to tell you the location of the will."

She looked at me as if I were stupid. "Don't confuse me with a carnival act. I only pass on messages given to me. I can demand nothing from the spirits. But I am sensitive to the constant flow of energy around us. And I see a connection between Everett's energy and yours."

"I think the only connection was that odiferous costume we both wore."

Katrina didn't find this amusing. "Two people are dead, Marlee. All because of the will. Do not tell me again that you don't hold the answer. You may not know where the will is, but you will soon." She paused.

"When you do, death will have its hand on your shoulder."

Without waiting for an answer, Katrina swept out of the shop like an elegant soothsayer.

"Merry Christmas to you, too," I muttered.

Only Christmas now seemed less merry with my death around the corner. I also couldn't figure out where the will was. Possibly in that third metal box I never had the chance to unlock. If so, the will was either a pile of ash, or in the possession of the sheriff's arson department.

And if Katrina saw death in my near future, I couldn't dismiss it. Especially since she may have predicted her own murderous response if and when I found it.

Whatever psychic sense I possessed told me that I was in serious trouble.

Chapter Twenty-four

After Katrina's unwelcome visit, I had a hard time feeling festive. Since I planned to drop off gifts to shopkeeper friends, I made an extra effort to spread Christmas cheer. Apparently, it worked. Everyone remarked on how jolly I seemed. That gave me a sinking feeling. Gareth was remarkably jolly right before his death.

I had just delivered a set of blueberry jams to Mia at Popping Fun—receiving a box of popcorn balls in return—when I saw Officer Davenport. If the sidewalk hadn't been icy, I might have fled in the opposite direction.

"Are you replacing Gareth as Santa?" Janelle eyed the cloth bag of gifts I held and the Santa cap on my head. "Although I don't think Santa wore raccoon coats. Reindeer coats, maybe. Not raccoon."

"I'm dropping off Christmas gifts to friends."

"Any for me?"

I couldn't resist. "I said 'friends.' "

"Yeah, I feel the same way. Even so I have a gift for you."

Her expression made me suspicious. "What do you mean?"

"Chief Hitchcock contacted Public Safety today to order a rush on the lab tests."

"The ones for those cookie fragments that killed the squirrel?"

She rolled her eyes. "Yes, the squirrel homicide investigation is underway."

"Why now? I gave him the cookies three days ago."

Janelle adjusted her police cap. "It seems Gareth Holmes was not killed by Piper's Christmas tree."

"Did something turn up in the autopsy? Was he poisoned? Maybe a deliberate blow to the back of his head? Were there markings on the body indicative of foul play?"

"Do you also want to know if someone shot him with an arrow?"

"That's not funny." Indeed, an innocent man had been murdered with a bow and arrow this past October. Janelle's mocking reference set my teeth on edge. "But I'm relieved Chief Hitchcock took my concerns about Gareth's death seriously."

"Oh, it had nothing to do with your theories. Two witnesses reported that before the tree fell, they saw Santa sitting alone on the park bench behind it. He was slumped forward, leading them to believe he was asleep."

"That's what Everett looked like when I found him on the bench in the museum."

Janelle nodded. "The chief and I thought this

seemed suspicious. Who falls asleep on a park bench during a cold, snowy night? Aside from the homeless."

"Then you suspect Gareth was already dead when the tree fell on him?"

"It makes more sense than Gareth taking a nap in the middle of a snowstorm. His death warrants looking into. The ME sent us the results of his autopsy today."

"And?" I suspected Janelle loved dragging this out.

"Poison."

I gasped. "Then the chestnuts *were* poisoned. But Katrina ate from the bag. I saw her."

"I doubt chestnuts were involved. What we do want to know is how methamphetamine crystals were found in his system."

"Crystal meth? Gareth wasn't a meth addict."

She gave me a patronizing look. "Of course not. If he had been a regular user, Gareth might still be alive. He probably ate something containing methamphetamine crystals. If you've never used the drug before, that amount can kill. In this case, Gareth suffered a sudden heart attack. He wasn't in great physical shape to start with. His death probably came quickly."

That meant Gareth must have been dead when Dean and I were waiting on the other side of the Christmas tree. Both of us unaware a man had been murdered only a few yards away.

"Does the autopsy show what he consumed that night besides the drug?"

"Old Gareth seems to have consumed about ten thousand calories during the Hollyberry Festival. You name it, he ate it. Somewhere during his food binge, a little poison got slipped in."

I thought a moment. "We just had that triple homicide in the county. And it involved a meth ring. Is there any way Gareth might have been involved with that?"

Janelle laughed so hard, she choked. "You never disappoint, Marlee. If there's a crackpot theory to spread, you'll be the first to do so."

"I'm serious. Because Gareth and crystal meth don't add up."

"The county is filled with meth heads. Anyone can get their hands on the drug." She wiped tears of laughter from her eyes. "Or maybe you've forgotten that your pretty ex-boyfriend was hooked on the drug back in high school."

I glared at her. "Should we blame Ryan for Gareth's murder then?"

"We don't have anyone to blame for Gareth's death. Not yet."

"A motive might be a good place to start."

"Thanks. We hadn't thought of that." She continued to chuckle.

"I can think of an excellent motive: Everett's will. The sooner it's found, the sooner you, Anthony, and Katrina learn which of you has inherited a fortune."

"I guess that puts me on the list of suspects. Fair enough. But as you like to remind me, Everett Hostetter was my father. And I know he felt guilty about abandoning my mother. Because of that, I'm certain he finally did the right thing and left everything to me."

"And what if the will is never found?"

She shrugged. "A court of law would view me as his closest living relative. It might take a while to contest any legal challenges Anthony will launch. Eventually I'd win. So why bother to knock off Gareth? Aside from the fact that he was an irritating blowhard."

"Because he did know who inherited. And Katrina thinks it might be her."

"Katrina lives in her own creepy world. God knows what rattles around in that strange brain of hers, other than ghosts and money." Janelle's smile turned sly. "Katrina and I had breakfast this morning. She believes you have the will. Her spirit guides have told her so."

"She told me the same thing. Sorry, I don't have the will."

"Katrina's spirits have a good track record. They're never wrong." Janelle turned up her jacket collar as the wind increased. "She's told me stuff she couldn't possibly know. To be honest, that weirdo scares me. And Anthony believes in her spirits as much as Everett did. If he thinks you have the will, he'll act on it. So if I were you, I'd start looking."

"Now I have to worry about Anthony as well?"

"We all worry about Anthony. He's a cunning pig. And he doesn't like you." Janelle seemed amused by this. "He refers to you as a loose end. And he likes everything all tied up."

I shot her an irritated look. "So do I."

"Then find that will. Everyone is getting impatient." She laughed again. "According to Katrina, your time is running out."

This time I did turn around and flee the other

way. A pity I couldn't speak with spirits. If I could, I'd ask Gareth who killed him. And what I should do next.

I refused to allow murder to spoil Christmas any more than it already had. When I returned home, the animals gave me a joyous welcome, which made me feel better. Dasha brought me her favorite rubber toy, while Panther raced about the living room. I put Minnie on my shoulder where she crooned her version of "Deck the Halls." In between verses, she tried to unravel the wool on my sweater. And the house smelled delicious.

This was due to Theo and Natasha's dinner preparations. I happily pitched in.

"I never knew you liked to cook," I said. "Or that you were so good at it."

"All Rostova women cook." Natasha pointed her knife at a pile of faded handwritten recipe cards. "These are recipes of my *prababushka*. She cook big dinner in Moscow for Stalin."

"I don't know if I'd brag about that."

"Is good I brag. Stalin kill many people, but he let my babushka live. All because she make best borscht and *golubtsy* politburo members ever eat. You taste tonight."

Assuming the meal was ever completed. Every pot, pan, and cooking utensil lay scattered about my kitchen. However, the aroma was mouthwatering.

Theo looked up from a boiling pot. "She has tiny fish eggs for us, too."

"You bought caviar?"

Natasha smiled. "Is gift from Alexei. We eat every night I have dinner with him."

"Does that include tonight?" The Russian architect seemed to have swept Natasha off her feet. If this became serious, I needed to vet him.

"*Nyet.* He has business dinner in Grand Rapids. Alexei is to build most fancy hotel. Tallest one in city."

"*Pozdravlyayu* to him."

"You speak Russian, too, Marlee?" Theo looked impressed.

"I teach." Natasha replied. "I am best teacher of Russian. And you can say *pozdravlyayu* to Alexei tomorrow. I invite here for Christmas Eve."

"How nice. I want to meet him." I quickly counted everyone expected for Christmas Eve dinner. I might need to run to the market tomorrow and buy another turkey.

Natasha swiftly chopped celery. "There is crutch in living room by fireplace. Does someone come for Christmas who has broken leg?"

I laughed. "The crutch is a prop from *A Christmas Carol.* It belongs to Tiny Tim."

"I like Tiny Tim," Theo piped up.

"Everyone does. And I used his crutch to help me escape from the fire at the barn. It helped save my life, so I'm keeping it. Before I left for work this morning, I put together that display devoted to Tiny Tim and *A Christmas Carol.* I love it."

The new Tiny Tim corner in the living room filled the last empty space I had in there. In addition to the crutch leaning against the short wooden stool, I'd placed an old-fashioned winter cap, a fake holly wreath, and my personal copy of *A Christmas Carol*. A pity I wasn't able to save the first edition that went up in flames last night.

"Katrina not tell me you will be in danger from fire," Natasha said. "She knows you are my friend. Why did she not pass on messages from spirits so I can warn you?"

"I wouldn't mind an answer to that as well."

"I am not happy with Katrina. First, she give me messages from cousin I hate. Now she not help me to keep you safe. For Christmas I give her something cheap."

"That will show her." I smiled. "And the only Christmas gift I care about is having my parents and Kit here. With luck, Kit will be back tomorrow."

"Because I won't be here for Christmas, I'll give you my gift tonight, Marlee," Theo said.

"We eat dinner before," Natasha ordered. "Then I have new *obraztsy kraski* to show. I change color of Peacock lobby. I need help to decide."

Theo looked bewildered.

"Don't worry," I told him. "And we have blinis and borscht to look forward to."

Three hours later, we finished dinner and came to a consensus on sea-ice blue for the lobby. Theo and I also exchanged gifts. He was thrilled with the three birdhouses I special-ordered for him.

But Theo's gift to me brought tears to my eyes: a heavy coffee-table book devoted to Charles Dickens's *Christmas Carol*. It included an annotated version, photos of numerous film and theater productions, and illustrations from dozens of incarnations of the classic story. Including the 1843 originals by John Leech.

I leafed through the pages. "This is wonderful! I can't think of a better gift. I am so touched, Theo. Thank you."

He looked pleased to have chosen so well. "As soon as you told me about being in the play, I ordered it on Amazon. Now you can put it in your Tiny Tim corner."

"Indeed, I will." I smiled. "First, I am going to give you such a hug."

As lovely as the dinner and gifts were, the festivities drew to a close soon after. Theo, who had been up since before dawn, headed off to the third-floor guest room. That I expected. As a baker, Theo was an early riser. But night-owl Natasha surprised me with her plans to soak in a bubble bath, then go to bed. I guessed Alexei had seen to it that she had gotten little sleep lately.

Since the past week had been draining, I welcomed some alone time before the holiday parties and family gatherings commenced. But once Theo and Natasha retreated upstairs, I discovered I was too agitated to read or watch TV.

A shame, too. It was quiet; a rare occurrence. Minnie had been retired to her sleep cage upstairs. Dasha was with her mistress. Even Panther had zoned out, curled up beneath her favorite white Christmas tree.

That left me to wander about the living room. Now that the police had proof Gareth did not die from natural causes, I had no doubt poison led to

Everett's death. But I'd assumed that from the beginning.

The killer must be one of the unholy three. But which one? And where was that stupid will? It had to be in one of the metal boxes in Everett's dressing room. Yet, Katrina and her spirit guides were positive I possessed the will. I knew it wasn't true, yet I couldn't shake the feeling she was right.

I understood how she frightened clients and manipulated them. Was that what she was doing now? Trying to get me to admit that I had the will? I felt as if her spirits were haunting me.

"Like in *A Christmas Carol*," I said aloud.

I stopped in front of the gas fireplace and stared at the flames. Actually, the unholy trio were the ghosts. Their harmful deeds haunted Everett, reminding him that he helped to make them the people they were.

"Janelle is the Ghost of Christmas Past," I said to Panther, who peeked out at me from beneath the white tree. "A past in which he fathered a child, then walked away. And she never escaped from that past. It turned her into a suspicious, unethical woman."

Panther let out a plaintive meow.

"Anthony lived with Everett in the present day, directly under his thumb and supervision. He's the Ghost of Christmas Present. But on steroids. A man who cared only for his own pleasure. Even if a friend had to suffer and die. And Everett convinced Katrina to lie about her spirits in order to take advantage of his sister. Unfortunately, when she relayed a message that was actually true, it led to the woman's death."

Maybe I had listened to *A Christmas Carol* too many

times. But Katrina could be nothing other than the Ghost of Christmas Yet to Come. A forbidding figure who passed on predictions of death and doom. And she warned that my death was imminent.

Despite my proximity to the fire, I shivered. If only I did have that will. I'd give it to them as fast as I could and let the three of them fight over it.

The strong winds whistled against my house. The walls creaked like a galleon on the high seas. I thought of the black garbage bag on my porch containing the Jacob Marley costume and the chain. I didn't want the bags to be swept off into the snow because I needed the chain. If the metal boxes had survived the fire, the keys would open them again.

I put on Natasha's raccoon coat and went out to the porch. As bitterly cold winds whistled about me, I fished the chain out of the garbage bag and hurried back into the house.

Once inside, I turned my home security system on, reassured by the green light. My house had been broken into this past autumn. Piper felt partly to blame, which induced her to install an alarm system. I rarely used it, but tonight I welcomed this extra security blanket. Especially with Katrina's prediction of my death.

The chain was long and noisy, drawing Panther's attention. He kept pouncing on the chain as I dragged it behind me. It must have seemed like a giant toy, one filled with keys, padlocks, and steel boxes. I sat in front of the fire and dangled parts of the chain for Panther to bat at with his paws.

The kitten especially loved the cash boxes. I held up part of the chain, swinging it back and forth for his amusement. Because it was so quiet, I heard a swishing noise. I swung the small box harder. Then shook it. Something was inside.

My heart pounded. It had to be the will. Only I dreaded the discovery. Because that meant Katrina had correctly seen the future. A future that held my death. However, if I was going to die over this will, I intended to satisfy my curiosity.

The box was locked. But it had a tiny keyhole, making it easy to find the tiniest key on the chain. I inserted the key and slowly opened it. A small square of paper lay inside.

When I lifted it out, I realized the square was comprised of three sheets of legal paper, as meticulously folded as origami. I carefully smoothed out the pages on the floor, firelight illuminating the text. I read all three pages, accompanied by the sounds of the crackling fire and Panther playing with the chain.

When I was done, I looked up. But I wasn't seeing the fire before me. Instead, I saw the disappointed and outraged faces of Janelle, Anthony, and Katrina.

Because none of them were left a thing in the will.

Chapter Twenty-five

Something woke me up. I stared into the darkness and listened.

It wasn't my cat. Panther slept beside my pillow. I heard only the gale winds beat against the house. The noise probably came from my carriage clock downstairs, which chimed the hour. Sometimes it did wake me up. Since it was now silent, I guessed it had chimed once to announce it was 1:00 a.m. Natasha hated the chimes and had threatened to remove the clock battery. I wished now that she had.

With a sigh, I turned on my side, hoping to fall back to sleep. After texting Kit to let him know about the will, I'd fallen exhausted into bed. Now that I was awake, my thoughts swirled around the three who expected to be named in Everett's will. Indeed, I wondered if one of them guessed what Everett had done and killed him out of anger.

If so, who? I was there when both Anthony and Janelle learned Everett was dead. Anthony seemed stunned, as though he didn't quite understand why his uncle sat lifeless before him. Janelle had been so startled by the news, she spit out her coffee. I didn't think she was a good enough actress to pretend that well. She hadn't expected to hear her father had died. Even if the revelation did also amuse her.

If only I'd been a witness to Katrina's reaction when she learned of her ex-husband's death. Maybe she already knew. Knowledge she would attribute to her spirit guides, or from having murdered him. Only why would Katrina murder Everett? She had far less reason to expect to be named in the will than his two blood relatives. Unless she knew Janelle and Anthony hadn't reformed, that both were the same unethical people who'd left wreckage behind in their previous lives.

According to David's friend Craig, Anthony's financial consulting not only cost Craig lots of money, but his credit card information had been stolen. My brief look at the files containing information about Anthony revealed he had been engaging in credit card fraud and identity theft ever since he moved to Oriole Point. As for Janelle, I had no doubt she'd found a way to engage in a little graft during her nine years on our small-town police force.

And *had* Katrina turned over a new leaf? Piper recently learned Katrina ended her current boyfriend's marriage after passing on ghostly revelations about his wife's financial activities. So Katrina was back to her old tricks. With her sights set on another rich husband.

Again, I heard something downstairs. Not a clock chime either. I clicked on the bedside lamp, but nothing happened. Trying not to disturb Panther, I rolled to the other side of the bed and tried the matching lamp. That didn't work either. The howling winds had probably knocked down a nearby power line.

I got up and peeked out the bedroom window. Tree branches shook in the wind, evergreens leaned to one side. And no light shone from my neighbor's lamppost. Douglas never turned it off. I craned my neck, but saw only darkness farther down the street. Including from those porch lights I knew were on timers.

Yep. The neighborhood had lost power. I reached for my cell phone on the bedside table, only to remember I'd left it downstairs in my home office to charge.

Another noise. Not loud, but in the silent house it seemed to reverberate. Maybe Natasha or Theo had gotten up.

After closing the bedroom door on Panther, who wanted to follow, I tiptoed into the second-floor hallway. I didn't need my kitty underfoot until I understood where the noises came from.

Natasha's bedroom lay across the hall. I put my ear to the door, but heard nothing. Minnie was safely covered in her sleep cage in the bedroom next to mine. Although she never woke at night, I peeked into the dark room to make sure. Next, I went up to the third floor, where Theo slept in the turret bedroom. His door was shut as well; I heard snoring within.

Whatever was making the noises, it wasn't either of my houseguests or the animals. Unless my friendly ghost Mary Cullen had decided to do something aside from clanging pots. But I feared this had nothing to do with ghosts.

My eyes had adjusted to the dark well enough to risk going downstairs. I knew which steps creaked and avoided them on the way down. Once in the foyer I looked over at the front door, which was closed. I also noticed the green light for my security system was off. No surprise given the power outage.

I heard the sound of a drawer being pulled out. Definitely from my home office, which had originally been a parlor. What to do? I didn't have a weapon in the house. And my phone was in the office.

Yet I couldn't leave, not with Natasha and Theo asleep upstairs. Nor could I return to my own bedroom in hopes the intruder would go away. Because I bet the intruder came here looking for the will. And would not stop from searching every inch of my house. Even if it meant harming the people in it.

My mind raced to come up with a way to defend myself. I had to confront this person—and soon. Eventually the intruder would realize no will was in there and come out. I heard another drawer open.

I pressed against the stairwell, trying to think. My fingers brushed against the head of one of the nutcrackers I'd placed along the wall. This one was a two-foot-tall sugarplum fairy. A nice heavy one. I carefully picked it up. Holding it like a bat, I prepared to clobber whoever was in there. No questions asked.

When I snuck closer to the open door of the office, a beam of light played against the wall. The person had either brought a flashlight or was using the one on their phone.

Once I reached the door, I stood off to one side, trying to quiet my breathing. From the room came the shuffling of papers. Yes, definitely on the hunt for the will. But who?

In a flash, I knew. I took a step back and raised the nutcracker, ready to swing.

But that one step on a noisy wooden floor gave me away. The flashlight turned its beam on the open door. No point in hiding now.

"Come out, Janelle," I called. "I know you're in there."

Silence.

Then Janelle replied, "You should have stayed in bed, Marlee."

Her flashlight blinded me. I raised my arm to cover my eyes, but too late. Janelle reached me before I could turn and run.

I swung the nutcracker at her, but she had the advantage. She knocked the nutcracker from my grasp, then twisted my arm behind my back. I winced in pain.

"I'd keep quiet if I were you," she said softly. "I know Natasha has been staying here. You wouldn't want your houseguest to come down. Then I'd have to hurt both of you."

At least Janelle had no idea Theo slept upstairs as well. Not that it was much comfort. It only meant I had two people to protect from this crooked cop. This killer.

"Looking for the will, I see," I spat out.

"I'll find it, too. Because you're going to tell me."

"Why would I? It's not like you're going to let me

live. Not when I know you're the one who killed Gareth." My voice hardened. "And your own father."

"I didn't kill my father." She twisted my arm tighter. "You've been nothing but trouble since you moved back to Oriole Point. Why didn't I find a way to get rid of you long ago?"

I didn't answer her rhetorical question. When she pushed me into the living room, Janelle swept her flashlight over the room. It was filled with more Christmas decor than Santa's workshop.

"I'm running out of patience. And you're running out of time. Where is the will? I know you have it."

"Because of Katrina's ghosts?" I gave a mocking laugh.

"Katrina swears you have it. She's never wrong. And don't make fun of ghosts. You'll be one soon."

I kicked backward as hard as I could, landing a solid blow on her shin. She let go of my arm and I scrambled over the loveseat to my right.

Her flashlight beam followed the sound and found me. "I have a gun, Marlee. And I will shoot. Even if I miss you in the dark, the gunshot will send your friend running downstairs. I'd have to shoot her, too."

I stopped. "How will you explain my dead body? And Natasha's?"

"I won't have to. The police will assume there was an intruder. Home invasions are common during the holidays. Thieves eager to make off with all those Christmas presents. And this power outage provides even better coverage."

"You won't get away with it. They'll trace the bullet back to your gun."

She laughed. "Not this gun. I have access to lots of contraband. Some of which never reach the police department."

Of course. Once a crooked cop, always a crooked cop.

"I'd rather not do this in the dark," I said in frustration.

"The power is out, fool."

"Not the gas." I slowly stepped back until I reached the gas fireplace. I flipped the wall switch. The gas flames whooshed and slowly grew larger and brighter.

Most of the room still lay in shadow, but Janelle was close enough for me to see her. And she did indeed hold a gun.

"Since you're not in uniform, I assume you're here as a criminal, not a policewoman."

"Why don't you assume I'm sick to death of you." She waved at the corner. "Sit in the corner where I can keep an eye on you."

I walked backward, never taking my eyes from her. Thankfully, the corner she directed me to held my Tiny Tim display. I removed the wreath, cap, and the Dickens volume Theo gave me from the stool and sat down. But I lay Tiny Tim's crutch at my feet, within easy reach.

Now that I was literally stuck in a corner, Janelle felt confident enough to come closer. The firelight revealed her grim expression. "Why do you have to make everything difficult?"

"And why do you want the will? I assume you've already found Gareth's copy. Did you get the will from him the night he died? The night you killed him?"

"No, the night I saw you and him at the Sandy

Shoals Saloon. I later ran into his bar buddies as they were taking him home. Since I was on duty, they didn't find it odd when I helped them. After they left, I went through every inch of Gareth's apartment until I found it."

"If you know you weren't left anything, why do you want the other copy?" The answer came to me. "You want it because you *aren't* named as heir. Better for you if no will is ever found. As his daughter, that gives you a legal claim on the estate."

She nodded. "I've done my homework on probate law. Someone dies without a will, the next of kin are most likely to inherit the estate. And I'm Everett Hostetter's next of kin. I've even got the birth certificate to prove it."

"That's why you killed Gareth. He was the only person who knew the contents of the will. He knew Everett left nothing to you or his nephew. Or Katrina."

Janelle snickered. "Katrina thought she was so much better than Anthony and me. She was convinced Everett had chosen her as his heir. But my father was far too suspicious to take people at face value. He kept an eye on all of us. That's how he learned she never stopped using her ghostly gifts to threaten people and enrich herself. My father respected—and feared—the spirit world far more than she did. That's why he left her nothing."

"But he still had a nephew."

Janelle shone the flashlight about the room, clearly looking for possible hiding places. "Everett hoped Anthony might become an honest man if he kept him under his thumb. Instead, Anthony stole credit cards and became adept at identity theft. When I found out about this, I passed on the proof to my father. Which is why I suspected Anthony wouldn't inherit."

"You really did believe you were the sole heir."

Janelle flinched, as if the thought that she wasn't cut deep. "I wasn't certain. But I should have been. He was my father. And he fired my mother when she became pregnant. Oh, but he did give her a check for fifty thousand dollars. I guess he thought that would cover child support for the next eighteen years."

Janelle moved closer to the fireplace mantel. I wanted to tell her she was wasting her time playing the flashlight's beam over my nutcracker collection. But the more time she wasted, the longer I lived.

"I don't blame you for being bitter." I decided to try being sympathetic.

"Mom and I moved way past bitterness years ago. He wouldn't even give her a job reference. And she'd been employed by his company over ten years. My mother worked two minimum-wage jobs to keep us alive. When I was in high school, she got me hired at the grocery store she worked at. So while my father lived in a mansion and flew on private jets, the two of us bagged groceries and decorated cakes in the supermarket bakery."

I thought back to Everett's cookies. "Where you learned how to make gingerbread man cookies."

My comment interrupted her search of the mantel. "Yeah, although baking's not rocket science. But I did bake those cookies. I didn't bother to bake for Gareth. He met his end with a big plastic cup of alcohol I gave him at the festival that night. One I had doctored."

"With methamphetamine crystals."

The firelight revealed her smug smile. "Amazing what too much alcohol and crystal meth can do to a man in his seventies."

"You're the one involved in that crystal meth ring." I felt as stunned as Janelle when she learned her father was dead. "The triple homicide Kit and everyone else has been working on. Is that how you got the crystal meth?"

Janelle pointed her revolver at me once more. "Don't waste your tears on those dead men. Fifth-rate drug dealers trying to keep all the money for themselves."

"That's why you weren't in the will," I said, more to myself than to her. "You just told me how suspicious your father was. How he kept his eye on all three of you. He obviously learned you were still a dishonest cop."

"He couldn't have. I made sure to cover my tracks this time. In Wisconsin I was reckless and got caught. But I've been careful since joining the Oriole Point police force. No one suspected. Not even Chief Hitchcock."

"Your father did."

Janelle shook herself. "It doesn't matter. He's dead. So is his lawyer. All I need is that will."

"Why did you say you didn't kill your father?"

"I didn't love the man, but he *was* my father. I'd have to be a monster to plan his murder. And I'm not a monster." She pointed her gun at me, which contradicted her statement.

Were two murderers involved in all this? Then I remembered something. "You were genuinely shocked when I told you about your father's death. I was struck by that. And then you seemed amused. I think I know why."

"Tell me, Nancy Drew."

"Those cookies were meant for Anthony. He had a sweet tooth, too. You wanted to kill off the only other blood relative, just in case Anthony was in the will." I shook my head. "That's why you went from being shocked at Everett's death to finding it funny. You expected to hear Anthony had died."

"So much for my foolproof plan. How irritating when it failed. But funny." She shrugged. "I have a dark sense of humor."

Quite an understatement. "Was that dark sense of humor responsible for the sprig of holly pinned to Gareth's Santa costume?"

"I thought it was fitting. Like those fools Scrooge talked about in *A Christmas Carol.*" She sounded pleased with herself. "I pinned it on him myself that night, right after I gave him his big cup of poison. He even thanked me."

To think that Janelle had walked among us for nine years as a police officer. I also realized that if Anthony had been her original target, Janelle probably had no idea her father's fortune would have been greatly reduced in a year's time. And I saw no purpose in telling her. She was already in a vicious mood.

"At least you handed the poison to Gareth. But anyone might have eaten those cookies."

"On the contrary. Anthony can't resist chocolate

or gingerbread. I baked him those cookies, put them in a plain paper bag, and left the bag in their mailbox. With a note saying, 'Merry Christmas to Anthony, from a friend.'" She smirked. "Despite his appearance, some women find him attractive. He would assume one of the idiots he dated left the cookies for him."

"But you had no way of knowing Anthony would eat them."

"Only Anthony and Everett lived there. And Everett's weakness was donuts; he rarely ate cookies." She looked disgusted. "Anthony probably never saw that bag. Everett must have picked up the mail first and decided to take the cookies to the exhibit to snack on."

Which meant she had killed her own father.

"You killed your sons' grandfather," I said softly.

She approached me in a fury and smacked me across the face with the butt of her revolver. I briefly saw stars and felt something wet trickle from my nose.

"It was an accident. The cookies were meant for Anthony. If you say I killed my father again, I will burn this house to the ground. Like I did the Calico Barn. In fact, it may be easier to do just that."

I touched my nose, then looked at my fingers. Even in the flickering shadows, I could see the blood. "You followed me downstairs at the museum the night of the memorial. And you heard me tell Odette that I thought I knew where Everett kept his will."

Janelle took a couple steps back. "I followed you to the barn, too. That's when I realized Everett hid the will in there. Only I didn't have the time or opportunity to search the building. So I used the dress rehearsal as a cover to set it on fire."

"Dozens might have died."

"People die every day."

"Janelle, you're mad. Or evil." Horror washed over me. "Or sick."

"I'm sick all right. Sick of my own father not caring if me or my mother starved. Sick of my cousin enjoying a soft life because of a Hostetter trust fund. One that might have been given to me. And I'm sick of being forced to live in this stupid town while an old man watched my every move. Living in fear that he'd expose my past to the police department that *he* forced me to join."

She aimed the flashlight directly in my eyes, blinding me once more. "And I'm sick of waiting for the life I deserve. But I'm almost there. It's within reach. Now give me the will."

"Move the flashlight first. I can't see."

With an irritated sigh, she turned the beam onto the floor. "Where is it?"

I played for time by wiping my bloody nose on my pajama sleeve. If I told her where the will was, she'd kill me immediately. If I didn't tell her, she'd kill me anyway, then set the house on fire. Which would kill Natasha and Theo.

"Marlee, where is it?" Her voice had turned cold. As if she was shutting her emotions off in preparation for killing me.

The only choice left was to throw myself at her. Dangerous with a gun pointed at me. I took a deep breath, getting ready. The only sound was the soft crackle of the gas fire. Otherwise, the house seemed as silent as a tomb.

Suddenly, I heard a loud clang from the kitchen. Janelle looked behind her. "What the hell was that?" she cried.

I grabbed Tiny Tim's crutch and swung at her midsection. The wooden crutch landed with a thunk and she bent over double. I stood up and struck her again, this time on the head. She fell to the floor and I jumped over her.

She grabbed my ankle and I went down. I kicked and kept on kicking. But Janelle clutched my legs to keep me from getting away.

"Let go!" I yelled.

I reached to the right and grabbed for one of my many floor decorations. This one a fiber-optic candy cane. Using it as a weapon, I jabbed her in the face again and again, praying one of her eyes might pop out. Something must have landed because she released me.

I scrambled to my feet, searching on the floor for the gun. I saw it at the same time Janelle did. We both leaped toward it, knocking it aside. Janelle and I began to wrestle, rolling back and forth on the floor.

If I could just keep her away from the gun, I had a good chance. Better than good. Because I'd tear her arms off to stop her from killing Natasha and Theo. Only the woman was strong and fighting for her life as hard as I was. I heard another clang from the kitchen. It felt like a cheering section.

Grunting and breathing hard, we wrestled our way right into the big white Christmas tree, which fell on top of us. Everything became more confused as we got tangled in strings of lights and crushed ornaments.

"What's happening?" someone said.

My heart dropped when I realized it was Theo. I had to get to the gun first. With renewed energy, I yanked Janelle's hair so hard, some of it came off in my hand. Then I got on top of her and punched her through the tree branches. She yelled out in pain.

I stumbled to my feet and ran to where I had last seen the gun.

"Marlee, what's going on?" Theo asked.

Frantic, I couldn't find it. I didn't see the crutch either. No, no, no.

In the flickering shadows, I saw Janelle scramble to her knees. With a victory cry, she grabbed the gun from where it had been kicked during our struggle.

I looked about for a weapon. All I saw was that coffee-table book of *A Christmas Carol*.

Before Janelle got to her feet, I grabbed the heavy volume and lunged for her. I swung the book at her outstretched arm, which caused the gun to go off. The gunshot was deafening.

As Theo yelled for Natasha, I next swung the book at Janelle's face as hard as I could. I felt something crunch when I did. And she dropped the gun.

Janelle tried to grab for me. But I hit her twice more with the book, the last time on the top of her head. That one knocked her out.

Out of breath, I stood over her. I wondered if Charles Dickens and I had actually killed Janelle. Then I heard her groan.

Before she revived, I picked up the gun. By this

time, Natasha had come downstairs. Dasha, too, if all the yapping was any indication.

"What is all this noise? It wake me up! Why are lights off?" Natasha demanded. "And who is dead woman on floor?"

Natasha sounded more irritated than shocked that a dead person was lying beside my fallen Christmas tree. "She's not dead. And it's that policewoman I don't like."

Natasha walked over and looked down at Janelle. "You must not like her very much to do this."

I felt an urge to laugh. But if I did, I might not be able to stop. A sign of shock. "She killed Gareth Holmes. And her father. She came here tonight to kill me."

Natasha gently turned my face to her. "You have nose of blood. Must wash."

"Not yet. Theo, please go into my office and get my phone. We need to call the police."

"Are you all right, Marlee? You don't look all right." He sounded frightened.

"I'll be fine. But please get my phone. I'm calling the state police, the sheriff, *and* Chief Hitchcock." I started to shake. "Maybe I should call the marines, too."

Natasha put her arm around my shoulder as she looked down at Janelle. "What we do with bad woman until police come? I think we tie her up. Maybe with lights of Christmas tree."

"I have a better idea."

When law enforcement arrived, they found a semi-conscious Officer Davenport restrained by a long chain filled with keys, cash boxes, and padlocks.

"What is this?" Greg Trejo demanded. "What's going on?"

I looked up from where I sat huddled on the couch with Theo and Natasha. With the power still off, the only light came from the gas fireplace and the police flashlights.

"I had a visit from the Ghost of Christmas Past." I felt too drained to say much more.

"Policewoman try to kill Marlee," Natasha said. "But Marlee strong like Siberian tiger."

"She's the one who killed the old man in the museum with poison cookies," Theo added.

Chief Hitchcock looked shocked to see one of his officers wrapped in Jacob Marley's chains. "Janelle? Is this a joke? Some sort of Christmas stunt?"

I shook my head. "Not a Christmas stunt. More like *A Christmas Carol.*"

Greg knelt before me. "What happened here tonight?"

"It's a long story. But suffice to say, Dickens was right. Ghosts can save your life." I looked toward my kitchen. "Especially on Christmas Eve."

Chapter Twenty-six

Later that day, the noise level in my house rose so high, it sounded like Mr. Fezziwig's Christmas party, minus the jig.

News of Janelle's arrest spread through Oriole Point as quickly as the fire had at the Calico Barn. Once everyone heard she had been charged with multiple murders, details soon followed. Those details included the break-in at my house, my physical fight with Janelle, and that I had knocked her out with a copy of Dickens. Then wrapped her in chains.

Small wonder a steady stream of townspeople came knocking on my door. All eager for gossip and a peek at the volume of *A Christmas Carol* that brought Officer Davenport down. I lost count of the visitors who dropped by. It felt like one of Piper's village-wide events. And everyone expected to be fed.

Thankfully, Gillian, Suzanne, Odette Henderson, Denise Redfern, and Diane Cleverly brought covered dishes of food to serve. Tess and David picked up rotisserie chickens from the grocery store. Natasha and her charming Russian architect put together remarkably good canapés. A shame I no longer produced cooking shows; I'd hire the pair to star in *The Russian Kitchen.*

Even Old Man Bowman came bearing food and drink: dried venison and a crate of home-brewed beer. And Piper and Lionel arrived with six bottles of Dom Pérignon.

I was just happy to be alive. And to have my parents and Kit with me.

Because I was the girlfriend of his brother-in-law, Detective Greg Trejo called Kit shortly after his arrival with the state police. When the phone was handed to me, I tried to reassure Kit that I was okay. He didn't believe me. Probably because I sounded as shaky as I felt.

So Kit woke his parents and drove them across the state at three o'clock in the morning. And he drove straight to my house. Although thrilled to see him, I had hoped for a different introduction to his parents. But they were the soul of kindness. Even if they couldn't hide their alarm at the sight of my swollen nose, fresh bruises, and bloodstained pajamas.

Had I known they were arriving so quickly, I wouldn't have fallen asleep on the couch, still holding hands with Natasha and Theo.

At least I showered and dressed before my own parents arrived. They walked through my front door at the exact moment the electricity came back on, which I found fitting. Mom and Dad had always been my guiding lights.

Of course they were upset to find their only child bearing the marks of a humdinger of a fight. The living room looked as if it had been in a fight as well. The big white tree had been put up again, half the ornaments broken. It was also permanently crooked. Dean claimed it gave him vertigo. None of the fiber-optic decorations worked. Three nutcrackers lay in pieces. And the police trampled over the blue Christmas tree in the front hallway when they half carried Janelle out the door.

But the newest holiday addition to my living room made up for all that. Because Kit knew how much Christmas trees meant to me, he and Greg went to the tree farm and chopped down a live Scotch pine. The scent of the fresh pine made me swoon, even with my injured nose.

I had no sooner hugged Kit and Greg for the lovely surprise when Greg's wife, Ivy, showed up with their three kids. This made sense since her brother and parents were already here. In addition to being adorable, the children insisted on decorating the latest tree. Which saved me a lot of work.

My greatest pleasure was watching Kit joke and talk with the ever-changing crowd. His parents and sister were as warm and friendly as he was. Even Greg loosened up and seemed to enjoy himself. Such a sharp contrast to my ex-fiancé and his insular clan. Kit and his family made it difficult for me to stand by my resolve not to rush into the next step in our relationship.

"Merry Christmas, Marlee," Odette said as she was leaving. "And happy birthday."

"I think it's safe to say my thirty-first birthday ranks as most memorable," I remarked to my father, who sat beside me on the couch, clutching my hand.

Dad was still upset. "This birthday was too memorable," he said softly.

"Also the most dangerous," Andrew added from his comfy seat on the club chair. Oscar sat on the floor beside him, eating a piece of birthday cake.

"Here's hoping you don't have another one remotely like it." Tess handed me a cup of apple cider. "With luck they'll all be dull by comparison. And safer."

She gave me a wink, then went around the living room with her tray of drinks. Because of my ordeal in the wee hours of the morning, Tess and my mom stepped in to play hostess. And they had their hands full. An outsider might assume this was a hundredth birthday. Or a wedding.

"They are going to put that woman away?" my father asked for the fifth time. "There's no chance she'll go free and hurt you again?"

"Don't worry. They charged her with the murders of Everett Hostetter and Gareth Holmes. She confessed the whole thing to me."

"But what if she doesn't confess to the police? She could hire a clever lawyer, and they might get her off. Convince the jury you were lying."

"I'd like to see them try. But she was also charged with three more deaths, men involved in a local drug ring. Kit was working on the triple homicide and they'd begun to make arrests. This morning, two suspects gave up names, as Kit predicted. One of those names was Janelle Davenport. And they have proof." I squeezed my dad's hand.

My mom heard this as she walked past. "Are you sure, honey? She won't go free?"

"Charged with five murders? With evidence she was a dishonest cop?" I shook my head. "Janelle will go to prison for the rest of her life."

"Thank God," my mom murmured, then went to the kitchen to fill her tray with more food.

Although happy and relieved, I also felt sad for Janelle's young sons, currently with their father in Milwaukee. Chief Hitchcock spoke to her ex-husband this morning to relay the news of Janelle's arrest. I hoped their father was more decent and honorable than Janelle, because those children would need a lot of emotional support.

As for emotional support, I had a marvelous excess. I smiled at the friends and family around me. Their warmth was greater than that of the gas fireplace, which had been crackling for far too many hours.

"Not another birthday cake," I said to Gillian, who set down a decorated cake on the coffee table before me. "We've already sung 'Happy Birthday' over the cake my parents brought."

Gillian laughed. "That was eaten long ago. This, and the one Theo is icing right now, should hold us until these people go. Some of them you barely know." She lowered her voice. "They must have their own Christmas Eve celebrations to go to."

"We can only hope," Oscar said. Since dating Andrew, Oscar counted himself among my inner circle of family and friends.

I sat forward and read HAPPY 31ST BIRTHDAY on the latest cake's buttercream frosting. "Tell Theo to hang up his pastry bag. We don't need any more cake."

Gillian shrugged. "You know Theo. He prefers being in the kitchen when there are this many strangers around."

"I feel bad he's still here." I turned to my father. "Theo planned to spend the holiday with his father, but missed his train yesterday. I promised to take him early this morning, but—"

"But a homicidal maniac broke into your home," Dean finished. He sat on the loveseat across from us.

"I still would have driven him, but he refused. Theo feels terrible he slept through most of what happened down here. He thinks he could have protected me." Although I cringed at the idea of Theo caught in Janelle's cross-fire.

"Marlee had to call his dad and arrange for him to take the train here instead," Gillian said. "And he'll be here in time for your actual birthday dinner. Which, by the way, I have to miss if I'm going to make my own family celebration."

"Then let me see you on the way. And give you a big hug." I looked at my father. "I need my hand back now. But I'll be close by. I promise."

With a reluctant expression, he released my hand. "Maybe you should move to Chicago. Your mom and I could keep an eye on you there. Make sure you're safe."

I kissed him on the cheek. "Haven't you read all the cakes? I'm thirty-one now."

It took another hour of pointed hints, but finally only my so-called inner circle remained: my parents, Kit and his family, Natasha, Tess, David, Theo, Dean, Andrew, Oscar, Piper, Lionel, Old Man Bowman,

Suzanne, and Alexei Fermonov, who never took his eyes off Natasha. I didn't blame him. Natasha looked especially fetching in a red skirt and sweater; the sweater, of course, trimmed with fur. Diane Cleverly was about to leave, but I asked her to stay behind.

We all assembled back in the living room. The Trejo children were safely tucked away in the sunroom, playing with the animals and watching a DVD of *Rudolph the Red-Nosed Reindeer*.

Diane seemed uncomfortable. "Marlee, you should be with your family and close friends. I only wanted to stop by to make sure you were all right. And to thank you for catching Everett's murderer. At the risk of your own life, too."

"Janelle didn't leave me much choice," I said. "Besides, I had a little ghostly help."

"Mary Cullen?" my mother asked. "Our kitchen ghost helped you?"

Those unaware of the existence of my ghost looked confused, so I explained. Oscar and Greg wore skeptical expressions, but everyone else seemed impressed.

"I got a ghost in my hunting cabin up north," Old Man Bowman announced. "He don't do much besides whistle on rainy nights. And hit me on the head if I snore too loud."

Since no one knew how to respond to that, Andrew said, "Well, I'm shocked to learn our local policewoman was a killer. Granted, she had a lousy personality and no fashion sense. But murder? She sure had me fooled."

"Marlee never like policewoman," Natasha reminded him. "Even before old man is killed. Shows Marlee has good *instinkty* about people."

"Especially murderers," Dean said with a grin. "She can smell 'em a mile away."

"Let's hope there won't be any more murderers for her to sniff out," Kit said.

Old Man Bowman lifted a glass of his own beer. "Here's to Marlee, one of the best trackers I know. She's so good, I might take her with me on my next hunt for Bigfoot."

"Marlee does not look for the Bigfoot." Natasha frowned at Old Man Bowman. "Is too dangerous. He may kidnap her."

"Okay, we can talk about me and Bigfoot later," I said. "Right now, I want Diane to hear what was in Everett Hostetter's will."

"Did he leave everything to her?" Dean whistled.

Diane turned white. "He couldn't have. I have no right to all those millions. He had a nephew."

"Who will be charged with identity theft and credit card fraud," Greg said. "As well as the crimes his business partner went to prison for. We found those metal boxes in the burned ruin of the barn. The ones Marlee said held information about Anthony, Janelle, and Katrina. Lucky for us, they were made of fireproof metal."

"Unlucky for the trio," Kit added. "Everett had proof that Janelle and Anthony not only committed crimes years before they moved to Oriole Point, but that they continued to do so afterward. Janelle is already in custody. And the sheriff's department arrested Anthony two hours ago."

Diane looked stunned.

"What about Katrina May?" Piper demanded. "I hope there's a warrant out for that ghoulish liar."

"What is this *ghoulish*?" Natasha asked Alexei. Since he shrugged, I guessed Alexei's English was as spotty as hers.

"They can't arrest Katrina," I said. "She didn't commit any crimes."

"But she used her so-called psychic gifts to coerce clients into giving her things," Lionel protested. "Jewelry, paintings."

"And handbags!" Piper said. "Now she's snagged another rich man. One she only caught because she and her spirits ratted out his wife."

"Unethical, but not criminal." I shrugged. "Sorry. Katrina remains free to pass on ghostly messages and convince clients to do her bidding."

"You've ruined Christmas for me now," Piper fumed. "I have to figure out a way to run her out of here. Maybe a few well-placed rumors."

Kit groaned.

"Leave her alone, Piper," I said. "Now that Katrina hasn't inherited the Hostetter fortune, I'm sure she'll marry this rich guy in Grand Rapids. You'll probably never see her again."

"I better not."

"Marlee, I can't accept all that money." Diane shook her head. "It isn't right."

I smiled. "You didn't let me finish, Diane. There was no single beneficiary in his will. Instead, Everett divided his money among every institution and charity in Oriole Point. The churches, the schools, the library, the hospital, the Green Willow Players—"

Suzanne let out a jubilant cry.

"Yes, Suzanne. Everett left your theater group twenty million dollars. More than enough to rebuild the barn and put on productions of *A Christmas Carol* forever. Only make sure the new barn meets every fire code."

This was too much for Suzanne, who collapsed in Dean's arms. He looked to his brother to help him out.

"He left the historical museum thirty million dollars," I told Diane.

Diane swayed on her feet. "I have to sit down."

My dad led Diane to the couch.

I looked out over the group. "There won't be a single person in Oriole Point who won't benefit from his largesse. Everett bequeathed money to everything, from clean-water groups to the Fourth of July fireworks fund to the local Audubon Society."

"He wanted to help the birds, too?" Theo asked me.

"It looks like Everett wanted to help everyone in Oriole Point. By the way, Piper, he left your Visitor Center a hefty amount of money as well."

For the first time, Piper was struck silent.

"Amazing, isn't it?" I said. "Everett sought to redeem himself just as Ebenezer Scrooge did at the end of *A Christmas Carol.* And he did it by giving his money away to help whomever he could. It's a shame Everett could only bring himself to do this after his death. He was never able to make the complete transformation Scrooge did." I sighed. "Some part of him remained Jacob Marley."

Diane burst into tears. "Poor Everett. He tried. At least he tried."

"Like Jacob Marley, he wanted to stop Janelle, Anthony, and Katrina from making the same mistakes he did," Tess remarked.

"Since Everett held so much store by *A Christmas Carol*," Kit added, "he probably thought they would reform their ways, like Scrooge had."

I walked over to my Tiny Tim corner and picked up the volume of *A Christmas Carol*. With a smile, I held it up. "We should drink a toast to Mr. Dickens. Not only did this book literally save my life a few hours ago, but it inspired our own Jacob Marley to better our town. And everyone in it."

Before people could raise their assorted glasses of cider, beer, and water, Lionel said, "Wait. This toast calls for Dom Pérignon."

So it was that we ended this Christmas chapter with raised glasses of expensive champagne. And a sense of wonder that Everett Hostetter had been such an unexpected and generous benefactor.

Although Piper still held a grudge. "If only we could punish Katrina."

"Don't spoil things." Tess gave her a warning look. "We're all in a good mood."

"And I have dream two days ago about pigeons," Natasha said. "Means Katrina will move away."

All eyes turned to me for an explanation. "Don't ask," I told them.

Piper let out an exasperated breath. "A shame this isn't the sixteenth century. We could have burned Katrina as a witch."

"Christmas means goodwill towards all," Lionel reminded his wife.

"Indeed it does." I raised my glass. "To Everett Hostetter!"

"To Everett Hostetter," the group echoed back.

"And may God bless us everyone!" I added.

Theo smiled. "Even Piper."

Recipes

NO-BAKE HOLLYBERRY CLUSTER COOKIES

After Theo points out the lack of holly pastries in the shop, Marlee searches on Pinterest for a recipe that incorporates a holly theme. This easy, no-bake recipe seemed perfect. Variations of this recipe call for shaping the batter into wreaths. Since the leaves and berries of holly are poisonous, real holly is not included. What you will find included is a lot of flavor.

½ cup butter or margarine
30 large marshmallows
¼ cup teaspoon green food coloring
4½ cups cornflakes cereal
⅓ cup mini red cinnamon candies, such as Red Hots

1. Heat butter in large saucepan or pot until melted. Add marshmallows.
2. Stir until all the marshmallows are melted. Mix in the green food coloring.
3. Stir in the cornflakes cereal, until all pieces are coated.
4. Drop by spoonfuls onto wax paper. Press 3 cinnamon candies into each cornflake cluster.
5. Let cool until set.

Makes approximately 24 cookies.

STRAWBERRY-GLAZED BAKED DONUT HOLES

Here are the strawberry donut holes that Marlee and Theo whipped up. Instead of berry-flavored candy canes, Marlee gave these away to the children who came to see Santa at The Berry Basket. You can see why this was a much better choice. A shout-out to alattefood.com for the recipe.

For the batter:
   1 cup flour
   1 teaspoon baking powder
   ¼ teaspoon cinnamon
   ¼ teaspoon nutmeg
   ⅓ cup white sugar
   2 tablespoons unsalted butter, melted
   ¼ cup almond milk (or any milk you prefer)
   ¼ cup Greek or regular yogurt
   1 egg
   1 teaspoon vanilla extract
   1 teaspoon almond extract

For the glaze:
   ⅛ cup strawberries, pureed (about 3 big
      strawberries)
   1 tablespoon heavy cream
   2–3 cups powdered sugar

1. Preheat oven to 350° and grease a 24-cup mini-muffin tin.
2. In a large bowl, mix flour, baking powder, cinnamon, and nutmeg, and sugar together.
3. In a second bowl, mix melted butter with milk,

yogurt, egg, and vanilla and almond extracts.

4. Make a well in the center of the dry ingredients, and pour the wet ingredients into the well.

5. Stir gently, until just combined. Batter will be thick.

6. Disperse batter into muffin tins evenly, about ½ to ¾ of the way full.

7. Bake for 7–8 minutes or until golden brown.

8. To make the glaze, puree strawberries in a blender or food processor. Mix with cream and 2 cups of powdered sugar, adding an additional cup of powdered sugar if the consistency is too runny.

9. Dunk donut in glaze. You can dunk the entire donut or just the top. Let glaze set before dunking a second time.

Makes 24 donut holes.

CRANBERRY WHITE-CHOCOLATE
PISTACHIO BARK

The Berry Basket's cranberry pistachio bark helped to calm Suzanne Cabot down after her play's Mrs. Cratchit wound up in the hospital. But don't wait until a stressful moment to try this delightful Christmas treat.

16 ounces white chocolate, chopped
¼ cup shelled pistachios, roughly chopped
¼ cup dried cranberries, roughly chopped
½ cup M&M's (using only red and green candies to give the dessert a Christmas touch)

1. Line a baking sheet with parchment paper and set aside.
2. In a small pot, melt white chocolate at 30-second increments. Stir well to prevent scorching.
3. When white chocolate is completely melted and smooth, spread on parchment paper into a rectangular shape.
4. Sprinkle chopped pistachios, cranberries, and whole M&M's on top. Place in the refrigerator for 10 minutes to set.
5. Break into pieces with your hands or a knife. Store at room temperature or in the refrigerator.

Number of servings depends on how many pieces the bark is broken into.